FROM BALTIC SHORES

Some other books from Norvik Press

Sigbjørn Obstfelder: *A Priest's Diary* (translated by James McFarlane)
Hjalmar Söderberg: *Short stories* (translated by Carl Lofmark)
Annegret Heitmann (ed.): *No Man's Land. An Anthology of Modern Danish Women's Literature*
P C Jersild: *A Living Soul* (translated by Rika Lesser)
Sara Lidman: *Naboth's Stone* (translated by Joan Tate)
Selma Lagerlöf: *The Löwensköld Ring* (translated by Linda Schenck)
Villy Sørensen: *Harmless Tales* (translated by Paula Hostrup-Jessen)
Camilla Collett: *The District Governor's Daughters* (translated by Kirsten Seaver)
Jens Bjørneboe: *The Sharks* (translated by Esther Greenleaf Mürer)
Jørgen-Frantz Jacobsen: *Barbara* (translated by George Johnson)
Janet Garton & Henning Sehmsdorf (eds. and trans.): *New Norwegian Plays* (by Peder W.Cappelen, Edvard Hoem, Cecilie Løveid and Bjørg Vik)
Gunilla Anderman (ed.): *New Swedish Plays* (by Ingmar Bergman, Stig Larsson, Lars Norén and Agneta Pleijel)
Kjell Askildsen: *A Sudden Liberating Thought* (translated by Sverre Lyngstad)
Svend Åge Madsen: *Days with Diam* (translated by W. Glyn Jones)

The logo of Norvik Press is based on a drawing by Egil Bakka (University of Bergen) of a Viking ornament in gold, paper thin, with impressed figures (size 16x21mm). It was found in 1897 at Hauge, Klepp, Rogaland, and is now in the collection of the Historisk museum, University of Bergen (inv.no. 5392). It depicts a love scene, possibly (according to Magnus Olsen) between the fertility god Freyr and the maiden Gerðr; the large penannular brooch of the man's cloak dates the work as being most likely 10th century.

Cover illustration: By Andy Vargo.

FROM BALTIC SHORES

Short stories

selected and edited by Christopher Moseley

Norvik Press
1994

British Library Cataloguing in Publication Data
From Baltic Shores
    I. Moseley, Christopher
    808.831 [FS]
ISBN 1-870041-25-9

Set in 11 pt Garamond antiqua.
First published in 1994 by Norvik Press, University of East Anglia, Norwich, NR4 7TJ, England
Managing Editors: James McFarlane and Janet Garton

Norvik Press has been established with financial support from the University of East Anglia, the Danish Ministry for Cultural Affairs, The Norwegian Cultural Department, and the Swedish Institute.

Printed in Great Britain by Biddles Ltd, Guildford, Surrey.

Contents

Introduction

The days when the Hanseatic League was an agent of cross-cultural fertilization between the cities around the Baltic littoral – Hamburg, Lübeck, Rostock, Danzig, Riga, Tallinn, as well as Stockholm and Copenhagen – are now long gone. In the centuries since then, new currents have swept into this basin of diverse cultures in Northern Europe, currents that have tended to separate rather than unite them. Alliances have been formed and broken, political boundaries drawn and redrawn, economic ties have flourished and receded, external powers have intervened and withdrawn, to such an extent that by the late twentieth century a situation has arisen where the cultures, languages and societies of Northeastern Europe are as diverse as ever, but they know little more about each other's identities than do complete outsiders.

Geographically, the territories of the Nordic and Baltic countries, taken together, make up a very considerable portion of Europe. In terms of population, however, the proportion is much slighter. With the exception of Sweden, and to a lesser extent Denmark, none of the countries in the region covered in this book has even been a great power in the political sense, let alone in the cultural sense. The political and cultural influences in the Nordic and Baltic countries have been overwhelmingly external – from Germany, from Poland, and of course from Russia. During the Soviet era, which is still a very recent memory, the Baltic nations were often dismissed by outsiders as merely a part, at best an adjunct, of Russia. The literatures of these countries have closely reflected these shifting currents. Of the countries covered here, only Denmark and Sweden can boast a written vernacular literature going back more than two centuries, and it is precisely these two countries that have in past centuries striven to exercise political hegemony in the region. The other four – Finland, Estonia, Latvia and Lithuania – developed a written vernacular literature very late in their long histories, as the majority of the population formed an uneducated peasant underclass, whereas the nobility, the clergy and the civil authorities spoke an alien tongue and drew on foreign cultural influences. All four of these nations were until the end of the First World War part of the Russian Empire, and at the beginning of the Second, a mere two decades later, three of them and a part of the fourth (Finland) were absorbed into the Soviet empire.

But in Finland the educated class spoke Swedish, and in Livonia (the duchy of the Russian Empire comprising the present-day states of Estonia and Latvia), the dominant, literate class was the Baltic German nobility, whose ancestors had settled in the region after its conquest by the Teutonic Knights, who imposed Christianity by force on their domains in the late 12th and early 13th centuries. It is for this reason that the Lutheran religion holds sway in Estonia and northern Latvia, whereas in Lithuania and southern Latvia, where the Knights did not penetrate, Roman Catholicism is the dominant religion. Lithuania was for centuries part of the mighty Polish-Lithuanian confederation, which at its height reached as far as the Black Sea. But after the partitions of Poland, which ended in 1795, the Lithuanian state passed under Russian hegemony. Russian Orthodoxy, however, has only taken root among the native Baltic peoples in the easternmost part of Latvia.

The sparseness of their largely rural populations has been both a strength and a weakness for the Baltic lands. On the one hand, they have been vulnerable to foreign influences and conquerors entering through their few large cities (and since these cities have all been seaports, these influences have been many and diverse). On the other, the rural populations have acted as a cushion against the spread of these influences and the uniformity and standardization they might have brought; instead these conservative, pious, reserved and hard-working farming nations came to preserve ancient folk traditions down to the era of their own national sovereignty.

And it is no coincidence that the phenomenon of the 'national epic' sprang up when and where it did: in the early nineteenth century in those Baltic lands which had yet to gain their political and economic independence. The ideas of Herder and the Enlightenment spread rapidly to the fertile soil of the Baltic German intelligentsia, and to the northern side of the basin as well. It was in 1835 that Elias Lönnrot, a country doctor in Finland, published the first edition of the *Kalevala*, an epic poetic narrative which he had fashioned from fragments of rhythmic verse preserved in the mouths of the many informants he found on his collecting journeys in Eastern Finland and Karelia. His example was soon to be emulated across the Gulf of Finland by his linguistic kinsmen, the Estonians Friedrich Robert Faehlmann and Friedrich Reinhold Kreutzwald, the compilers of the *Kalevipoeg*, which thenceforward came to be known as the Estonian national epic.

Some decades were to pass before a similar venture was undertaken in Latvia by Krišjānis Barons, who methodically collected over ten thousand of the characteristically Latvian *dainas*, oral poems dealing with every aspect of the cycle of human life and death. Barons' *Latvju Dainas*, too, have come to be regarded as the literary treasure-house of the Latvian nation.

The Baltic littoral is a very diverse ethnic and linguistic region. At the mouth and on the western flank of the Baltic we find the Danes and Swedes, speakers of a Scandinavian offshoot of the Germanic branch of the Indo-European family of languages, fairly closely related to the German spoken by their southern neighbours. Swedish speakers also make up less than one tenth of the population of Finland, to the east, whose own majority language is quite unrelated.

The Finns and Estonians speak almost mutually intelligible variants within the Baltic-Finnic branch of the Finno-Ugrian family of languages. It is uncertain when these peoples first arrived in their present territory from beyond the Urals, but it is reckoned to be at least ten thousand years ago. The only other major European language which is at all related to the Baltic-Finnic languages is Hungarian, but other small pockets of Finnic languages are found to the east in Russia (Karelian, Ingrian, Veps, Vote), and to the southwest in Latvia (Livonian, now on the point of extinction).

At the southeastern end of the Baltic we find Latvian and Lithuanian, the two remaining survivors of a once larger branch of Indo-European collectively known as Baltic. Some linguists believe there may once have been as many as ten members of this branch, but what is certain is that a third member, Old Prussian, died out as recently as the late seventeenth century. The Baltic languages have many features in common with the Slav tongues, but form a distinct branch within Indo-European.

Space does not permit any but the sketchiest outline of the

literary history of the Baltic littoral nations. To do them justice, a full volume on the subject would be required. As we noted earlier, Denmark and Sweden can boast rich literatures going back to the times when their respective languages diverged from the Old Norse in which the sagas were written. Historically, Copenhagen was the metropolis of a kingdom which included Norway until 1814 (whereafter Norway formed a dual monarchy with Sweden until 1905), and the Danish language served as the literary language of Norway as well during that period. What has served as the medium of instruction has naturally also been the accepted literary language throughout the region. In both Denmark and Sweden, the traditions of poetry and drama were firmly established before the novel became an accepted form, and in this, the Nordic countries broadly followed continental European trends.

Fiction writing, especially short fiction, is in the Nordic and Baltic countries a relatively recent phenomenon by continental standards, however. The short story is by and large a genre of the twentieth century. In Denmark its precursor was Steen Steensen Blicher (1782 – 1848) with his tales of the Jutland heathlands. Apart from Hans Christian Andersen's fairy tales, which first appeared in 1835, the next significant works of short fiction from Denmark were to come well after the middle of the last century, from the pens of Jens Peter Jacobsen (1847 – 1885) and Herman Bang (1857 – 1912). By the turn of the twentieth century, the short story was well established in Denmark, as it was all over Scandinavia. Few twentieth-century storytellers have been translated into English, however, one notable exception being of course Karen Blixen, though even her best-known works were written in English and do not deal only with Danish themes.

In Sweden the pioneers of the short story were more famous for their works on a larger scale: August Strindberg (1849 – 1912) and Selma Lagerlöf (1858 – 1940). They were followed by numerous others: Bo Bergman, Hjalmar Söderberg, Hjalmar Bergman, Dan Andersson, Jan Fridegård, Eyvind Johnson, Karin Boye, Artur Lundkvist, Lars Ahlin and Lars Gyllensten to name but a few of the more important ones. Again, few of their works have been made available in English.

In Finland, the first acknowledged novelist and storyteller was Aleksis Kivi (1834 – 1872), whose major work *Seitsemän veljestä* (Seven Brothers, 1870) paved the way for Finnish vernacular literature. Juhani Aho (1861 – 1921) was another major story-writer before the turn of the century, but as elsewhere in the northern countries, it was only in the early years of this century that the genre came into its own, in works by writers such as Volter Kilpi, Aino Kallas, Joel Lehtonen, Maria Jotuni, and above all, two giants of twentieth-century Finnish fiction, F.E.Sillanpää and Mika Waltari. The post-war period has produced fine short-story writers of the calibre of Paavo Haavikko, Eeva-Liisa Manner, Hannu Salama, Erno Paasilinna and Sirkka Turkka. But again, most of these marvellous writers remain a closed book to the English-speaking reader.

Finland is a bilingual country, however. Swedish is currently the first language of some seven percent of the population, mostly concentrated on the southern and western coasts, and Swedish was of course the literary language of Finland even after 1809, when Finland passed out of Swedish sovereignty. The Swedish-speaking community has produced a large number of distinguished writers, starting with Johan Ludvig Runeberg and Zachris Topelius in the early nineteenth century, continuously down to our own day. Among those who have written short fiction we might mention Elmer

Diktonius, Tito Colliander and, in our own day, Lars Huldén.

Vernacular literature in the Baltic republics only became possible when a sufficient number of writers and readers were literate in the native languages, and we must bear in mind that even the fundamental question of orthography was still being thrashed out even in the early years of the first independence period between the two world wars. Even so, it is worth noting that literacy in the Baltic lands in the eighteenth and nineteenth centuries was more widespread than in most of the sovereign nations of continental Europe.

In Estonia, the pioneers of the short story were Friedebert Tuglas (1889 – 1971) and Oskar Luts (1887 – 1953). As in the other northern countries, the flowering of short fiction had first to await the passing of the period of national awakening, which found expression first in poetry (firstly epic and heroic, later lyrical and romantic) and then in drama. While the more prominent authors, Anton Hansen Tammsaare and August Gailit among others, were working on a larger canvas, the Estonian short story matured in the hands of others such as Karl August Hindrey and Karl Rumor.

With hindsight it might be said that the process of maturing in Estonian fiction was almost complete when the Molotov-Ribbentrop pact of 1939 consigned Estonia and the other two Baltic republics to the Soviet sphere of influence, with their resulting annexation and invasion in 1940, German wartime occupation and reconquest by the Soviets. By 1944 many of Estonia's leading writers had fled abroad, mostly to Sweden, which became a centre of Estonian culture in exile. Within Estonia, literature under the Soviets entered a decline into uniformity, and only works which corresponded to Soviet literary ideals saw the light of day. The diaspora in exile were few in number, but there were some beacons of cultural independence, such as Bernard Kangro's publication *Tulimuld*. But by the nineteen-sixties a bolder, more independent approach was discernible in the pages of the Writers' Union organ *Looming* (Creation), which flourishes even now in independent Estonia. The country's position at the western fringe of the Soviet Union made it susceptible to Western influences, notably from kindred Finland.

Since the restoration of independence in 1990, the freedom to write has not yet been matched by the economic incentive to publish. The early nineteen-nineties in the Baltic lands in general have been a time of reclaiming the past, of rediscovering what was once forbidden, of getting acquainted with foreign literature, as much as, if not more than, of experimentation with the new. Publishing outlets have been slow to privatize, and the funding for literature in the new free-market economy is simply not there. Gone are the days when a mediocre time-serving author could enjoy the patronage of a Soviet sinecure. Thus the process of finding outlets for publication for the modern Estonian writer can be a dispiriting one, even without the shackles of Soviet conformity and censorship.

In broad outline, the same processes apply to Latvia, Estonia's southern neighbour. The period of national awakening stimulated heroic and folk-based poetry, and not until 1879 did the first true Latvian novel appear – *Mērnieku laiki* (The Time of the Land-Surveyors) by the Kaudzīte brothers. The early part of the century, up to the first years of independence after 1918, was dominated by the figure of Jānis Rainis (1865 – 1929), whose plays, poems and novels would surely be better known in Europe had he written in a better-known language. Rūdolfs Blaumanis (1863 – 1908), though more famous as a playwright, was also an important writer of stories. Short fiction in the brief twenty-year period of independence was produced by notable authors such as Eriks Ādamsons and Jānis Ezeriņš.

As in Estonia and Lithuania, the outbreak of war brought the end of political and cultural independence, and the flight into exile of writers who matured abroad. In Sweden Mārtiņš Zīverts and Veronika Strēlerte, and in America Anšlavs Eglītis, made exile literature as significant as the home-grown variety if not more so. But this was true only of the previous generation of writers, and in Latvia, as in all the Baltic countries, the centre of literary activity is now returning to the homeland.

In Lithuanian literature, poetry was overwhelmingly the dominant genre almost up to the independence period. The recognized classics of Lithuanian writing from previous centuries are almost all in verse: from Donelaitis and his *Metai* (The Seasons, 1770), through Baranauskas' *Anykščių šilelis* (The Anykščiai Pine Forest, 1861) to Maironis' *Pavasario balsai* (Voices of Spring, 1895). Poetry continues to be an important strand in Lithuanian literature even today, but in the early decades of this century many talents emerged in the field of fiction, such as Vincas Krėvė and Juozas Grušas. Writers such as Petras Cvirka were tackling social issues in the last years of independence. But the loss of national sovereignty brought with it the flight into exile or deportation to Siberia of many of Lithuania's most gifted writers. The USA became a particularly important centre of cultural activity in exile. But in Lithuania itself the dead hand of socialist realism began to be lifted after 1956, and poetry especially experienced a new freedom of expression, followed gradually by an explosion of new talent in the field of fiction. Even before the restoration of Lithuania's independence in 1990, its literature was bold, vital and diverse. But as in its neighbour countries, there are fewer economically viable outlets for writing in the emerging free market economy than existed under the subsidized patronage of socialism. This is a problem whose solution will come in time, and in the meantime we can only hope that translations such as those in this volume will encourage Baltic writers by letting their voices be heard outside their own borders.

A word or two about the scope of this book is in order here. The range of countries covered in this book might have been extended to include Poland and Germany, but their populations and literatures are so vast that the inclusion of only three or four writers from each of them would smack of tokenism. More importantly, those countries' capitals and cultural centres are not located on the Baltic shores. Norway, though in every sense part of Scandinavia, does not have a coastline on the Baltic, and therefore it, too, was omitted. Thus the symmetrical choice of three Nordic and three Baltic countries seems fitting for a volume of this size.

The writers chosen to represent these countries are all living and active, most of them still quite young. We hope that a small taste of their work will whet the English-speaking reader's appetite for more. The stories were chosen because we hope they convey the flavour of life in the lands on the shores of the Baltic, both urban and rural. The present day is generally the setting, but there is an element of timelessness as well. The twenty stories selected for inclusion here are intended to sharpen the curiosity of the inquisitive reader to find out more about the rich literatures they represent.

I would like to thank my fellow contributors, Romas Kinka and Professor Glyn Jones, for their painstaking and faithful renderings of three of the stories in this book: the former for the stories by Juozas Aputis and Romualdas Lankauskas, the latter for the story by Svend Åge Madsen. For the rest, I must thank the native speakers whom I pestered with questions;

their unstinting help and freely given advice was of inestimable help, especially Tiina Tamman, Reinis Mertens, Ivans Belevičs, Algis Chveikaouskas, and last but certainly not least, my wife Kristina. My grateful thanks also go to Janet Garton and James McFarlane for patiently and helpfully seeing a complex project through to fruition. Without help from these many hands, this anthology could not have come to pass.

Biographical details of the authors

Juozas APUTIS (Lithuania) was born in the village of Balčiai in Western Lithuania in 1936. He graduated from the University of Lithuania in 1960, and since then has devoted himself to literature and journalism. He has been involved with the leading literary periodicals in Lithuania, and since 1990 has been editor-in-chief of the magazine *Metai* (The Seasons). Unlike most of the authors in this anthology, Aputis has specialized in the short story genre almost exclusively. His first collection of stories was published in 1960. The story included here comes from the collection of the same name, *Horizonte bėga šernai* (Wild boars running on the horizon, 1970).

Orvokki AUTIO (Finland) was born in 1941. Her works, including the collections *Timanttihäät* (Diamond Wedding, 1970) and *Sininen kaappi* (The Blue Cupboard, 1972, from which 'Thirty Pennies' is taken) describe the lives of people in her native Ostrobothnia, on the north-western coast of Finland. In addition to fiction, she has written drama for television and the stage.

Alberts BELS (Latvia) was born in 1938. To date he has written nine novels and three collections of stories. In addition to his literary work he has been active in politics; until 1993 he was a deputy of the Supreme Council of the Republic of Latvia. The story in this anthology comes from his collection *Sainis* (Package, 1980).

Suzanne BRØGGER (married name Suzanne Preis Brøgger Zeruneith) was born in Copenhagen in 1944. She was educated in Denmark and South-East Asia. She has been an actress and a news correspondent, working in the Soviet Union, the Middle East and the Far East. Her written output, beginning in 1973, has been very varied, encompassing drama and children's books as well as fiction and reporting. She has won numerous awards and stipends in Denmark and abroad, and has been translated into 13 languages, in addition to being a translator herself. The story included here comes from her collection *Den pebrede susen* (The peppered whistle, 1986).

Bo CARPELAN (Finland) is the only representative of Swedish-speaking Finland in this volume. He was born in Helsinki (Helsingfors in Swedish) in 1926. For most of his working life he has been on the staff of Helsinki City Library. Chiefly noted for his poetry, he has published numerous collections of verse since 1946 – most of these have been translated into Finnish as well, as have his short stories and novels. The story included here comes from the collection *Jag minns att jag drömde* (I Remember that I Dreamed, 1979).

Per Gunnar EVANDER (Sweden), was born at Ovansjö, in Gävleborg province, northern Sweden in 1933. His literary career dates from 1965, and though most of his output is fiction, he has worked extensively as a drama producer on the stage and in radio and television. The present story first appeared in the Swedish anthology *Gåspennan* (The Quill Pen, 1984).

Romualdas GRANAUSKAS (Lithuania) was born at Mažeikiai in northern Lithuania in 1939. Up to 1972 he worked on a variety of jobs, but since that year he has lived permanently in Vilnius and devoted himself to writing. Apart from stories, he has written screenplays and translations. The story reproduced here originally appeared in his collection *Baltas vainikas juodam garvežiui* (A white wreath for the black locomotive, 1987).

Marie HERMANSON (Sweden) was born in Sävedalen near Gothenburg in 1956. She has worked mainly as a journalist. This story comes from her first collection, *Det finns ett hål i verkligheten* (There is a hole in reality, 1986).

Valentīns JAKOBSONS (Latvia) was born in 1922. He spent the years from 1941 to 1956 in prison and exile in Siberia. His writing, which he began in his fifties, is mainly based on his memories of the years in prison camps, and the example which appears here is taken from his second book, *Brokastis ziemeļos* (Breakfast in the North, 1992).

Romualdas LANKAUSKAS (Lithuania) was born in the port city of Klaipėda in 1932. Though best known for his short stories, he is also a novelist, children's writer, translator and painter. He studied at the University of Vilnius but did not graduate, having refused to attend the obligatory courses in Marxism-Leninism. He has worked as a journalist on a variety of publications, but has mainly devoted himself to creative work. In 1989 he set up the Lithuanian chapter of the PEN Club and was its first chairman. He has translated several of Ernest Hemingway's works into Lithuanian. The story here dates from 1983.

Rosa LIKSOM (pseudonym; Finland) was born at Ylitornio in the far north of Finland in 1958. She has lived in many parts of Europe and held numerous jobs. In addition to her fiction she has written journalism for newspapers and magazines, and a film script. The bulk of her work has been short fiction, and the story included here comes from her second collection, *Unohdettu vartti* (The Forgotten Quarter-Hour, 1986).

Einar MAASIK (Estonia) was born in Narva in 1929. His career has followed a more orthodox Soviet path than most of the authors represented here. He graduated from the University of Tartu in 1956 and from the Leningrad Higher Party School in 1970. He has worked on the Writers' Union monthly *Looming* (Creation). He has published numerous works of fiction since 1966. The story in this volume dates from 1973.

Svend Åge MADSEN (Denmark) was born in Århus in 1939. He has been writing novels since 1963, as well as stories and plays for radio and the theatre. *The Man who Created Woman* is taken from the collection *Mellem himmel og jord* (Between heaven and earth), published in 1990.

Eeva TIKKA (Finland) was born at Ristiina in 1939. Since 1973 she has published novels, stories and volumes of poetry. Much of her work is set in the eastern province of North Karelia. *The Aluminium Rings* is the title story of a collection published in 1984.

Göran TUNSTRÖM (Sweden) was born in Karlstad in 1937. He has been a published author since 1958. His work includes radio and stage plays and numerous volumes of fiction. The story translated in this volume comes from *Det sanna livet* (True Life), 1991.

Mati UNT (Estonia) was born in 1944 and educated at Tartu University, in which city's theatre/he worked from 1966 as a producer. He has written many volumes of prose and has been a prolific short story writer – the present story, dating from 1972, comes from *Valitud teosed* (Selected works, 1985). He is one of the few Estonian writers whose work has been translated into several languages.

Aija VĀLODZE (Latvia) was born in Riga in 1957, the daughter of Regīna Ezera, another distinguished writer of short fiction. She has worked in journalism and the film industry. Though she has had individual pieces published before, the collection from which the present story is taken, *Sveiks, mans maziņais* (Hello, My Little One, 1992) is her first full volume of work.

Arvo VALTON (Estonia; real name Vallikivi) was born in 1935 and educated at Tallinn Technical University. From 1949 to 1954 he was deported. He worked as a film director from 1975 to 1988. His work consists mainly of novels, stories and aphorisms. The story translated here comes from his *Valitud teosed* (Selected works, 1984).

Dorrit WILLUMSEN (Denmark) was born in Copenhagen in 1940. Her first collection of stories was published in 1965, and she has been a prolific writer ever since, with novels, poetry, plays and stories to her credit. The present story comes from the collection of the same name from 1978.

Mārtiņš ZELMENIS was born in 1956 in Riga, where he still lives. In 1982 he graduated in philology from the Latvian State University, and subsequently worked as a translator for what is now the LETA news agency. He has also worked as a librarian, and as a journalist on the literary and arts newspaper *Literatūra un Māksla*. Since independence, and until recently, he has been Editor-in-Chief of *Pilsonis* ('The Citizen'), the organ of the Latvian Citizens' Congress. He now divides his time between writing and photography.

I Live as I Write and I Write as I Live

Suzanne Brøgger
Denmark

I can't tell you how I write – because I don't know how; instead I can tell you about my way of life, since in my case it is almost the same: 'I live as I write and I write as I live.'

I live in quite an inconspicuous place, one that progress has passed by, and I'm happy with that. Instead, perhaps, some god of tears was passing through here once, at the dawn of time, for it's a sort of desolate place, where both houses and tree-trunks are green with moss, moisture and tears. It's a humble place, one that you can find only on quite special maps.

Yes, it's quite an insignificant place, but when you look more closely, or open yourself up to it, it reveals secrets and unveils strange curiosities, just as a piece of skin is full of mountain ranges when you look at it through a microscope.

Instead of bread, I'm bringing you a stone. It's seven thousand years old and it comes from the centre of culture, Mullerup, which is an old kitchen-midden from the early Stone Age. You keep coming across stone axes all over the place, and everywhere the earth is littered with arrowheads.

I live only a hundred kilometres from Copenhagen by train – but thousands of kilometres away in time. I live in a swamp, where there's a mist on the ground – or, as we say, 'the bog-woman is brewing' – and I write books; which may amount to the same thing.

From my window I can see where the world ends. It ends on the other side of the river, over the hill; there's a Bronze Age king buried there, and a little further on there lives a bachelor of about 60. He's lived there alone all his life, and they say he's put a big rock on his armchair, one that he talks to and drinks a toast with when he has a snaps. He's very entertaining and sensible. I've met him twice in the course of thirteen years in the swamp. He isn't intrusive.

Five kilometres away – if you're a bird – is Trelleborg, the best preserved Viking monument in Europe, and perhaps the most mysterious? Is it a fortress? A prison for slaves? Or the centre of a cult? We don't know, but it's probably been all of those things.

Every week I take the train to Copenhagen where I have my piano lessons, and on the way home I pass a former town, where the earth is fat with Swedish corpses. They say that a farmer can't put a spade in the ground without bringing up a shovelful of Swedes. These are the bones of all the Swedes that died in the battle of Havrebjerg during one of the Swedish wars. I don't know if they lost or won, but dead they are.

At Løve, a couple of kilometres away, is the site of the old Thing, from where the region was governed. Today this old democratic stone circle has become a glamour-park with menhirs, where the names of the noblemen of the district are engraved and their portraits shown. Here lie farmers, parish officials and schoolteachers side by side without the slightest trace of humour.

At Løve the king kept his horses, so that was a resting

place. King Valdemar Atterdag in the thirteenth century. But ah! Hans Christian Andersen had no horses; he had to walk on his poor feet through Løve to Sæbygaard, where he was given lodgings, and, let us hope, was given a little attention and wasn't teased.

The place where I live was once, in the early Middle Ages, a royal castle, and from here the Lady of Løve ruled over the peasants, at the same time as the building functioned as a fortress against the enemy. Down in the left-hand corner of my garden you can ascend the remains of an old tower, which today serves as a look-out post, if the hawthorn hedge hasn't got the upper hand. It needs persistence to keep it down, that hawthorn hedge; otherwise you run the risk of falling asleep for a hundred years.

It sometimes happens that a group of local amateur historians knock on my door to dig for a royal sword among my potatoes. 'That's quite all right,' I say, but so far they've found nothing but potatoes.

I no longer live in a mediaeval castle, but the address is the same, and it is not without satisfaction that I receive letters from the wide world with the short and pithy address: S.B. Løve.

I have written a little book about what it means to live in Løve, and if it had been translated into English the title would have been precisely 'Love from Løve'.

The house I live in had later become a rural school. Now it is closed down, and the building is a good hundred years old and has 28 windows. I'm always meeting people, like the painter and the carpenter, who laugh when they visit me, because they went to school in my house and know every corner, almost better than I do, and then they ask me, as a joke, whether I can teach them something.

In those days there were only two classes, one for the big

ones and one for the small, and they went to school either in the morning or the afternoon; the rest of the time they had to stay home to help on the farm. They had to lend a hand at the school too, for the teacher was always sending the children out to weed or cut firewood – that was part of the teaching. Isn't that what they now fashionably call 'integrated education'? The school was closed down some time in the fifties, when they were centralizing the country and the whole process of depopulating the countryside in favour of the towns was gaining ground. But at the same time there was a counter-current, of more or less marginal people who felt they could no longer stand the nuisances of the city, moving out to the country, often as collectives, and they now took over the old institutions that had closed down. Nowadays the old village schools, homes for the aged, workhouses, dairies, mills and stations are inhabited by artists and swindlers – all sorts of people who are not necessarily dependent on a particular line of work, and are therefore slightly different from the old rural population. It is by no means uninteresting to see how this social life develops among people with quite different backgrounds.

Knudstrup was once a proper village, with a school, a shop, carpenter, smithy and mission hall. Now it's just a little handful of people who have nothing in common other than living there in the swamp. But that isn't so little either!

Diagonally opposite lives the cat-maker. If he had only ten cats we would call him the cat-man, but he has a hundred and forty cats – in cages – so we call him the cat-maker. He loves animals so much that big tears run down his cheeks when he talks about 'pussies'. But the mere thought of a cat slipping out of its cage fills his face with fear. He used to be a drunkard, but he lives so ascetically now – on one loaf of bread a week, which he bakes himself. And if someone gives him a chicken for some service that he's done – for he's very helpful at doing our hedges and so on – then he boils the chicken and gives it to the cats, and has the broth himself, which he can make last a whole week. He lives on welfare, but all the money goes on the cats, several thousand crowns a month.

On Reersø, a little peninsula in the vicinity, there live some more funny cats, and these are very rare, because they have no tails! It is said that the tailless cats can thrive only in Reersø; otherwise they die. They originally came from the Isle of Man. A ship from the Isle of Man sank, but all the tailless cats swam ashore and since then have not wanted to be moved, even though the health authorities come and say that tailless cats shouldn't hang around the inn when there are guests. But the people of Reersø, like their cats, are too proud to take orders. They still talk about the time the King came past on his way to Kalundborg, and after the King had washed his hands he dried them right in the middle of the towel. The innkeeper's wife got so annoyed at the King drying his hands in the middle of the towel instead of using the edge that she gave him a proper tongue-lashing. Shortly afterwards, so history tells us, the King sent the innkeeper's wife twelve new towels.

But I mustn't forget to tell you about my own cat, The Empress, the tyrant of the swamp, with her tiger-eyed charm, fourteen years old, a sovereign named after the Empress of Persia, la Shahbanou. Since the fall of Iran, there is only one Empress left in the world, and she lies on my velvet bed, licking herself in the sunshine. She loves being on television; the spotlight is her natural element. Recently a history of Danish literature appeared, with a picture of la Shahbanou with the caption: 'La Shahbanou occupies a prominent position in the author's works.' She purrs every time I read that bit to her.

Right opposite, on the other side of the main road, live my

neighbours, Axel and Signe. She is a housewife and he is a factory worker. For fourteen years I've drunk coffee with them at four in the afternoon, when Axel comes home from work. We talk about the animals – Signe looks after Shahbanou when I'm away – and look for new buds on her potplants. Sometimes we discuss politics, but that's mostly Axel, for he's a raging Red, but lives an utterly conservative life according to the same pattern, year in, year out. He accuses me of being conservative, even though he thinks I live a wild life, against all the rules. When they'd read my autobiographical book 'Creme Fraiche', they just said: 'You have a lively imagination!' My way of living from writing books is something they don't appreciate. They just can't take it seriously. And when I come back from, say, Paris, and tell Signe about some television programme I've taken part in, she becomes quite distant, shakes her head imperceptibly about 'such nonsense', and looks out the window with her head on one side to find out whether the wind is blowing enough to hang out the washing.

For Signe and Axel, what counts are completely different qualities and norms in life: whether you can get the crackling to go crisp or the bread to rise, whether you can make a sauce that's neither lumpy nor curdled. Further, it conveys a certain status to make your garden neat and get things to grow without taking over.

It's typical of rural people that they actually don't care about nature.

'Shouldn't you clean up your garden?' or 'Try and get that bit of land cleaned up' they say, as if weeds were dirt or filth.

This last thing has been an ongoing controversy between us over the years. I would like to have a garden that grows wild, but Axel couldn't accept that. Everyday as he took a walk in my garden with his dog, he would always start criticizing a bush or a tree which in his opinion ought to be cut down or pruned. Gradually it developed into something almost sexual – in the mythical sense – between us: he was always the one to prune and cut, putting out poison for the moles and weed-killer on my gravel paths. It had become his function to keep life down and mine to make it grow – out of defiance. Experience has since taught me that both are equally important!

One's relationship with a garden and working in it are not romantic. It's a question of a physical relationship with life and death. Not just because one is dependent on pulling up a carrot out of the earth – . Earlier, I showed you eternity in the form of a stone. Now I want to show you transience in the form of a cranium that I found in my garden at Easter.

'Where did it come from?' I asked Axel.

'Ask the dog.'

It turned out that Signe had boiled some brawn for Easter and had put in my garden the remains of a pig's head, a real Easter gift. My garden has become a Golgotha, which in Hebrew means the place of skeletons or skulls. And if you think that sounds grotesque, then remember that Jesus required of his disciples that they should eat him. We call it the Holy Eucharist, but in a sense it is nothing other than the rhythm of regeneration based on the theme of life and death, which occurs in any garden, in any place where people gather round a table to eat and live.

Signe calls her husband 'my lord and master', and when she has cleared the window-sill of pot-plants so that la Shahbanou can take up her place like an Egyptian statue, and we are sitting with the retriever waiting for her lord and master to come home, listening to the clock ticking, it's so still. And if a car comes past, we sit for a long time talking about who it might have been and where the car might be going.

Her wedding ring is quite ingrown into her finger and is stuck so fast in the flesh that she can't get it off at all any more, even though she's lost the little piece of red glass that was her precious stone. Her lord and master would never agree to wear a wedding ring, for he says it's too impractical, that it would be in the way when he's working. He says he has a devil inside his body, but that he doesn't dare let it out, because his wife wouldn't like it. She doesn't want confrontation. Signe is always happy and content as long as he doesn't criticize her food, but he does, if she tries some new recipe from a women's magazine that's going around. Her housekeeping is a model of diligence and order. Axel shoots pheasants and hares in the bog, but all the other meat they eat she wins at cards. Her hands are never at rest, for that would be a sign of laziness. And last winter, after knitting three tops with beads and wings on them, she started a bit of crocheting.

'What are you crocheting?' I asked.

'It's something to lay the cards on.'

'Really?'

'Yeah, then you've got more control of the cards.'

Her pantry and cellar are full of jars and vessels with fine labels on them, preserved and pickled fruits and vegetables and salted herring. She would never dream of buying something ready-made or throwing a pig's-ear away, for you can always put it in a soup. It was from Signe that I took the title 'A pig that's been fighting can't be roasted'. During a struggle, enzymes are released which harden the muscles. Signe possesses plenty of that – forgotten wisdom. People didn't particularly care for that book, even though Signe was proud that it said she'd won a lot at cards. Winnings always go on food and meat, and they have three chock-full freezers for two people. Food is the highlight in their life.

We have a friend in common, an old clog-maker, who has

been trying hard for the last twenty years to drink himself to death, but his heart is too strong.

The old rose-gardener was paralysed a few years ago from the waist down. His rose garden at Løve is famous all over Europe, because it cultivates the old roses. Modern roses can boast their beauty, but they have no fragrance. At Løve they cultivate the old roses of Chinese, Persian and Lebanese origin, and they are exported all over the world. The old rose-grower, who spoke fluent French, because he had spent part of his youth in France studying landscape gardening in the Versailles tradition, but who later lived modestly in Løve on porridge and gruel, had to retire when he became paralysed, and the nursery has now been taken over by an artist, a painter, who has become such an expert on roses and so enamoured of them that he actually handles them as if they were women. Last autumn I let him plant fifty old roses in my beds, and they're all named after famous queens and baronesses. But so that it wouldn't get too nauseatingly virtuous I put a few bastards and less decent mistresses among them.

My garden is surrounded by a hawthorn hedge and high trees and runs down a slope covered in violets to where the fields of barley, rye, or wheat begin. Cows also graze there, and I think it gives a quite special sense of luxury when you go for a walk and twenty cows come running delightedly toward you. I well understand the psalmist Kingo, who lived in the Løve district and wrote an ode to a cow. That cannot be done too often.

Apart from lilacs, wisteria, laburnum, jasmine, apple and plum trees, I have a big copper beech in my garden, to the right of the two rockeries. There are usually two nests here. Uppermost is a hawk's and below it a little wood-pigeon's nest. You could say: Uppermost is the Pentagon or the Kremlin, a nest of stones, gravel and concrete, and below it, the dove of

31

peace in its thin little nest of straw, grass and leaves. No sooner has she hatched her eggs than the hawk swoops out of the air and snatches them all. All the same she stays there, year after year building her nest under that of the bird of prey. So if the garden reminds you of life and death, you also come to think of futility. A bird of prey and a dove in the same tree; it can never turn out well. But it keeps on going.

The hens examine the ground for delicacies, doing their charleston steps as though they'd all attended the same dancing school. You can't help feeling sorry for them with such small heads – and wonder why their eggs are so big!

The garden is set out like an old school garden, with symmetry and order for the eye. And I'm now trying to continue with it in the same old style. But I have allowed myself a couple of frivolities, such as placing two stone lions in front of the house, a Greek goddess under the lilacs and a little white marble table in the opening onto the fields and the bog. The rose-grower gave me the idea, because he had seen such a table at a similar place – Holberg's at Tersløsegaard manor nearby. It's a good place for contemplation and well-being. Yes, it turned out to be a happy place, because one day I looked down at the ground and found an ancient Egyptian coin showing a sphinx and two pyramids!

I begin each morning by practising yoga. And after that – fasting on a lemon – I set about writing, which is only another form of yoga. Writing is an excellent ritual for training the concentration, memory and observation. It is an exercise of the capacity to dream and associate, and not least a training in truthfulness. For I agree with Saul Bellow, that one knows immediately if a sentence has come from the right layer of one's consciousness. If it has, it straight away begins to breed and flourish on the paper, in that it gives birth to and attracts to it a whole mass of other sentences. If it is a lie, or you write from a shallow place in your consciousness, then sooner or later you go stale and can write no further. Sometimes this morning ritual is a catharsis of tears and laughter. In any case it is an extra dream dimension to everyday life, which allows a person the rare privilege of bathing twice in the same river. Still I wouldn't attribute to 'writing' any greater importance than to baking bread, knitting a shawl, planting asparagus, or playing the piano.

I read quite a bit. As a rule, one book a day. At the moment I'm studying Tibetan Buddhism, because at some time in the future I might go to Tibet. I subscribe to various magazines: The New Yorker, The New York Review of Books, and Revision, edited by Buckminster Fuller, Marilyn Ferguson and Fritjof Capra. I've cancelled my subscription to 'Literaturnaya Gazeta' because my Russian has faded, and I've given up reading French magazines because I think the French have overdeveloped their talent for blowing up balloons.

Nevertheless I travel every spring to Paris to let myself be irritated by the Parisian intellectuals, but actually to visit my friends, who unfortunately are French. But I've been corresponding with them in French since I was 16.

I try to include a poor country in my travels every year, for I think it distorts your perspective if you only travel in rich ones.

This autumn I'm going to Turkey, where my first book, *Deliver Us From Love*, has appeared and is much discussed in the Turkish papers.

In the summer, I have several guests in my garden. Sometimes I have the feeling it's like Epicurus' garden, where one 'laughs and philosophizes'. 'Bene vixit bene latuit' – he who lives in obscurity lives well – said the same Epicurus. But

33

I feel I live in a state of withdrawal which is not separation. For as I see it, through contemplation I live in freedom and in peace and in connection with the world.

In the winter I have a 'salon', in the red room, to which I invite a few friends. I might also think of inviting people I don't know. But we are never more than the Muses or fewer than the Graces, that is, at least three, at most nine, people. Before lunch I serve elderberry juice from the garden with snaps or tea with rum, for they go so well with the sounds from the stove. After that the guests each have five minutes to present what is currently in their hearts or on their tongues or on their minds: a song, a shanty, a fixed idea, a dream, a dance, a recipe, a challenge, a thought or two – And five minutes silence is not to be sneered at either. It's my experience that when the guests themselves have been asked to contribute, then a specially intimate and intense atmosphere arises around the table, because no-one feels excluded, people get to know each other better, for everyone has their turn to introduce themselves and be present, and all have received attention. Attention is the real thing that's missing these days.

At my last 'salon', which I held just before I went to America and immediately after my return from Iceland, where I'd been reading my epic 'Tone' to the Vikings up there, I'd invited an incarnated lama from Tibet, Tarab Tulku, and three female friends whose common experience was that they had all just come home from India. My sister, who is an anthropologist, has been living for half a year among the hill tribes of southern India. Another had just come home from a freezing Gandhi ashram in the Himalayas. I also sent an invitation to Klaus in Cairo, where he was clambering around the pyramids. Still he managed to reach Løve in time. Nini is a psychologist, at the moment working in Norway, where she is doing research on security precautions at atomic power

34

stations. Laurits was a Dominican monk in Paris until he revolted at the monastery during the cultural revolution of May 1968. He is occupied with and knowledgeable about so many different things that I will content myself with calling him an intellectual catalyst and guide. Finally I had invited Mischka, who calls himself a Sufi, and who had come back to Denmark after spending a few years in America and Puerto Rico. His contribution to the 'salon' was to teach us all belly-dancing.

I bet we were the only people in the neighbourhood doing belly-dancing that morning!

But afterwards we ate roast pork, and I wouldn't be surprised if in that way we were following the same ritual as most others in the district: eating pork for Saturday lunch.

We were both a part of our environment and at the same time very alien. And perhaps one could say that it is typical – not only of me but of Scandinavians in general – that we don't live on the basis of Either/Or (Kierkegaard has never been accepted as a prophet in his native land), but on the basis of Both/And. We are quite a small people, which has kept its distinctive features – even its language! – while at the same time being open to world culture. That's apparently how it's been since Viking times. And this Both/And is not necessarily an expression of compromise, but an instinctive knowledge that there are many realities to be taken into account and profited from. Perhaps that isn't a specially high-minded, idealistic attitude, but rather earth-bound and pragmatic. That attitude is also reflected in our economy, which is both capitalist and socialist. It is this Both/And that one might call the 'Scandinavian solution'. In my own life it finds expression in both living in obscurity on the local level in a mini-society in which I participate, and feeling a part of world culture.

One might also call it an 'aristocratic' solution – both living in the country in a pact with nature and in towns as an exponent of culture.

But it also feels like an 'erotic' solution, because my life is not based on marriage, family or other exclusive models. Instead I am nourished through the more 'inclusive' *Wahlverwandtschaften*, as Goethe called them. I have connections, but without conditions. Perhaps that is in fact a 'poetic' solution – to belong everywhere and nowhere.

Anyway, it's not a solution at all, but just a way. My way.

1 April 1983

The Man Who Created Woman

Svend Åge Madsen
Denmark

'There are admittedly various obscure points in the story of Vero, the man who never once in his life met a woman, but who must be considered the source of some of the most beautiful descriptions of love the world has ever seen. However, by uniting the undisputed facts with the most fortunate guesses and charming additions it is nevertheless possible to create a coherent story out of it.'

The woman sitting opposite me was silent for a moment. She looked closely at me. Slowly she drew her hand across her lips, flashed a smile at me and began her story.

'The setting for the first episode is bay after bay of bulging shelves characteristic of the huge library. It is an autumn day many years ago. A few rather faint sounds seem to be coming from the books; otherwise that heavy silence reigns which is peculiar to illustrious old libraries.

Two rather unusual people were going around searching and hesitating, afraid to disturb the established pattern. It was the young man, a weaver who had as yet not completed his training, who was most embarrassed at the situation, forever stroking his short, refractory hair. He had a receding chin and wandering eyes, and his hands were sweating. The girl, heavy and uncomprehending, followed in his footsteps. Pregnant she certainly was, but no one knew how close to her delivery - too late had the young couple begun to concern themselves with what was fermenting in her stomach and causing it to distend. When the more imaginative versions of the story tell us that the girl had got into this condition without the assistance of the man, this is doubtless a spill-over from another well-known myth; this detail appears to have no foundation in fact.

The couple scarcely knew why they were in this place. In their distress, however, they had been persuaded to accept the claim that the solution to all problems can be found in books. However, they had not envisaged there being so many different problems as the number of books seemed to indicate. There they stood without any idea of where to begin; to read right through all the books was obviously an insuperable task. All around there were librarians standing motionless behind counters, but they couldn't address themselves to them. Naively, then, they allowed themselves to be attracted by the reddest spine, but on closer examination this turned out to be outshone by another one further away. But now their eyes alighted on another yet more exciting shelf. With a series of rapid, jerky movements the young man made his way deeper and deeper into the forest of books, lost his way, found new possibilities, enthused, was disappointed. Patiently gawping, his vital burden lumbered after him.

When the violent pains overwhelmed the girl they were in a distant corner of the building where people seldom ventured. The young weaver considerately led her into a convenient cubicle. Before long the pains merged with the distended stomach and turned into a child.

38

The two grown-up children looked at the alien being to which they had given birth, the girl in despair, the boy scared on account of the stain they had left on the august floor. Meanwhile, their long association with books had resulted in a certain eloquence on the part of the weaver, and without any difficulty he persuaded the girl to get up, and as soon as she had found her feet again they fled from this collecting ground for all learning, leaving behind them the consequences of their ignorance.

The story could well have ended here, for it really was a place abandoned by Man in which the child had laid itself down. The room was filled with books with damaged bindings in need of repair, and the general pressure of work meant that there were no immediate prospects of improvement. It must be considered a miracle that the child was found while still alive.

The librarian responsible for this corner of the collections was a middle-aged woman, sere and unmarried, and with few friends. One curious feature about her was that she looked just as though cut out of cardboard - a hunched, angular figure with a pointed nose. Although she had spent most of her life in the library, she had never managed to wrest anything but dust from the books. And so her amazement knew no bounds when she went into the broken bindings room and found on the floor a tiny infant which had apparently originated on one of the shelves.

The child's tears softened some of the cardboard, giving rise to certain hitherto unknown feelings. Almost immediately, the woman felt herself growing mightily, and she conceived the idea of keeping the child, of grasping this opportunity of enfolding in her arms a more living fragment of reality than those everlasting books. She was aware that she would lose the child if she declared it. So as to keep the thing she had found, she had to leave it in the safest hiding place imaginable, this

39

final resting place for mouldering volumes.

She made a bed for the child on the shelf where there was most space, and tended it with yet more care than she lavished on the other works, even if it must be assumed that she had already become so stiff and brittle by nature that she showed but few signs of affection.

It was under these distinctive conditions that the child now grew up, always shut up in that far-away cubicle, most of the time left to itself. At first the old woman was together with the infant as often as she was able, picking him up and imagining that that was how it would feel to enfold life in her arms. But it was not all that different from holding an untidy stack of books in her embrace, and soon the child grew so big that the cardboard arms had difficulty in lifting him. The woman's interest in this tender life was now limited to that of the observer. Now and then she would stand and watch him crawling about; later he toddled around; the child grew bigger and bigger, but she herself had no greater share in life.

The child appeared to thrive. He dragged books off the shelves and used them as toys. He explored his world, clambered up as high as he could, went all the way along the rows of shelves lining the room, teased all the secrets out of this strange universe. He built towering mountains of books, mountains which he only climbed with great difficulty, after which he slid down again with a squeal. He built houses of them, caves in which he could hide from the light; he spread them around on the floor and hopped across from one island to another. It is known that when he reached the highest point of his technical achievement he was able to plait them into each other so securely that the books could hang together of their own accord, allowing him to make a quite substantial bridge of them stretching from one row of shelves to another.

The book-nurse watched the boy at play, but she took no

part in it, for she did not understand it. She taught him to speak, but she did not talk to him, for she did not understand him, could not conceive of the fantastic world in which he lived, as her own consisted entirely of those prosaic books. She faithfully replaced the books on their shelves, brought food for the boy, and otherwise was content to observe him.

It is not clear at what age the boy began to take an interest in the black symbols he found in all his playthings. It is not even known whether it was the librarian who taught him to read. One theory, for which there is plenty of support, is that in his urge to understand everything in his world, the boy latched on to the differences between the symbols in the books, and by means of a quite stupendous process of deciphering slowly acquired the ability to read. Among the books on the shelf there were admittedly two reading books for beginners, but even if by some improbable stroke of luck the boy had come across them, they cannot have made things noticeably easier for him in his efforts to ascribe to the different combinations of letters a significance which he could only know from other books. Indeed, most scholars appear inclined to the view that the woman must have helped him to make a start on his reading, but they are in no doubt that he was left to his own devices at an early stage, as is indicated, among other things, by some rather odd misunderstandings.

The lad soon gave up using the books to form mountains and islands, as he discovered that inside them there were far more magnificent mountains and mysterious islands to be found. (It is known that for a long time he was deeply engrossed in the book about Robinson Crusoe). It is, of course, impossible to imagine what thoughts the child had on seeing such words as ship, sun or tree, but it is likely that on the basis of the various contexts in which he came across these words he gradually formed a fairly accurate idea of the nature of these things. Coming to understand this had a particularly strong effect on him, as he realized that the way in which he had hitherto been playing with books and exploring his limited universe was childish and misconceived, that the real world was to be found inside the books, that real houses, real mountains, real bridges existed there, and that in his play he had only constructed random unreal embodiments of things, the true existence of which were the concepts created by the words in the books.

As far as is known, he managed to get to know over half the books collected in his little, but tightly packed space, works differing greatly in character. He was particularly taken by a short story telling of a man who decided to dream another human being into existence; the condition of the book makes it perfectly clear that Vero returned to it time after time.

It was evidently not the librarian who first set him writing. By the time he had already read quite a lot he began to see himself as a kind of excrescence, a root sucker growing from the books (possibly a reminiscence of the early days when he had lain on a shelf), and he saw it as his task to become the root source of new books, perhaps because he believed that all the shelves in the room were to be filled, and there were still quite a number of gaps here and there.

On the basis of some of the books he wrote it is possible to gain an impression of the world view he formed in his isolation. Naturally, it is only with considerable reservations that his philosophy can be formulated in our language, but perhaps a summary and a translation of his reflections can give us some impression of the views he gradually evolved.

'The real world is this room, which I can traverse in a few steps. But it owes its status as the real world exclusively to the fact that it encompasses countless other worlds within its outer limits. Irrespective of which book I take and open, a new, quite different world will be unfolded, narrow and limited in its way in so far as it must be contained within the confines of the book, and yet truly colourful, populated by countless figures milling around, riding or sailing away, grieving or hoping, all on the assumption that their world is the real one, the proper world. And here I sit, the only person to know the truth. I can smile at the people in the books, talk to them, hear their dreams, understand their feelings, but there is one thing I cannot do: I shall never manage to convince a single one of them that the world in which he finds himself is not the real world. If I were to tell him that there was a totally different world just beside his, he would not even shake his head at my assertion, but without hesitation would leap on to his horse or dash up the stairs, or confront his opponent with his rapier, continuing the activity in which I interrupted him with my mis-placed superior knowledge.'

Vero, as he is called by one of the names he ascribes to himself in his books, was particularly interested in a certain type of account. Perhaps he might read somewhere that the heroine was sitting at her sewing table with her hands in her lap. Her eyes then fell on the book lying open before her. She began to read and was soon so absorbed in the story that she was oblivious of everything else. At first Vero's thoughts centred on what the heroine's book might be like. He tried to imagine the story she was reading, and what thoughts it instilled in her. At the same time he sincerely hoped - though he knew it was in vain - that the liberating thought might strike this woman that she could experience her place in another book, the one in which Vero was reading about her; that she might look up and glimpse Vero's world; that she so to speak might even step into the space in which he had his being. But of course this hope was never fulfilled; this woman, too, was obliged to have her being in the book which was her fate. Never did any of his fellow human beings from the shelves catch sight of him, their own reader; never were they able to step out of their own mini-world into Vero's sphere.

From other accounts it emerges that the solitary young man could not occasionally help wondering what it might look like outside his world, outside these four walls. He came to the conclusion that just as his world was garlanded by all his potentialities, all those fictitious worlds of his, so, too, in a circle around this, there must be the worlds of all his heroes and heroines, the tales in which they could allow free rein to their thoughts. These must be the sources of the faint, undecipherable sounds which he occasionally caught. But otherwise, these dreamlands were inaccessible to him. In this way he saw his world surrounded by ring after ring of ever more distant, ever more unreal universes, crust upon crust of fictions' fictions. In time he even concluded that the whole of this cosmos in some remarkable way turned in upon itself so that he, too, his life and his place, were a story told in another world.

It is quite strange to think that the fantasies in which this poor eccentric had to indulge in his isolation should come to preoccupy quite a number of scholars, and that in the course of time numerous theories have evolved to demonstrate that the world view which Vero developed in the worst conditions imaginable in actual fact was enormously far-sighted, indeed that it provides us with a much more comprehensive understanding of the state of things than the many conjectures formulated by scholars with all possible access to the phenomena of the world.

It is remarkable that nowhere in Vero's papers is there any mention of the old librarian. All indications are that Vero was quite unable to think of her as a human being; she was too far removed from the creatures described in his books for this. For him she was much rather a law, a principle governing his world, not a living being. When he let go a book it fell to the floor; in exactly the same way it was subsequently put back in its place. With the same regularity as hunger made itself felt, food was provided. Thus he experienced the woman as a quality with which the world was equipped, not as a being resembling himself. The word 'human being' was for him reserved for the people populating the book he was reading. It seems palpably incorrect to draw from this set of circumstances the conclusions arrived at by certain scholars. One believes that Vero was blind and therefore never saw the old lady, who on the other hand read the books aloud to him. This view is more curious than well-thought-through. Others have been of the opinion that the woman was of a quite unusual appearance, or that she never really entered Vero's room. But these attempts to explain away things seem to be superfluous; it seems quite natural for Vero to have come to the conclusion that all real things and beings were spiritual, immaterial concepts. When he became aware of the woman's physical presence, he must have thought of her body as something non-existent; she occupied the same place in his world as figments of the imagination occupy in ours.

In yet another respect Vero's way of thinking has been of outstanding interest to scholarship. As, merely by opening a book, he was able to place himself in the Middle Ages, and by opening another could move several centuries forwards or backwards, he was naturally led to the view that time, in our sense, does not exist, that all phenomena occur incessantly, that everything is contemporaneous. Of course, he had no reliable method of discovering an absolute point in time which he could call his own: on which book's publication date should he place the greatest reliance? No, his room existed as the sum of

45

all ages. In complete accordance with this view, and on the basis of precise calculations, the conclusion has been reached that if he had acceded to our way of measuring time, he would have been unable to achieve what he in fact did achieve.

Research continues to reach a detailed understanding of the world in which Vero lived, though there is no prospect of being able to gain the ultimate objective; it will never be possible fully to acquaint ourselves with the incorporeal, to our way of thinking, dreamlike existence in which he found himself, an existence far removed from this world of ours which is filled to capacity with cumbersome objects with which we are constantly in collision, even though we are really aware that they are non-existent, only a swirl of insubstantialities.

It was an unusual event that brought the story to light. One morning an elegant young woman arrived at the library. She addressed one of the figures behind the counter and asked to borrow a particular book. The librarian looked into it and was able to tell the woman that the library only owned a single copy of this work, and that it had been sent for repairs. The woman insisted, but the young librarian took his stand on the regulations and remained dismissive. Perhaps the woman was particularly stubborn, perhaps it was her elegance and self-assuredness that decided the outcome - at any rate the upshot was that the young man took her in to the Head Librarian, who was otherwise reluctant to be disturbed. An old man, he was writing some words in a little book as they entered, although he could scarcely see.

The woman explained her errand. The old man looked up in surprise, but was only able to see the outstretched hand with a ring too tight for the finger wearing it; the woman herself was lost in mist.

Tour Ticket

Oslo   Monday July 6, 1998

OSL-2 Norway's Viking Explorers

Please see Silversea Chronicle for departure times

SILVERSEA

'I remember the book. I set great store by it,' he nodded. 'The binding split, and so it has been put aside. But I have my own copy in my private collection at home. I would be delighted to give it to you; I am an old man and would like to know it is in good hands.'

Strangely enough, the woman refused the offer; she preferred to borrow the library copy, despite its poor condition.

'As you like,' said the old man. 'I will take you to the book. I am the person most easily able to find it. The lady in charge of that department died quite recently, and we have not yet appointed a successor.'

The Head Librarian went first into the room where the damaged books were stored. It seemed to him that there was something peculiar about the place, but he was not able to decide the source of this feeling. Perhaps it was the smell, which could not only be coming from the many old books. All the works were in their places, and as far as his weak eyes could determine, there was nothing in the room that should not be there.

On this point, too, there are two theories. Many tend to the view that Vero died in this cubicle of his (the cause can only be a matter of conjecture). The old woman then dragged out his dead body one night - she had her own key to the library - and buried it or threw it into the sea. Soon afterwards she herself died of grief at the loss.

But a group vigorously expressing the opposite view maintains that the order of events was the reverse. They believe that the woman died first. Naturally, Vero soon had to follow in her trail when one of the most important principles in his world ceased to apply. But at the time of his death he had become so incorporeal as a result of his constant preoccupation with fictitious beings that after his death he left very little in the way of a body. What the first theory contains in the way of physical impossibilities (the feeble old woman could scarcely unnoticed drag the dead body of a young man out of a public building), the second contains in the way of unreasonable assumptions in conflict with our wholesome belief in the indissolubility of solid bodies. And so it has also been maintained that the truth must lie somewhere between the two views.

As already noted, all the books were in their rightful places, and so the Head Librarian had no difficulty in finding the book he was looking for and handing it to the woman. It was, incidentally, the very book containing the story about the dreaming man by which Vero had laid such store.

As they were about to leave the room the Head Librarian's weak eyes lighted on a book which he did not think he recognized. He took it out, opened it and was amazed. It was written in a meticulous but strange handwriting which with great accuracy reproduced normal printed lettering. The Librarian did not know this book, and neither did the library catalogues admit to possessing it. Not even a thorough examination of the catalogues covering all publishers and libraries threw light on this work. The book was a short novel incorporating a young man's sensitive and hesitant praises of a wondrous, but distant woman, written in a dreaming language which seemed to have some difficulty in sustaining its substance.

Several critics immediately threw themselves over the book. They were fulsome in their praise of its incredibly realistic narrative. But the scholars only became seriously interested when yet another work was found in the same bay, but on a completely different shelf, and written under a different name. Here, too, the handwriting was meticulous, but far firmer in character, imitating a different print type. This book described the lonely poet who in some strange manner received visits from a woman who was portrayed in such vivid detail that readers could not help feeling that she was sitting before them. Despite the similarity in theme, it diverged notably in style from the first book to be found, so much so that it was difficult to believe they could both have been written by the same person.

Now a systematic examination of the damaged books was set in motion, and before long a considerable number of new and hitherto unknown works saw the light of day. Some of them were such deceptive copies of printed books that they were at first put back on the shelves because the researchers really thought they were printed. All in all sixty-two works were discovered, a few of which, however, were in several volumes. They are written under a large number of different names. Some of the authors' names appear on two or more works, and one is responsible for eight. They are written in different handwriting and in radically divergent styles. Similarly, the contents vary greatly, ranging from essay-like reflections, through historical novels to fantastic fairy tales. Careful research has demonstrated that none of them contain any words not found in any of the printed books in the room; likewise there are no styles not already represented in the room, and neither are there any sentence structures, elements of intrigue or genres not present there. And yet every one of these works is original and independent; the majority of them must without question rank among the major works of world literature.

The love stories are those which enjoy the greatest favour. And indeed, these are among the most masterly in the collection. They describe various aspects of love life, and a couple of them are even crudely pornographic - though these diverge so much in style that some leading critics doubt their authenticity, assuming that they must have been smuggled in while the examination of the room was still at an early stage.

Vero shows his supreme mastery in his portraits of women. There are portraits of every type, written with such a sensitive hand that most women really existing pale and seem unreal, dreary and vacuous in comparison with them. From this it can be seen that women in fact can only be described by people who have never met them, and that everyone else ought to refrain from the attempt.

As a result of the success achieved by Vero's female portraits it was not long before the most prominent women chose a specific character of his as a model and made an effort to behave, speak, dress and think as she does. They quickly achieved such assurance that they were soon able really to resemble their models, becoming the embodiment of an ideal. Woman after woman followed this fashion on discovering the beneficial effect the experiment had had on the first ones, and before long there was not a woman left as she had originally been created; they all went around as the corporeal shadows of a lonely man's fantasies.'

The woman fell silent. Throughout her long story I had scarcely noticed her presence, merely let her words pour over me. She smiled at me with a look which I was unable to interpret.

'Do you think – ' I said hesitantly. 'Do you think it is this man who has made all women so distant, so unapproachable?'

I had sat silent through her account, fascinated by the unreality she was disseminating. Only slowly did I begin to collect myself. It was some time before she replied; it was obvious that she, like me, was trying to retain the story.

To give her time I elaborated on my views. 'I often have a feeling as though women are quite ethereal beings totally beyond my grasp. Even if I am sitting opposite a woman, as I am with you now, I feel as though she is not there at all, that it is not her herself I can see, touch, talk to. She is a name, a body, a smile, a movement, a few words. But when I stretch out my hand it is nevertheless not her I touch; when she answers me, the words don't come from anyone, but are only present in space.'

'I think it is only you who feel that way,' she replied. 'It has doubtless had its effect on women that they have had to live up to Vero's ethereal descriptions of them. But I am of the opinion that he has given them substance, colour, different forms. Were they not paper thin before he brought them to life in his unique way? Only now have they become ordinary beings, firmly planted on the ground.'

I had to agree with her. I studied the hand she held out to me and noticed how tight her ring had squeezed the skin on her finger. Once more I felt her presence before I slowly closed the book and allowed her and her story to live on in her own world. For a time I thoughtfully contemplated the red book with the tattered binding into which she had disappeared.

With my usual care I put it back in its place, looking around in the little room to see what changes her words had brought about.

Suddenly I am overwhelmed by a terrible shock. For a brief moment it is as though I can feel the eyes which are reading me, the hand turning over the pages in my story. I feel like a little word in a narrative, feel the story encompassing me. Am I smiling, or am I shouting as I feel the pages pressing close upon me as my book is closed?

If it really was a film

Dorrit Willumsen
Denmark

The most embarrassing thing about it is that they're always looking at him that way. And talking about him. Sometimes as if he were some sort of major figure. And sometimes as if he weren't there at all. They call him: the accused, the lodger, swindler, violent criminal, husband, thief. They run through his days, backwards and forwards on a spool. As if it were a film they're not really satisfied with. And as if there's something they're trying to put right.

But it's not just that that makes him uneasy. It's their movements as well. Their crabbed way with clothes, hands, bags, skin. A strangely stuffy, yet solemn bearing they have.

Sometimes they also try to drag words out of him. And sometimes he really does speak, because otherwise the pauses would be far too long. But he doesn't care about that.

If only the judge would stop looking directly at him, just for a bit. If only the defence and the prosecution would just stop referring to him so openly and demandingly. If only he could sit in a soft, dark room, with velvet chairs and a fine, smooth screen, on which everything happened.

If it really was a film. How simple and easy it would be. For it is in fact films that he likes most. The cosy, protective darkness and the women, so beautiful, so delicate, so moving. And they do everything. Much more than he could imagine. And they don't object to him watching. They're never offended. Not even when he talks to them.

Once he simply whispered to Catherine Deneuve that he thought she had ugly legs. And she didn't respond with a single acid remark. She just smiled – a little, nervous smile. Then she walked in amongst tall subtropical plants. Haughty, thin-legged and beautiful.

In fact he's never been unhappy with anything on film. Perhaps the action wasn't always to his taste – but then he would just close his eyes and let it go off on some other track. And even on the unhappiest days, he's never had the slightest trouble with Sarah Miles or Charlotte Rampling. He's looked them in the eye without blinking, without having to apologise for his appearance, his breath or the faint but unmistakeable smell of sweat.

Apart from that, not much has been a success. Not even his marriage. But he always remembers how she looked.

She packaged layer-cake bases. Her sheepskin coat was greasy at the neck. She never shaved under the arms. They had a car and a two-room flat with a toilet on the landing.

They took turns in buying something quick to take home. They would eat at the kitchen table. She would stuff her mouth as though she wanted to eat with her fingers. Afterwards she would sit for a long time with her elbows propped each side of the plate. No children, luckily.

They would read the sex-problem letter page together. Especially her. She'd read it aloud. Slowly and clearly, as if it were a lecture. It didn't mean much to him. There were no pictures. She would furrow her brow while she read. There was something angular about her elbows and legs. And something southern about her hair and the fur bristling in her armpits. She herself wasn't actually that much inclined to sex. If they did actually have it, it was always in the same position. The missionary position. As far as he knew she wasn't religious in any other way. Her knees poked obstinately up toward the ceiling.

But she didn't love him any more, she said, one evening when, just for once, she sat knitting. The needles clicked up and down.

Deep down he thought she never had. All the same, he jumped up and went to the kitchen cupboard. He took the bottle of snaps down to the car. As far as he could see, she went on with her knitting.

First he drank a little. Then he drove out to the harbour and stood there, glaring. The water looked strangely dull and half-dead, with oil-slicks and rubbish.

Yet it made him sentimental, filthy or not. There was something about water. Cold, fluid darkness. And you could die of it. He saw himself in slow motion. Jump – no, more likely slide, over the edge – and down, deep down. As if in a dream. Small clear bubbles of regret on the surface. A cry, locked inside the water. A secret, closed up within his body. He hurried back to the car and drank most of the bottle.

Perhaps she was still sitting there knitting. Or tapping her teeth with the needle. Thoughtful – with tears running down her cheeks. 'Don't love you any more.' No – tears were not her style. Only when in physical pain. The time she hit her knee. And the time she was stung on the thumb by a wasp. It was his fault, she said. He had hit out at it.

They had never been happy together. Not for long.

He drove. While everything was quite calm and clear in his

head, the car, with a fine gliding motion, drove up onto the pavement. One or two frightened shadows cried out and pressed themselves against the buildings.

He found a parking space. He wanted to stop. But something happened. There was a sudden crash and a shaking. There was a darkness and a great stillness within his head. A soft fall through round, swaying rooms. And something warm ran down over his throat.

And out of these swaying rooms. Out of the soft, dizzy darkness came the image of Helle. Something gaily illuminated. Something pinkly glimmering, something amused and warm, and pale blue near-sighted eyes behind pale blue glasses.

He could still drive. He and the car, they were invincible.

He rang at Helle's door. He also rattled the letter-box a bit. She came out, barefoot and heavy with sleep, in something of transparent pink that clung to her body. It looked as though she was walking into a red spotlight. Her hair was damp with sweat. She held her watch up to her nose. 'It's half-past two,' she said. And her pupils were surprisingly dark.

He tumbled in against her. In an embrace, or a fall, they rolled onto the carpet without really hurting themselves. The pink lace scratched his face. He was giddy, and all those sex letters ran through his head. She was full of orifices and sleep and damp pink skin. She had beautiful slender legs and little veins of delicate blue. He wanted to find her clitoris with his tongue. It would be pink – like a sweet. Somewhere. His glasses bumped against her knee. She had a soft, slightly stuffy smell. She began to fumble for his zipper with sleepy indecisive fingers. Her dog had woken up. It stood beside them, looking on. It was a big mongrel with wispy fur and a long lupine snout. 'She must do this often,' he thought. 'Since it doesn't bite or do anything.' Her cunt had long fur, like the dog. They tumbled onto a vase on the floor. The dog moved reluctantly.

The legs of his trousers became wet. He pushed the shards aside with his foot.

He turned toward her face. She let out a small cry. 'Perhaps she's having an orgasm,' he thought, with both wonder and relief.

'How do you come to look like that?' she said.

It was she who looked like that. He must have bumped her nose with his knee.

'Go and look at yourself in the mirror,' she said. They went out together.

It was him the blood was coming from. From his chin. A thick dark streak oozed slowly down his neck.

'You'd better go to casualty', she burst out, at once hysterically and practically.

She poured some Nescafé into a cup. He couldn't drink it.

'What did you really want from me?' she asked, when he was on his way out the door.

He didn't drive to casualty. Driven by a quite absurd curiosity he made his way back to the parking place. And it was overwhelmingly big and full of confusing white lines. The dizziness and nausea rose up in him again. Everything was slipping. And if it hadn't been for the owner and the police standing there with sharp, swinging spot-lights, he would have banged into the same car again from behind.

They took care of him.

They gave him three weeks in the can. Three stitches. And concussion. He lost his licence too. In a way, it made everything seem rather distant.

It was harder to begin again. After the dizziness eased off. After there was only a thin white scar. And after someone else had taken over his job.

Just finding a room. The landladies' suspiciousness. 'And not too much noise in the kitchen. And no socks in the bathtub. And not too many visitors.' And if he doesn't fall out with them straight away, he will in any case when they discover that he sits around the house all day. And that he eats without a knife and fork and keeps his shoes, sheets and socks in the same drawer. In the course of two months he lives in one yellow, one mauve and one grey room. He's flung out of the grey one because the landlady finds a woman's hair in the butter-dish. That's a lie. It's a hair from the middle of his own head. But he has indeed cut the odd pat of butter.

That day he's standing there again with his things in a blue shopping-bag. Light snow is falling. The cold makes him at once furious and depressed. He gets to think about his former wife, to whom he is in fact perhaps still married even now. Her secure life, barricaded by yellow cake bases and knitting-needles. Perhaps she still reads the sex letters pages aloud. He dismisses her. He has to start again. He's got to keep moving. That day, too, will be a sort of beginning.

Luckily a bus comes. He is so close to the bus-stop that he only has to run a couple of steps. He steps into the warmth and buys a ticket. Soft and secure, he is driven through the glimmering whiteness, without any actual plan. And he enjoys it, until he suddenly goes dizzy and hollow, and remembers that he hasn't eaten a thing since half past six this morning, when he buttered a dusty Dutch rusk with a pat of borrowed butter.

He gets off in an area of summer cottages. The snow is falling more thickly. There is already a thick blanket of it, squeaking under his shoes and hanging in clumps under the soles. He drags his feet onward. He turns his toes inwards. He is indifferent. No-one notices how he is walking. He sneaks around a bit, looking at the expensive, locked-up houses. Through the shutters he can see only darkness. The locks are substantial, and he fiddles with them without expectations.

Suddenly one of them gives way. 'For visitors,' he thinks; 'an annexe.' He finds a switch, and he is standing in a gigantic, ice-cold lavatory with showers and mirrors and gilded taps. In wonder, he cleans his glasses on a thick towel. Outside, he pushes against a spruce-tree. But it pricks him back, and tips a load of snow down onto him.

Later he finds what he must have been looking for. A lock with a fragile fastening. He eases the knife in, and the lock falls into the snow. He opens it. It's a doddle.

It's freezing cold. But what has he not heard about these houses. Cash. Cigarettes. Transistors. Fat, dark cigars. And perhaps a secret hatch in the floor, where you just stick your hand down among precious bottles. He lifts the carpet. And pulls out the drawers. Half a packet of Kings and 27 crowns in a matchbox. 'A middle-class house', he thinks, and sits down in the kitchen with a quilt and the cooker on at 250 degrees. He reads through old weeklies without distinguishing between novels and recipes. Every now and then there's a gorgeous woman in a thin bra. He gets impatient, looks around again and spies the freezer.

He's not really expecting anything special from it. He's never bought anything but pork sausages, spring rolls and frozen cod. But when he opens it, there is an orgy of great frozen lumps of meat, which he heaves out onto the floor. There are also packets of spinach, beans, liver paste and strawberries in plastic bags. 'Strange,' he thinks. 'They must be strange, to have all this. A road accident, a divorce or even a trip – it must be just about impossible with all that frozen meat.' Then he breathes on his hands a couple of times and flings some pork into the scorching oven. He tosses all the rest back into the freeze-box.

He walks around a little, with the quilt over his shoulders. He looks like an Indian in the mirror.

On the chest of drawers there are some photographs. Must be of the ones that own the house. Nice-looking people. Friendly, as far as he can see. Children, grandchildren, lunches. Wet bathing-clothes and laughter. Bottles and glasses. Well-fed hips and stomachs. They could have been his parents.

But he had his own mother. His elegant, single mother, and her gentleman visitors. Usually they'd hand him a crown and shut the door. But where was he supposed to go with one crown? He would wait outside. Finally she got tired of him always standing there. He was shuttled back and forth between her and an aunt. Once, when they were both tired at the same time, he spent half a year at a children's home. She had her life to live too, she said, on the couple of occasions she visited him.

The roasting pork smells a bit funny. He checks it. The plastic has melted off it. A dull white bubbly film is spreading over the baking-tray. Of course, he should have thought of unpacking it properly. But apart from that, it looks like a good, hot sizzling roast. He finds plates, knives, forks, glasses. There's something festive about this. If only he had something to drink. Roast joint with water. Roast joint with Nescafé. Roast joint with camomile tea. Roast joint with elderberry juice. That is what the house has to offer.

But what he wants is red wine, blackcurrant liqueur and snaps. It's Friday, he remembers. He has enough cash. And from the bus he had noticed the sort of phosphorescent light that might almost mean a supermarket.

But what if someone suspects? He looks at himself in the mirror. Supermarkets don't have suspicions, and apart from the quilt there's nothing unusual about him. He has another look at the roast. It looks almost ready. He sets the table for two, because somehow the table seems to invite him to.

Outside, the cold hits him harder. It's glassier than he had expected. But he's made up his mind. His shoes are leaky. But he wants to walk through the ice and glass. And afterwards there will be the warmth, the fat meat and the wine. He is blinded by the snow and believes he's going the wrong way. But suddenly he's standing right in front of the market. The doors open when his shadow falls on them, and he walks in among the washing-powder, stockings and fruit.

Luckily he's not alone. He follows a young couple with a shopping trolley. A delicate blonde woman in a long-haired fur. Wolf, perhaps. She stretches out her arms to all the shelves. She takes tins and meat, cosmetics, butter and nappies. Her lips are a shiny red. She has pointed canine teeth and a gold filling. She carries on lifting goods down off the shelves and putting them in the trolley, while the fur makes her movements shaggy and significant.

He walks just behind them. He is expecting all the time that the man will notice the mountain in the shopping trolley and say that will be enough. He sees her provide herself with six bottles of white wine and a half-bottle of brandy. Then he is distracted by his own purchases. A bottle of Portuguese with a screw-top and one of blackcurrant liqueur, which is on special. He glides up to a cash-desk where the girl has deep dimples. And it's over and done with.

The way back is easier. He has a following wind and he can follow his tracks. 'My tracks,' he thinks. 'As if they were something to follow.' But he is quickly back there. He wants to sit down soon with incredible amounts of steaming hot meat. He wants to eat and drink until he falls over. He wants to let himself collapse into bed and sleep heavily, numbed by food and wine. And too bad if he drops grease and hairs on the kitchen table.

There's the hedge. And the lamp in the narrow kitchen window shines cosily and warmly. He looks at his tracks. But suddenly there are three tracks: his own, which point toward him, and two strange ones. Two fresh new tracks, weaving in and out of his own. One pair of shoes is slightly smaller than the other. He stops. Before him he sees two figures, well wrapped up in scarves and coats. The man with a soft hat and the woman with an imitation fur cap pulled down over her ears. He doesn't believe it at first. They turn right at the low spruce-hedge and go straight up to the house without turning round. Just two heavy, lumpy shadows. Then he hears a sharp little cry from the imitation fur cap. But that is the only uplifting thing he hears. For he runs back to the bus-stop with a bottle in each hand. And those two – of course they'll go right in and plant their broad behinds on the kitchen chairs and eat up the whole roast. Embittered, annoyed and nervous. The woman would be nervous, anyway, and stare uneasily out into the darkness while she cuts the meat up, and drinks Nescafé or camomile tea with it. This last thought only occurs to him when he has seen that it's one and a half hours to the next bus, and not even a shelter. The Portuguese wine is bitter and icy cold. Still he empties it. He falls asleep in the bus, and wakes to find himself talking in his sleep with a thick, rough voice. At the last stop they shove him out. And there's most of a night to go until the cafeteria opens, and he can read the paper and begin to ferret about for a new room.

He takes the cheapest one, with a woman with wise, toad-like eyes and loose, brown-flecked skin.

'Partly furnished,' she says and points at a flat bed. 'Don't you have any bags?'

'They're in storage,' he says.

'Three months in advance,' she replies.

'One,' he says, and rustles his two hundred-crown notes a bit.

She smooths them carefully before they vanish into her apron pocket.

He says he's a seasonal worker.

'What sort of seasons?' she asks.

But he shuts the door and falls asleep immediately.

Three days later, he gets a job delivering newspapers, and he creeps out the door at four in the morning wearing a balaclava helmet and an imitation leather jacket.

By eight o'clock he's home again.

'You're like some sort of robber – you could almost frighten people,' giggles the landlady.

On some staircases he saves himself a flight of steps by crossing over the attic.

He runs along narrow crooked corridors, where everything is dusty and dry. In one place, the doves fly freely through the attic windows and breed, shit, coo and die. There's a fluttering and rustling of wings and beaks. And a stink of shit and eggs dropped prematurely.

In other places there are lumber-rooms. Rusty, frail locks separate him from boxes of cups and glasses, tattered books, copper ware, heaps of coke, prams, wash-stand frames, treasures and junk piles up together.

'Recycling' it says on the front pages of the papers.

'Recycle' throb his feet, as he runs down the stairs.

He knows those attics inside out. He knows where the switches are. Where the exits are, where the nooks are to hide in, if anyone comes. 'The evening,' he thinks. 'The evening will be safest.'

He chooses a lumber-room where a transistor can be seen through the chink. In the morning he takes note of everything. Sober and clear.

But it's different in the evening. Even on the steps, his heart is fluttering like a bird. And even though he's wearing rubber boots, there's a strange, lively squeaking in the wood around him.

Only when he stands before the lumber-room does he feel safe. His hands are not shaking. The knife loosens the hinges quite easily. He pushes the door open, and the torch picks out the objects in the dark. The transistor, a gas mask, a meat-safe, a pile of newspapers. The objects get very close and significant, and he touches them one by one, very softly, as if to reveal their essence. He is going to sneeze. Three – four – five times with his hands pressed against his nose. He feels giddy and is about to run away. But he turns off the torch and forces himself to remain standing in the close, living darkness. And no-one comes running to investigate his intrusive sneeze.

He quickly stuffs the transistor down into a nylon net. He also takes a candlestick which might be made of silver, and a little blue plate.

When he is standing on the street, he feels a kind of relief, which for a moment he confuses with a good conscience.

At home, he tries out the transistor. It works.

'Well,' says the landlady, 'it's got quite homely. You've got some music.'

She invites him to coffee.

The blue plate and the candlestick earn him 30 crowns with a second-hand dealer.

Standing there with the money in his hand, he feels for the first time in a long while a sense of having succeeded. Later on, it becomes a habit.

Two times a week. And never at weekends. In the mornings he picks out a loft. At eleven in the evening, just as the midnight film showings are going to start, he slinks out. His landlady is a heavy sleeper. He can hear her thick, heavy snoring. Snoring like a toad, muffled under an eiderdown. She is hard of hearing too – perfect in every way. He makes a present to her of a vase of lilac-coloured glass and a white porcelain dog, for which he can't get anything anyway. She

63

takes hold of it with broad, gentle fingers. He had never even thought of wrapping it.

Gradually he learns what is worth taking.

One night, he takes a box of fragile old glasses, wrapped in newspaper. He doesn't take a single wrong step.

'Where did you get all that from?' says the second-hand dealer, looking curiously at him with reddish eyes in a fine mouse-like face.

'- My mother -' he says. 'She didn't want it any more.'

Cautiously the dealer unpacks the glasses and looks at them against the light. He puts them on the table, as carefully as if they still contained wine.

'If your mother's got any more like this -'

Those glasses bring him 300 crowns.

The summer is heaving with heat. Buzzing flies, thick grey dust and midnight film-shows. He can afford to sit in the pavement restaurants and drink cool draught beer. He goes to cinemas with air conditioning. He walks in light clothes. In the afternoons he carries a grass-green towel in his shopping-bag. In the park, he carefully takes off his clothes and lies down to read magazines. Occasionally he eats at a cafeteria or a grill. He looks at the girls. Their thin T-shirts and their long smooth legs. He sniffs the odour of their lotion and shampoo.

He expands his territory. In a suburb where he has never so much as delivered a handbill, he fetches 50 French preserving jars. It's a game. He carries them down two by two. He has to take a taxi home. It's foolish and wild. He gets 100 crowns and goes off to Sweden in the afternoon. He gets drunk and touches up a girl with small Swedish breasts. He doesn't understand what she says. Otherwise everything is in order.

It's towards autumn when he gets carried away.

He sees an attic filled with tools. A chain-saw. A drill. Heavy, hard things. He's seen in the papers what that sort of stuff is worth.

He goes for two weeks without taking anything. He gets restless and can't get to sleep. Every time he shuts his eyes, all those valuable tools appear before him, shiny and dangerous as a hook pulling him back up into daylight. And he gets up. He walks around the streets to tire himself out. He looks at the couples clinging to each other. He sees a very tall girl, almost transparently pale. Dressed in tight-fitting cowboy jeans and a worn leopard-skin jacket. She walks like a beast of prey, sinewy, slender and muscular. He goes past her quite close. Her jacket is open. Her blouse is of glistening black. Her belt is a dog's collar. He tries to catch her eye. But she walks on. As unapproachable as a billboard.

He has neither his torch nor his knife with him. But he can't wait any longer. It must and shall be now. He rummages in his pockets. The comb. Perhaps he can use that. Anyway he just wants to sneak up and see. Just see one more time. That will make him more certain when it's serious.

He turns the corner. He moves purposefully, paying no heed to people or facades. There is a thumping inside him as if it were the first time. Then the kitchen stairs enclose him in darkness, soft and soothing. There are only his almost noiseless steps. And way above him, the wind, whistling through the cracks in the roof and the small rustling sounds of the pigeons. He shoves the comb into the lock. It gives way, willingly and gently. The door opens almost by itself. And the chain-saw and the drill are overwhelmingly heavy in his hands.

He doesn't turn on the light when he goes down. Perhaps that is what's wrong. He is used to light and fragile glass. But the weight of the tools makes him uncertain. It seems to grow in the dark. It's too big, too cold and too smooth in quality. For a moment he supports himself against the wall. He begins to count the steps. That's what goes wrong. If only he hadn't

65

counted them. If only he hadn't counted on six and been surprised by the seventh. He stumbles in the dark. He twists his ankle, but gets up and continues. Then it's suddenly light all around him. Blinding and white. It cuts into his eyes, right into his head.

'What the hell!' says a gigantic man.

And the chain-saw falls down the steps with a deafening crash.

The man presses him against the wall and says nothing more than 'What the hell', as he glares at him, as if he were some kind of strange insect that he is irritated at not being able to kill properly.

The rest is just routine. Almost a relief, when the giant's wife gets the police. In the car, he can breathe.

He's done this before. But that time he was almost numb. This time everything is quite clear. The steel comb. The light. The saw that fell down the steps and the drill that he was idiotic enough to keep holding onto. No matter how hard the giant pressed him.

He is ripped out of his darkness. Up into the cold smooth light. He sees a man at a desk. The man looks healthy and sunburned. He must have a wife, children, a flat. Perhaps a house – a car – a pension.

The man looks at him. Much more kindly than he feels he deserves. And it's easy to confess about the drill and the saw.

The typewriter rattles it down.

'But there must have been other things – what's your speciality?' It sounds almost polite and interested.

'French preserving jars' -

'Address?'

If only he himself had such a perfect nose. Such light, smooth, glossy hair. Such confidential eyes, without structural faults. And then that height!

'And you were in the vicinity between 2300 and 2330 hours?'

He sees no reason to deny it. The man smiles, as if they were somehow friends. Or at least as if they could be.

'You know Miss Marion Levinsen?'

And it's easy. It's like that time with the car. The same twinkling giddiness and slackening. Of course that must be her name. She comes towards him, walking like a fine, tamed beast of prey. With her delicate nose up in the air. With her tight, tight trousers. Her platform boots, which make her walk artificially provocative and troublesome. Weighed down, even though she is light. She is transparent and hard, like a piece of glass. Cool, slender and delicate. The long slim neck, lifted high above the worn leopard-skin collar. The bleached blond hair with an artificially phosphorescent glow. Raw. Brittle. Beautiful. With dark, half-opened lips.

'It was you who killed her. The theft of the drill and the chain-saw was just to create an alibi. We'll overlook the preserving jars.'

That must be it. Once again he sees her before him, with the dog-collar around her thin, fragile waist. An ice maiden. Stretched out. Cool. Without desire. Without sweat. Without sticky pink tinges. Without movements. With her arms stretched over her head. With smooth armpits. Fleeting dark shadows around the eyes. Long, glossy, reddish-brown nails. And otherwise white. White translucent bones under white, delicate skin. The clear outline of the hip-bone. The dark hollows over her collar-bone. Blows against her loins. Teeth in her breasts, in her bitter white skin. The moth-wings of her lips. A moment trembling in the light. And she is gone.

'And there have been others?'

There is a strange air of confidentiality that he must make himself worthy of.

Helle emerges from her pink light. The Swedish girl's breasts. His wife's monotonous schoolgirl voice, women who scream in films and then, with a quite simple and well-executed movement, become quite still.

The man is looking at him all the time, interested and without reproach. And he talks and talks, until his brain is empty of images, and he is led away.

The cell is not that much worse than his room. But he feels worse. The regularity of the meals is tiresome. He skips some of them and gets thin. All the happy people are outside. Outside, they're still driving buses on the streets. Outside, the old broken sound of the transistors continues. And any time you like you can slip into a cinema and find a glow of success and luxury. Or you can buy a beer at a pavement restaurant and just for a short while feel elevated above all those going by. He yearns to get out. He longs to get on with things.

He hopes to be summoned to the big desk.

One day a defence lawyer comes.

'I don't believe you,' says the lawyer, looking at him with mild reproach. 'I believe you want to deceive us.'

He is just about to say that he doesn't care for that tone. But on the other hand he doesn't want the man to go either.

The lawyer's pullover has come unstitched a bit at the edge. It occurs to him that if he were very cautiously to take hold of the little thread and pull, while the other one looks straight ahead with his mild distracted eyes, perhaps he could unravel the whole sweater.

'You have admitted nine cases of violence. I've talked with your wife. With your landlady and one of your female acquaintances. They say it couldn't possibly be you.'

'What do they say?'

'Your landlady says you're a nice sociable person.'

'She doesn't understand a thing.'

'Your wife says you aren't capable of anything of the sort. Your former girlfriend says you have a problem you can't really put into words. As far as Miss Levinsen is concerned, no-one has seen you near her. And none of her acquaintances have ever met you.'

He's giddy.

'Withdraw your confession,' says the little insignificant man. 'You made a confession under duress or in confusion. You were out of your mind.'

'At the time of the crime -' he says, relieved.

'No,' says the lawyer, almost annoyed. 'You haven't done anything. You're just a very ordinary thief.'

One day, Helle comes.

She looks at him with round, gentle eyes from behind the fish-scales of her new contact lenses. She's put on weight. Her breasts are heavy under something clinging and pale mauve.

'The papers are writing such a lot of shit about you,' she says.

'What are they writing?'

'So much – But I don't believe any of it – I just think there was something you wanted.'

'What would that be?'

'I want to help you,' she says.

He looks at her too round, over-large breasts.

'Don't you think you put too much flour in the sauce?' he says. Later they fetch him.

They put questions to him while he sits right up in the front of the room with the little rustling noises of the public behind him. He gets a headache, as usual when he sits too near the front.

He hears the dry, tiresome voice of his defence lawyer, just calling him an ordinary thief.

They also call him: the accused, the lodger, swindler,

violent criminal, husband, murderer.

They contradict each other.

They roll his life backwards and forwards on a spool. His wife, his landlady and Helle are there. And he wishes they would turn off the light so it would just be dark and soft.

One day the defence lawyer gives him a picture of a blonde woman with dark lips and a smile at once reserved and hard.

'Who is that?' they ask.

It feels curiously flat in his hand. He doesn't know how to answer.

But he notices that they are longing for him to say something. So that the film can go on rolling.

He has the sense that everything around him is tense. He is like an arrow in a bow. In a moment he will say something. He will give in to the pressure and fly toward unknown landscapes. Unresisting and hard.

He has to say something.

Summer Rhapsody

Einar Maasik
Estonia

I

When Karl climbed bottom first down from the loft, the world was still in the twilight before the dawn. At some immeasurable height above his head the airy strips of cloud glowed pink, but the yard, the hedge of fir trees, the house, the fields and the distant rows of the forest were as grey as could be. It's good, the thought passed through his head, bloody good, that I got up so early. He had no more time to think; he was balancing on the ladder, keeping his equilibrium with one hand, with the other spasmodically pressing a black instrument case under his arm. The leather soles of his sandals were worn smooth from walking the dry, thorny forest paths, and any second he risked tumbling down.

Having got down safely after all, he leaned the violin-case against the rungs of the ladder, put on the coat he had thrown over his shoulders and sat down to do up his sandal-buckles. Dew had fallen in the night; the meadow of wild plantain and camomile glistened a dull silver, like fish-scales. Before I get to the main road, my feet will be squelching, thought Karl. But so what? The sun's coming up, it'll be as dry and warm a day as yesterday and the day before, my feet will get dry. Why abandon my efforts just for nothing?

He felt in his coat pocket for a piece of paper, took out a pen and wrote a rough message right away, leaning on the violin-case. It went, word for word, like this:

Õie!

Instead of wasting time arguing with Roobert I'm going off for a walk as long as he's here. I'm taking the instrument with me so when I get back I'll have pockets full of money. There are still accordion-players in a few villages but no fiddlers any more. I wouldn't have gone otherwise, but it upsets me that you even take your brother's side so much that you let him say nasty things to your own husband's face. If the boy's still got a cough, give him some lichen tea with honey mixed in. One of the men in our band said it's the best thing for a cough.

He drew a big K at the bottom of the letter, though there was no need to. In the small breast pocket of the coat he felt for a chewed-up piece of chewing-gum, pressed it between his fingers, broke it in two and pressed it into the corners of his missive. He crept down below the south-facing window of the house and pressed the letter against the pane. The room was quiet; the curtains were still drawn. Of course they were both still asleep - Õie and Mauno. Let them both sleep on - better that way, you can go without quarrelling!

You sleep too, Roobert - perhaps your bitterness will lessen while you're resting, and you won't be the only one who thinks you're human!

He took the violin-case off the ladder and set off up the former cattle-track in the direction of the village. The cattle-track was bordered on the left side by a stone wall overgrown with blackberry bushes: on the right was the cornfield of the collective farm. The heads of the rye were already starting to turn pale and droop. The heart of the summer is almost over, the best time to take a look around, thought Karl, as if to comfort himself. What if you do find yourself in some strange place at night without shelter - you can always find some haystack or clover-rack to nestle down in. You can still catch a fish nicely too, there ought to be enough rivers and lakes here in Estonia for you always to be able to stumble on one.

Karl hurriedly passed the abandoned dairy, the plaster on its walls glowing and the thin sheet-metal chimney stretching like a mast up toward the pink clouds. There were no people here but before him stood the village, the collective farm; he had to go through that before he actually got to the main road. They know him there and they're sure to stand around looking, saying look, there goes Oraku Liine's son-in-law with a violin-case under his arm. Karl thought it perfectly possible that they would regard him the same way as Roobert did - with a working man's healthy contempt for an idler and a grasshopper.

He increased his pace, and no longer looked so carefully in front of his feet; the spear-grass had made the legs of his trousers wet through, and his sandals were squelching. That Roobert, yes, his brother-in-law, schoolmate, old friend and ancient enemy... It wasn't because of the instrument that he hated him, that wasn't the reason why he'd started finding fault with him yesterday, that he'd come to get fat on other people's bread.

They both know how things stand, but when Karl spoke out about it yesterday, Roobert flew into a rage, his chin even started trembling and... he swore a lot.

73

'You might be grateful to me,' said Karl.

'What the hell for?' asked Roobert, a querulous tone in his voice.

'For not letting you escape across the bay.'

'Oh, to hell with you,' Roobert laughed maliciously, mockingly.

'I suppose it's because they threw me out of school. That they - bullied me - dragged me off to interrogations - That I did time in the nick?'

'Of course that's why... Now you're a top-notch worker, clean record. Even got your picture on the roll of honour at the plant. What would have become of you there? An empty ragamuffin! A refugee without a homeland.'

'A man like me!' Roobert laughed again, even more malevolently.

A man like me - that had been Roobert's slogan even then. Here they don't know how to appreciate a proper sportsman, but there... There they'll see what he's capable of.

He himself hadn't got outside the republic's borders with his own records. Megalomaniac, mad! Now he did his work spitefully, to show what sort of man he is. And it hadn't even got him... any further than the roll of honour at the repair works. The most ordinary men! The sickest kind of hatred! The most... everyday story.

And still Õie goes on defending her brother!...Karl got to the main road. Far off on the serrated ridge of the fir-grove a sliver of sun could already be seen, the world around him was starting to get more colourful, from somewhere among the trees the wind brought yesterday's air, which through the filter of the night had been cleaned of dust, but retained within it a hint of yesterday's warmth.

Karl leaned his violin-case against a kilometre-post by the side of the road and started waiting for a chance car.

II

'They're all Rooberts, one way or another,' thought Karl spitefully, when he had got up yet one more time, waved his hand in the direction of an oncoming car and sat down again by the edge of the ditch as it passed. There was not much traffic yet, mostly cars. At least that man in the Zaporozhets had looked at him and gesticulated with his hand - then he'd turned off at the bend between the fields. But the Volga rushed past him and the man at the wheel had pretended not even to see him. I'm a little grasshopper, why ever look at me?

Then came a refrigerated lorry, big, tall, a refrigerator like a wagon behind it. You can't get one of those just to stop like a horse - whoa there! Karl just sat there, but when the lorry drew near him and he noticed that the driver was looking at him, he raised his hand as if he were in a classroom having to answer the teacher. The truck slowed down, pulled in to the roadside and came to a stop twenty metres or so ahead of him. Karl grabbed his violin-case, and when he'd run up to the lorry, the driver had opened the cab door. 'Where do you want to go?' he was asked by a hoarse voice, a round swarthy Gypsy-like face with brown eyes. 'The main thing's just to get out of here,' said Karl. 'Hop in, what you waiting for?' he barked, and Karl perceived that here was a man used to giving orders. Not commanding, just giving orders. 'Put the case on the back seat,' Karl was ordered. 'And pull the door shut properly!'

After that the driver was busy with his lorry for a while and only when they were on the other side of the bend did Karl notice that he was being looked at.

'What sort of bloke are you?' asked the man behind the wheel.

'Human,' Karl replied.

'I can see that,' replied the driver. 'But there's every kind of human. Even thieves and scoundrels are human.'

'Is that so?'

'So you think there aren't?'

'Of course there are.'

'You see,' said the driver with satisfaction. 'You pinched some decent musician's instrument and now you're trying to get away as quick as you can. So you're human, eh?'

'It's my own fiddle,' Karl replied.

'If there's an instrument inside it, that is.'

'Why wouldn't there be?' answered Karl. 'If you want, I'll show you.'

'You can show me later,' the driver responded. 'But if the fiddle is your own, you ought to be able to play it.'

'I can play it, too,' said Karl.

The driver was following the road and paid no heed to Karl. Who knows whether he even heard what he said.

'So who was it you wanted to get away from so quick?' asked his neighbour unexpectedly. 'Wife upset you did she?'

'Almost,' answered Karl. 'That's almost it.'

'But not quite? Let's have another go. Of course, the mother-in-law too!'

'Mother-in-law too...' admitted Karl.

'There, you see? I know about life and people.'

'But you didn't get the main character in it all.'

'Is that right?'

'The main character is the wife's brother, Roobert. The others are what you might call the chorus, but Roobert's the soloist.'

'You don't say!' cried the driver, surprised. 'I've travelled around a lot, and I've heard all kinds of stories too. But always something new turns up. One long endless variety, this life!'

Karl agreed that life really is full of infinite variety.

'Why does it gnaw at your soul so much... ' asked the driver, not pesteringly, but, well, once you've started telling a story you might as well finish it. Karl had nothing against finishing it.

'He says I'm just a good-for-nothing grasshopper, see. Whether you're sawing at a bit of wood or a fiddle, there's a big difference in his eyes.'

'But there is a big difference!' cried the man behind the wheel.

'Well, yeah, but he thinks sawing wood is much more important.'

'Aha, now I understand. So he's a thick one.'

'He might be a thick one as well, but there are other things too.'

Karl wondered whether he should tell everything or nothing at all. Õie certainly wouldn't have wanted him to talk about family matters to a complete stranger. But he had a grudge against Õie, for one thing, and secondly, if you talk to an acquaintance or even a friend, you're gossiping; if you talk to a stranger, you pour your heart out... And Karl chatted even about the old things.

The driver listened and nodded, nodded and listened, his eyes fixed on the road.

'Well, you're a good boy for telling him, for saying what you think to his face. This brother-in-law of yours is stupid - where would he have got to ? Nowhere! I know that, nowhere. I was a border guard myself for a while.'

'Yeah, he wouldn't have. But how do you know what could have happened...'

'All sorts of things, of course...' agreed the driver.

'But now he calls me a traitor and who knows what else. Grasshopper too, of course... because of that old thing.'

'No matter what he says' - the driver was getting heated, so that his eyes even left the road. 'Grasshopper... well, that's a good one, that's the best thing about this. I love musicians and singers.'

'First you looked at the violin-case and only afterwards at me,' said Karl.

'That's right, that's it,' admitted the driver.

'But all that about it being stolen and me running away, you made that up to start chatting about it.'

'Right too! And why else! You see, some people are a bit closed-up like... You pick them up to make the time pass a bit quicker, to amuse yourself... I don't take money from passengers, on principle... But what do you get? Quiet as a mouse, got to pull a word out of their mouths with tongs!' He glanced at Karl, his eyes full of merry laughter. 'So you think, there's got to be some chip on this bloke's shoulder. So you give that a poke, and that sure sets their tongues going.'

'You sure got to the chip on mine pretty quick,' laughed Karl.

'That was no chip, that was a violin-case,' the driver retorted.

'Well let's get acquainted anyway, and if Fate wills it, we'll be friends too. My name's Vasya. But it doesn't come from Vasily, it's from Vasil. I'm from down there, between the Black Sea and the Danube.'

'Moldavia, you mean?' asked Karl.

'Moldavia or Bessarabia, as they used to call it in the old days. Anyway, what I do know is that it was a poor area and my mother was the poorest woman and she had the most children in the village and my Dad was killed by the kulaks. And that's the story of my life.'

Throughout this tale Vasya had been looking ahead, hands on the wheel; the traffic was getting thicker on the road and there was less time for talking.

'My name's Karl,' he said.

'Nice name,' said Vasya.

'Vasil's a nice name too,' Karl came out with a delayed compliment.

'Vasil...Ion...Stass...Veronica...Nadina... Ion was blown up by a mine, after the war, you know, everywhere was full of mines. Younger he was, the youngest of the boys, I was supposed to keep watch... But you've got to keep your eyes peeled all the time. You know, when I start to think about it, it hurts my soul even now. What can you do? Stass was a younger brother too - he served his time in Berlin. Stood on guard at the tomb of the Unknown Soldier. Suddenly some sort of bandits come up to him, take pistols out from under their coats and... cut my younger brother down. And for that too, my heart hurts to this day.'

'But how did you get here?' asked Karl, so as to lead the conversation elsewhere; he wasn't much of a comforter.

'With the army, see? Doing my time...' answered Vasya; in front of him was a sharp bend, he slowed down, steered a little to the left, crossed the centre of the road, and turned neatly out of the bend.

'I got to know a girl here. Name was Ellen. Well, I stuck with her;' - that is not what he said, but rather he specified what he meant by 'stuck'. But it didn't sound cruel or rough at all. 'Got two kids now. The boy's in eighth grade, the girl's in sixth grade. Anyway before I go off on a long trip, Ellen always cooks me a soup - our way, Moldavian-style. And the girl, Nadja-Nadina, takes the concertina and plays her little heart out to her Dad. Just last night - I was sent out of the house with a Pioneers' march!'

'That's really nice!' said Karl.

'Reckon I'd put up with all this otherwise? The journeys

I've got to make! The Caucasus, to my homeland, to Ashkhabad, to Tashkent! ... Two weeks at a time we're on the road. So then - there's got to be something warm inside you from home!'

'Something warm from home, yes, you need that,' agreed Karl somewhat ambiguously.

They were travelling through an Estonia that had woken or was waking up, and now and then they both looked attentively out of the window, following the roads, the oncoming traffic, those behind them, the commands and prohibitions by the roadside, the curves, and in places the corners of their eyes picked up other impressions: a group of horses eating in a pasture, a woman tethering a cow by the roadside, smoke coming from the chimneys of the houses, windows reflecting the sun, straight firebreaks disappearing into the depths of the forest. From all this something of the morning's freshness and calm poured into Karl's heart, somewhere deep within him a sort of quiet brightness began to take on life and expression, the anxiety of the morning before dawn evaporated into the winds, melted in the sun's rays, crumbled into the roadside ditch - among the roots, the burdock and the willow-bushes.

Vasya started singing. At first he hummed, then he started trilling, next came the words and the tune got going. His voice was hoarse, but he sang along with his whole heart and his corpulent body. They were unfamiliar songs to Karl, obviously from his childhood, emanating from somewhere along the banks of the Danube, the rhythm was different, more varying, faster; it reminded him of Gypsies, of herds of horses galloping across the steppes, the mountains... One melodramatic song which he heard for the first time stuck in Karl's mind. Vasil sang it somehow with a special nuance of feeling, as if it were for him, Vasil, of some specially deep, unique significance.

A young girl asks a man to take her with him far away and

start to call her his wife.

The man replies that he can't do that, because his wife is waiting there far away.

Then the girl asks him to take her with him and call her his sister.

The man replies that he can't do that either, because he already has a sister there far away.

So the girl asks the man to take her with him far away and start to call her his mistress.

The man replies that he can't do that, because there is no place for a mistress there far away.

As if he himself had some darling whom he wasn't able to take away to those distant places, thought Karl.

There probably wasn't - he launched straight into trilling the next one, which had nothing to do with its predecessor.

They were approaching the outskirts of the settlement of V.; up ahead loomed houses, a church tower, chimneys, and a whiff of smoke in the sky.

'Well, are you coming with me? Shall we go and see how the beauty of Minsk is getting on?' asked Vasil.

'No, I'd like to stay right here,' replied Karl. 'I want to go through Estonia and look around.'

'If you won't, you won't,' Vasil consented. He drove the truck to the side of the road and stopped. 'Now, get your fiddle out! One tune, that's all I ask!'

They got out of the vehicle, Vasya to stretch his legs, Karl with his violin-case. By the side of the ditch he took the violin out of its case, tried the strings, tuned them, took the bow in his hand, raised the instrument to his chin - and started playing, legs splayed, on the road. He wanted to surprise Vasya, and played a Moldavian tune he had heard from a friend.

He saw that the surprise hit home.

Vasya swayed his fleshy body in time to the music, his hands started moving, he stamped his feet; Karl bent over the violin, as if nodding with Vasya, his eyes glowed; he had never experienced anything like this before, a concert by the highway like this, with only themselves as the audience.

'Oh, boy that was good!' sighed Vasil. 'But perhaps you'll come with me after all? It's a shame to let you go. We'll ride along, I'll tell you anecdotes, I've got an endless store of them. We'll rest on the road, you play, I sing, what's wrong with that?'

Karl shook his head apologetically: 'I can't, you know I can't!'

'Okay then, if you won't, you won't. At least take my address, write it down. If you come back from your holiday, I'll be expecting a visit. Ellen will cook some soup, Nadja will play the accordion. You're an expert, listen to her, perhaps one day she'll be such an artiste that -'

Karl agreed to this. Vasya swung his body, heavy from so much sitting, up into the cab, started the motor; slowly the great lorry turned into the road. Vasya waved. Karl waved back and stayed there to watch. Only when the vehicle was far away and looked like a little beetle did he bend down to put his fiddle back.

III

From the buffet Karl ordered two cups of coffee and a couple of pies: he had to save money as he hadn't earned any yet. The woman put the pies and the cups of coffee in front of him on the counter, took forty-eight kopecks for it, put it straight into the till, resumed leaning her elbows on the counter and remained with her chin in her hands listening to the mumble of the men's conversation. She was fat, good-natured, and inquisitive; this was a tea-house in a fishing

82

village, the cat there couldn't be bothered with the mice, the dog with a bone, nor the tea-house-keeper with the kopecks. Or else she was such an old hand that she could tell by the smell of them who was honest and who wasn't. Karl's round face, grey, peaceful eyes and slightly hooked nose might leave a somewhat honest and aristocratic impression, and then there was the violin-case - that was his trump card, of course, it came before his passport and his work-card in precedence.

Karl took the coffee-cups and pies to the table, then came back for the violin-case, put it beside him leaning against a vacant chair and sat down to eat. Fishermen were sitting at a neighbouring table - they had come from the sea, wearing rubber-boots and sailcloth jackets, one younger, with a craggy face and arrogant look; the other older, but just as strong and heavily-built; both had ruddy faces, and had before them glasses of stronger stuff than tea, and evidently they were trying to prove or explain something to each other. They cast a glance at Karl too, the older one's eyes slid over the violin-case, but then they returned to their own concerns.

He ate slowly, chewing each mouthful carefully, taking pleasure in swallowing, and stared with a thoughtful, self-absorbed expression at the pattern on the table.

When the edge was taken off his hunger, he began to listen and look around. He remained listening to the men's talk at the next table; it was the nearest and the talk was the loudest. He saw that they were in dispute about something, throwing single words at each other in an odd way, like snowballs; the words did not seem nice, and they didn't raise their glasses together, but alternately.

'I said what I think,' stated the older one and looked toward Karl. His eyes again strayed to the violin-case and rested on Karl, not as if to stare, but just out of curiosity, and did it only seem so to Karl or was he really winking at him?

'Your own affair,' declared the younger one.

'So go on your own,' said the older one.

The younger one picked between his teeth with a match, spat on the floor and made no reply.

Karl noticed a cat manoeuvring between the tables - a chubby pussy which had eaten and rested; it came up to Karl, sniffed, looked at him, rubbed its side against his trouser-leg and raised its tail upright like a mast. Karl broke a bit off the side of his plate and put it under the cat's nose. The cat sniffed - and proceeded on to the next table.

'I've got to eat it and it's not fit for you!' thought Karl. 'Looking a gift horse in the mouth...'

'Schoolmaster' was the word disdainfully hissed by the younger man beside him.

'You didn't have a father...' said the older one.

'Schoolmaster,' the younger one repeated stubbornly, placing on this single word a whole load of disdain and - well, hauteur.

'... there wasn't anyone to give him a good beating.'

You could feel the annoyance in the older man's words, but when he looked toward Karl, again it seemed to him that he was winking.

'Look for another man for your boat,' the younger one spat out with the same haughtiness.

'Are you on the make?' the older one shouted. He said no more to his junior companion, but turned half-around toward Karl, and exclaimed: 'Why are you sitting alone? Come and sit with us men.' And he shifted his wine-glass with his elbow - as if half by accident or as an insinuation - in the direction of the empty seat.

Karl didn't know whether to go or not. He had just been thinking that he ought to somehow engage the men in conversation; they'd suddenly want to hear his instrument.

Karl made to get up slightly, still in two minds.

'Come on, come on, bring your fiddle over here too, look, men are eyeing your place,' the older one repeated good-naturedly.

Karl looked: yes, there were men standing at the counter, bottles and glasses in their hands, and they were looking around for a place to sit. He got up, took up his coffee-cup - he had eaten his pies by now - lifted his violin-case from its place resting against the chair and sat down. Immediately a more manly and assured feeling took over the men's table. The older one stretched out his hand. 'Johannes Sootma, boatswain.'

Karl gave his own name too, and glanced at the younger man, who was sitting with his back half-turned to him and taking no notice.

'This is David, David Suits,' the older one introduced him.

'Pleased to meet you,' said Karl.

David looked askance at Karl and made no reply.

'Nothing in that to be pleased about,' commented Johannes. 'A boy child was born into the world. His father proudly gave him the name David. His mother gave him the pet name Davey. The boy grew up, became a man, and changed into only a Goliath. He's got plenty of strength, but he doesn't know how to do anything sensible with it.'

David darted a glance at Johannes, raised his glass to his mouth, drained it, wiped his sleeve across his mouth, said 'Rubbish!' and stood up. 'Listening to your garbage here! Got heaps of work to do at home.' He picked up a heavy bundle from beside the chair; the cat, which was creeping around, got a kick, intentional or unintentional, so that it yowled and scampered some way off.

'Customers are waiting, money's waiting,' said Johannes, looking at the departing David. 'So you've got to hurry. And also because a stranger was listening while I criticized him.

He's ashamed!'

'His face wasn't like that,' said Karl.

'Can't tell from the face, of course,' explained Johannes. 'The face doesn't tell you anything. I know him on the inside too, that's how I know.'

'Well then,' said Karl.

Johannes' tongue was loosened.

'Nobody's ever made a god out of money yet on our bit of coastline. There's been plenty of it around for ages, whether it's from fishing or carrying booze. In the old days there were proud men too - take that same David Suits' grandfather: at his son's wedding they were watering his street with champagne. Built the first house, a two-storey job, with a sheet-iron roof, and a tower on the corner like some castle. But - he didn't make a god out of money. He had some, so did others too. If he had a party, the whole village had a party.'

'The grandson doesn't take after his grandfather then?' asked Karl, mainly to encourage the other man to talk.

'Ah, David!' Johannes returned from the world of memory. 'David builds as well. Builds and buys. Built a new house, even put up a sauna. Bought a car. Then bought another, in his wife's name. Now he's probably getting the money together for a third - for his daughter you see. But - it's not the same as his grandfather. His spirit's broken and miserable. You think he picked up the bill today, do you? It's like this: I said let's go by the tea-house. David says to me: well, if the money's itching in your pocket and you pay for it, then we can. The hell it was itching, I thought. Right, I'll take you and turn your soul inside out like an old coat. Perhaps I'll still find some... bit that isn't moth-eaten...'

Johannes took a gulp from his glass and put it back in front of Karl.

'Well, so you found one, then?' asked Karl.

'The hell I did!' replied Johannes curtly. 'Perhaps I did find a little, but I don't know myself what to do with what I found.'

'Got into a squabble while you were at sea, did you?' asked Karl. 'I mean, when you were in the boat.'

'You don't quarrel at sea. The sea won't stand for squabblers... But ...to tell the truth... there was a bit of a quarrel even on the boat. We took the fishing-nets out, and there were a few small fry among them. The kind that the law says you have to let live. I looked: David was happily picking them up... into his own bag. You know, he wouldn't take them to the delivery point, but he takes them home - you can find men to sell them to - who knows how much they'll pay! Well, we've all done something on the sly when needs must. But what needs does he have, to... without saying a word to the men... Then I said, David, you've gone too far with the fish... He wouldn't even listen...'

So there have to be Rooberts like that everywhere! This Goliath is not a real Roobert, but he's Roobert's half-brother.

'I do know... Goliaths like that. Words don't help with them at all,' said Karl.

'Yeah, you're probably right,' said Johannes thoughtfully.

'My own wife's brother... Completely stuck-up. I and people like me are... just grasshoppers to him.'

'Is that so, grasshoppers?' said Johannes.

'Well, we do the same useless scratching away at strings.'

'Useless, eh? I read in some paper somewhere that even fish get together to listen to music...'

'Could well be.'

'What's that instrument of yours there? Fiddle is it?'

'Fiddle, yeah.'

'So you're an artiste on the violin.'

'Don't know about artiste...'

'But you do play...'

'I play in an orchestra.'

'Oh, an orchestra, really.'

'In the theatre, when they put on an opera or an operetta.'

'And yet your wife's brother calls you a grasshopper?'

'That's what he calls me.'

'So he's a... sort of Goliath too, is he?'

'Reckon so.'

'Never mind. Don't even think about it. Better off playing something. Or does your fiddle only come to life... in the orchestra?'

'Everywhere.'

'Listen, play something, really. Strike up a tune, I'll make it worth your while. Look...' Johannes bent down under the table and lifted a shopping-bag onto his knees. He pulled it open, and as if expected, the head of a sea creature poked out of the bag. Johannes pushed the fish back into the bag and closed it again.

'You'll get such a fish soup that you'll never forget it.'

Actually Karl had been waiting for the moment when he could take his instrument out, finger the strings a bit and set the bow on them. Both for the sake of playing and for earning his bread. But now he looked around him, doubtfully, suspiciously.

'It's cramped...'

A lot of men had gathered there, loud voices could now be heard from several tables and Karl did not want to play - to him it was just as repugnant that drunken people might intervene in their camaraderie or make fun of him or downright mock him.

'So let's go to my place,' Johannes suggested.

'But perhaps we could go to the sea-shore,' it occurred to Karl.

'That would perhaps be the best.'

'Agreed,' Johannes approved, and got up ready to go. 'On the sea-shore, yeah, that's the most appropriate. I've never yet heard a violin played there, and I bet I never will again.'

They stepped out of the tea-house, Karl with his violin-case, Johannes with his shopping-bag in his hand. Johannes went ahead, turned off the road onto a footpath which led between some houses straight down to the stone jetty. The air was still, the sea was calm, the sun was dozing in the sky and a slight wave lapped between the rocks.

'If it's a payment, then it's a payment,' said Karl, 'but I'd really like to let these small fry back into the sea.'

'Listen, they're not undersize, you know,' Johannes uneasily hastened to say.

'Not because of that... But I've always wondered: if you let a fish into water, you don't know what it'll do: will it swim off straight away, or stick around for a while to listen to the music,' said Karl, in a pleading tone.

'Oh, that's why...' Johannes understood. 'So it's just to look at what they do. Well - are you going to put it in the water, or...' And Johannes busied himself opening the bag.

'Let me play.'

Johannes lifted the fishes one by one out of the bag and released them on the spot into the shallow water among the rocks. Karl played - played while watching the fishes himself. As they got into the water, they vanished between the rocks like grey shadows - they didn't have time to listen to a violin or anything else, they just drove themselves ever deeper.

Johannes remained sitting on the rocks with his head in his hands, looking ahead, at the same place as Karl did - at the surface of the bay, as sunbeams danced on the gentle waves, at the gulls wheeling above the fishing-harbour, at the little islet that rose further out in the middle of the sea, and further still into the yellowish haze of the horizon.

IV

By this morning Karl was somewhere in the heart of Estonia by a lake, dipping his fishing-line. In the meantime he had been wandering here and there, travelled in one or two vehicles, played at one funeral and two weddings, he even had money - more than when he left home. He'd eaten too, and drunk. But he'd spent last night down here in the meadow, amid fresh hay in an old hay-barn. In the evening he had looked for worms under the rocks and among the piles of rotting wooden tiles beside the barn, cut a rod out of a slim nut-tree, tied a line, a sinker and a hook on the end, so as not to delay too long when the best time came to strike out.

He stood at the mouth of the river, with a wall of reeds reaching over his head behind him, the cork floating restfully in the open-water among the lily-pads; the sun hung far off on the other side of the meadow, low over the forest.

I ought to go further out, thought Karl. Here he had caught four tiny perch, then some roach had come; it seemed that the shoal of roach was moving further out, as for quite a while not a single fish had nibbled at his line. He took the rod in his hand, and was planning to pull the line out when the cork started playing again. It slipped half under the water, rose straight up again, started making slow circular movements. Got you, you bugger! A roach, was it? A perch pulls greedily, a perch doesn't play like that. It pulls, swallows and goes... The perch strikes suddenly and acts decisively, it doesn't have time to play. Once a thief always a thief! It's either a roach or - a sprat. Then the cork bobbed under the water, sank, vanished, and didn't come up again. Karl pulled, pulled so hard that the rod bent, something bright flashed in the water, something big and silvery, the rod suddenly got away, the fibre whizzed through the air, the empty line flew behind his back into a thicket of reeds. 'Damn the bugger!' swore Karl.

'It was a bream,' said somebody's voice behind him.

Karl looked toward the source of the voice: up on the roadside stood a man in uniform. Karl actually took fright; it was so unexpected to see a uniformed man here in the creek between the lake and the river, so early in the morning. It occurred first to Karl that the man standing there was a forest patrolman or some other sort of official, some inspector or something. But he wasn't; on closer inspection he recognized an officer's shirt and he could even read the rank, from the green epaulettes. The stranger was a major, and he likewise had a pole in one hand, a plastic bag of fish in the other.

'That was a bream, yeah,' repeated the stranger. 'Your bream drags the cork to the bottom, with the worm between its lips. And then you can't be sure whether it will swallow or not.'

'I thought it was a sprat or a roach,' said Karl.

'No, it wasn't,' the major assured him.

'Never mind,' said Karl. 'At the moment I've got so many fish that I can stave off hunger.'

The major stepped down from the roadside toward Karl. Karl lifted his bag of fish for the stranger to see. 'Well yes, you've got quite a fish soup there,' he affirmed.

'Won't be fish soup, you've got to fry it on coals,' said Karl.

'Fish soup's better,' said the major.

'There's no pot to cook it in. What's the point of cooking, when there isn't even any salt? To say nothing of the bay leaves, onions and dill.'

'I thought you were from these parts,' said the stranger.

'No,' replied Karl. 'I'm from further away; at the moment I'm travelling around the country.'

'If that's so, then come to my place. We'll put our fish in one pot, and make a real, proper fish soup,' said the major. 'I live right here, on the other side of those pines' - he waved his hand at the hillock.

'I don't know...' said Karl doubtfully. 'I don't dare to sort of barge in. I'm sure you've got a family there and ...'

'There's nobody there. An old invalid in bed, otherwise not a soul.'

'As long as I'm not disturbing you,' said Karl.

The major dismissed that with a wave.

'So few people come here that once in a while you want some company. Specially in winter.'

'I guessed you were only here for the summer,' said Karl.

'No, I'm here all year round,' replied the major. 'For a pensioner it doesn't matter where you are. And you can't leave an old person alone.'

'It's your mother there is it?' asked Karl.

'Wife's mother,' replied the major.

They wound the line around the rod, took the bags of fish, and by the barn at the edge of the meadow Karl asked the stranger to take care of his rod and fish as well, and picked up his violin-case; the major showed no interest in what it was, why he had an instrument-case with him; silently they made their way up to the pines, through the grove to the edge of a corn-field and then up to a little grey house.

It might once have been either a fisherman's hut or some newcomer's dwelling - it wasn't important enough to be a farm. Everything here was too small - the kitchen, the room, the other room, the pantry, even the well in the yard, so that a bucket hardly fitted down into it and had to be thrown on its side. Everything was small and old and had the appearance of being tended or put there by a careful hand - the glistening patches on the roof, the new doors and windows...

'We'll have to fend for ourselves, there's no woman here,' said the major, returning to Karl. He'd been changing out of his uniform, and was in jogging bottoms and a vest; Karl noticed that it was an ordinary old faded blue vest, with a triangular patch torn out at the back and rather inexpertly sewn up.

'The wife's away from home then?' said Karl, not concealing his sense of relief. 'Bachelor life's always better.'

'The wife's in town,' said the major.

'In this kind of weather only a fool'd be in town. Sitting there is like being in hot soup.'

'Well, the soup she's sitting in right now is not all that hot,' said the major, as if grateful for Karl's solicitude. 'If she's sitting, then she's doing it at Klooga or Pirita or Võsu, by the seaside. And she'll be up to neck in cool water.'

'Is that so?' responded Karl.

'Don't bother to clean your catch, I'll take care of that, but you do the cutting and gutting - here's the scissors, and run them once through water.'

The major made short work of dispatching the catch; Karl found it hard to keep up with him. When they went into the kitchen, with tubs of clean fish, the water in the pot was already boiling on the stove.

'Now, the onion and the herbs too... in a quarter of an hour the fish soup'll be as ready as can be. We've got bread, butter too. Want to try some fresh mushrooms?' the host asked Karl.

'I always want to,' said Karl.

He brought a jar of mushrooms from the pantry - marinated chanterelles, boiled in their own juice in a light vinegar.

'This is really the wife's work,' Karl ventured.

'Wife's! The wife is sitting right here, opposite you.'

93

Karl ate hungrily, but at the same time he started thinking that there must be something here of the kind that had made Vasya say 'I've seen a lot, but never anything like this.' There is a wife and there isn't. There are mushrooms, but prepared by the man of the house. There's a wife's mother, but it's her son-in-law that looks after her. There is and there isn't... there is... and as if reading the other's thoughts, the major said thoughtfully:

'That's how it is in life... Together we conquered the enemy, but alone, each one for himself... not many men have conquered themselves. I had a good friend, a company commander. Intelligence company, now there a man had to have a calm mind and cool blood. Got through the war in one piece and intact. About three years later I heard that he'd started drinking. And then a year or so later I found out that he'd shot himself and his wife. First the wife and then himself. What with? His own weapon, that he'd got in the war. It has a silver plaque on it engraved: *Za muzhestvo*, "For bravery".'

'But you...?' Karl broke off.

'What about me? You want to ask if I've conquered myself?' inquired the major, more in the intonation than in the words. He didn't answer, slurped calmly and meditatively at his fish soup, and when he did take up the conversation again, it was on another subject.

'Excuse me,' he said, getting up from the table. 'I have to go and look after the old person now, and I'd promised to go and help out in the chaff-mill today. I help out at the collective farm here - as much as I can. I give the pension to my wife, and earn my own pocket money at the collective farm. So if you want to have a rest, go ahead, I leave the house in your hands.'

Karl replied that he didn't want a rest, and really he ought to get going, as it was still a long way home.

94

They went together to the end of the road, where the major had to turn to the left, Karl to the right. They shook hands in farewell and each turned to go his own way.

And he never did tell me whether he had conquered himself, thought Karl, as once again he made his way along the gravel road, his violin-case under his arm.

He has, he obviously has!

That's why he didn't say he had. You had to figure it out for yourself!

It doesn't matter what it was about, and at what price the victory over himself had come, but come it had.

And a tune started playing in Karl's head - peaceful and yet solemn, and somehow naturally optimistic.

V

Karl gave up hope of getting home that day, and so he had enquired at the Five Ways Food Bar whether there was anywhere to stay the night round those parts. The local aristocracy - in the persons of a tractor-driver, a sawyer and a peat-maker, all equally hairy and dirty - had explained to him that there wasn't a single hot-hel, mot-hel or brot-hel in the vicinity of Five Ways; there was one at Supsi-Mari, but not here. Karl had explained that he wasn't after any comforts - no room with a soft bed and white sheets, nor a bathroom with hot water. In the past week, for instance, he'd slept in a loft, in a hay-barn, a trawler cabin, an empty summer cottage and on the floor of a boiler-room. He'd even been prepared to settle for a barn, a hay-rick or a clover-patch, but since there was nothing but tall spruce groves and primeval mossy forests hereabouts, he did not have any hope of either hay or clover.

The men conferred with each other using their eyes. Then the sawyer said that about eight kilometres away in the forest there lived a woman called Veera, and there he might actually

95

get a bed.

Karl flinched. Eight kilometres is a lot. All right if his hands were empty, but look, he had an instrument and that weighed quite a bit.

The men held another conference of eye contact, and then the tractor-driver said that he might be going that way himself and he could take the stranger with him.

It takes a fair while by tractor, Karl opined.

Oh it wasn't by tractor, he had his very own three-wheeler, explained the tractor-driver.

'Ah, what's the use standing around thinking about it,' the sawyer interposed. 'Bring a bottle to the table and Edgar'll take you.'

Karl asked weren't they afraid of traffic inspectors.

The men replied that nobody had been seen there at that time of night.

And off they went on the three-wheeler through the forest, until the tractor-driver let Karl out beside a field and said: 'See, there's an old house with white window-frames. That's where Veera lives. If she's in a good mood, she'll let you in, if not she'll chuck you out. Remember - nothing ventured, nothing gained.'

The door to the entrance-hall was open; from inside, some coarse-voiced cursing could be heard: 'I'll flatten you, so help me! Who gave you permission to go into Mum's pockets? Just you wait...'

Karl thought that it was high time to intervene; he knocked on the door.

Everything went quiet inside. Quiet as the grave.

Karl knocked again.

'Come inside, you'll make a hole in the door!' - the voice resumed at its previous high volume.

Karl pushed the door open and stepped into the room.

In the middle of the room stood a woman, with a broom in her hand; she looked toward the door, her eyes screwed up with anger and her face red.

This must be Veera. And an inner voice told Karl that the men who put him here had been taking her for a ride as well.

'Hello,' said Karl, as though nothing were wrong and he had heard nothing.

'So what's your business here?' asked the woman in a decidedly unfriendly tone.

'I came to see if you needed any help,' replied Karl.

'What bloody help?' answered the woman. 'If you want to help, take your belt off your trousers and give this girl a hiding that she won't forget for the rest of her life.'

Now Karl noticed the other occupant of the house. A girl aged six or seven was sitting on the sofa, her legs tucked under her like a tailor, her hands in her lap, her face pale, her eyes full of dark defiance.

'What for?'

''Cause she's been at her mother's purse. As if she was short of something - got clothes on her back and a full stomach.'

'Perhaps she didn't mean to.' Karl was conciliatory.

'Didn't mean to! It was on purpose.'

'I didn't want Mummy to bring wine and get drunk,' came the clear and matter-of-fact explanation from the girl on the sofa.

'Took the last tenner and chucked it in the fire,' commented the mother. 'And anyway, stranger, what's your business here?' she asked again.

'About a room for the night.'

'What room for the night?'

'Well, the men back there at Five Ways said that you might put me up for the night.'

'What kind of men?' demanded the woman.

'There was a tractor-driver. Walked with a limp. He even brought me here on his own motor-bike.'

'That was Limping Karla,' the girl interposed.

'You shut up!' yelled the mother at her daughter and adjusted her dress, the shoulder-strap of which was broken. Karl noticed that she had an ugly triangular scar on her neck. 'Limping Karla wanted to come here himself, but I threw him out.'

'Mummy had an axe in her hand and she was screaming: Whoever comes will get cut to bits,' said the girl, laughing.

'I'm a free woman and I know myself who I'll take and who I'll leave,' said Veera proudly.

'But how's it going to be with me?' asked Karl.

'I'll heave you out that door,' said Veera with assurance, adding as if by way of an excuse:

'You aren't even as much use to me as Limping Karla! At least he knows how to give the kid a fright - you can't even do that!'

'No, I can't frighten her,' said Karl helplessly. 'Got to be a father to do that.'

'I threw her father out the door too,' said Veera.

'Well, and now you're in trouble?'

'Trouble or no trouble, what business is that of yours, stranger?'

'No business. It's just that I can see you're a strange woman. You act first, think later.'

'What would I think for? I'm not about to be a share-farmer.'

'Ah, that's how you are,' Karl went on. And not knowing what else to do, he got his violin-case open, took the instrument out, ran the bow over the strings and let fly with a tune. He stood in the middle of the room; the sounds filled its sparsely-furnished space, which was too cramped for them;

they bounced off the wall, the wardrobe, the table, the benches; they cascaded over the child sitting in her tailor's pose on the sofa, listening to his playing with her mouth open; they penetrated Veera's thin printed cotton dress, the broken strap of which had again slipped down. Veera didn't notice that; she was looking at the player; her expression dissolved, her breast rose and fell in its breathless rhythm... and miracle of miracles, the walls fell away before the sounds, they vanished; Karl stood in the middle of a field and called forth a warm summer rain to pour forth from his fiddle onto these two naked human beings.

He remained standing before the girl, bent down on one knee and played her something good, joyful and - encouraging. When the sound had finally died away, a deep silence reigned in the room. They were all still under the spell of those notes, perhaps also under the spell of having been offered and given without asking something for which they felt a greater need than for their daily bread. Evidently people had always been coming to this house just to help themselves.

'Oh Lord, I've been all eaten up inside,' sighed Veera.

Karl got up, and put the violin cautiously and tenderly back in its case. He didn't want to admit to himself that he was just as moved as the woman sitting on the edge of the bed, whom a wanton and wild life had not managed to render insensitive to music after all.

'I've got nothing to offer you,' said the woman. 'But if you really do want a place for the night, then stay. Just don't play any more...' - her voice was pleading.

'You can play for me,' the girl's voice called from the sofa.

'None of your lip!' barked the mother. 'Thank your lucky stars you escaped the father of a hiding!'

The spell of the music was broken.

'I wanted to get to N., but I saw I wouldn't get there today.

Not a single car was going that way from Five Ways,' said Karl.

The woman looked him in the face thoughtfully. 'Who have you got there? Got someone waiting for you there?'

'A wife, name of Õie. And a son too.'

Veera got up, looked at a clock lying on its side on the table and said:

'What are you waiting for then? There's a bus going in half an hour, goes through N. You'll just make it to the Forest Guards' bus stop.'

'Is that true?' asked Karl.

'True, why would I lie to you? If I wanted to lie, I would have kept quiet.'

'I'll go then,' said Karl, getting up.

'Go, you heart-eater! And don't come back!'

The grey house was swallowed up in the green embrace of the birches; he could no longer see the girl's floral skirt or the mother's dress - perhaps they were still standing on the steps, but the birches enfolded that strange house and its people.

Karl walked along the pine-strewn path to the bus-stop. As he walked he hummed the tune he had heard from Vasya the truck-driver. About the girl who asks to be taken far away and be called the man's wife, sister or sweetheart.

And about the man who can't do anything about it, because he already has a wife and a daughter and... a sweetheart, all in one person, all in that one dumpy, round, ever-balanced, thick-spectacled Õie.

VI

The road loomed dimly through the night as Karl made his way home. Barely a week ago it would have been much lighter at this time; now the abandoned dairy with its stick of a chimney had sunk into the hem of the darkness. The heart of the summer was broken, and Karl was walking home again. More by instinct, more by touch than by sight did he find the place where he had to turn down the cow-path. The night air smelt humid and heavy - of ripening rye and mown hay, of potatoes and the collective farm's cow-shed, whose lights gleamed up on the hill. Far off a corncrake cawed, and something flew almost silently over his head - it came out of the darkness and vanished into the darkness. A bat, thought Karl.

The farmhouse slept in the bosom of darkness. The windows were dark, everything was still.

Karl felt with his hands for the ladder to the loft, held the side of the ladder in one hand, with the violin under the other arm, and hopped up. Slowly he opened the hatch to the loft, his head bowed so as not to knock it, and climbed into the loft.

The rustling of a mattress was heard, and then the beam of a torchlight fell on Karl. He blinked.

'Look, the wanderer of the world has come home,' Õie's voice was heard to say - with irony, but Karl soon noticed that the irony was a pretence, and somewhere deeper down there was something more - satisfaction or even joy that her husband had come home. Be diplomatic now, thought Karl, be diplomatic and try to make the irony go away and let the satisfaction and maybe even the joy reign in full power over people's feelings and... actions.

'The tour's over,' replied Karl, and started taking off his coat.

'Plenty of money in your pockets then,' Õie's voice came from the darkness, still ironic and ready to launch into a monologue about what a horrible way to behave, leave your wife and child and go wandering off into thin air, while at home there's so much to do and look after, weeding and berry-picking and a thousand other things...

'My pockets are empty,' said Karl.

'No money at all?' Õie feigned amazement.

'Well, I just played a bit, for bread and for fish and...'

'... and you mostly failed, didn't you?'

'It wasn't like that,' replied Karl. 'No, it wasn't like that at all.'

The sound of Karl's trouser-belt buckle in the darkness led Õie's thoughts elsewhere.

'How can you come between clean sheets like that, all dirty and sweaty... just like some big workman,' said Õie, half out of concern, half out of spite.

'Just this afternoon I went for a dip in Mustjärv lake,' said Karl. 'The bank was muddy, but afterwards I washed my feet in the stream. And now I smell like a water-lily.'

'Is that what I've got, a water-lily?' said Õie, and Karl felt that he was almost forgiven.

He crawled onto the mattress. Collecting his thoughts for a moment, he started chatting about what he had seen and heard and what he'd been thinking about. It was probably the best thing he could do now.

'And you know, I've even got a feeling that I've got over that Roobert business. Now that bastard doesn't bother me any more,' he said conclusively.

'Well, at least some good's come of it then,' said Õie, now actually quite conciliatory and even concerned, it seemed to Karl.

'Yes, and everything else too,' replied Karl. He might even have said that that something else was the most important to him. He had been tired, easily upset, and he had begun to think that the whole world consisted only of Rooberts. Now he realized that most of them out there are quite different people, anti-Rooberts, and they are the ones who provide the basic notes of that musical tune called life. In a major key, definitely. He could have said that, but that was what he was talking about all the time, what else?

He stared into the darkness, but before his eyes was still the radiant rainbow of the past few days.

'Tomorrow we'll go into the forest for blueberries,' he said to Õie.

'Well, if you're up to it,' replied Õie.

'I am,' replied Karl.

His hand sought its way around Õie's waist - cautiously, testing the surface, to see if he would be pushed away or not.

He wasn't.

Oh my homeland! My home, wife and child!

And the blueberry forest.

And the people around you.

And the violin-case.

And the lump in the chin caused by resting that same violin there.

A lump that your wife feels tenderly, as if it contained inside it love and fate and the homeland and the future.

And the night, the smells of the night and the corncrake's call.

You never know if ...

No, no, don't think, don't think now, think in the daytime!

Just feel now.

It's summer, and ahead lies autumn.

Autumn will come, but right now it's still summer.

Still summer.

And holidays ...

And ...

Saturday in the Sauna

Mati Unt
Estonia

Tõnu really was a very fat man. I myself was only nine years old, and I believed with my child's understanding that he was the fattest man in the world. I reckon a tape measure would have hardly gone round him. The men were sitting under the big birch-tree and drinking vodka in honour of Miners' Day. There weren't any miners among them, but a holiday is a holiday. Tiina, the neighbours' girl, was just running around too; she wasn't old enough to drink, she was still small, the same age as me. They used to say that Tiina was my wife to be. My story has now started to concern Tiina, but it was meant to be about Tõnu. Now Tõnu was sitting under the birch too, drinking vodka, and Father said we'll all be going to the sauna soon. The birch they were sitting under was very tall, and as dusk fell, its soughing was stilled. Our neighbour Ivi, Tiina's elder sister, called the cow home, and Totsi mooed back from the bushes, but still didn't come. Tõnu and the other men drank their vodka and mooed as if Ivi the neighbour had been calling them. Tiina stroked Tommi's head. Tommi was our dog. Tiina stroked him and Tommi didn't bite her, or growl; he was an old dog, and a year later he was to die out in the barn, but I didn't know that then, and I looked at Tiina and Tommi. When the clock struck ten and the sky turned dark green, Tõnu got up and said, 'Now we're going to the sauna.' Tiina left Tommi after stroking him, but Mother said, 'Better let the men go first.' Tiina went on stroking Tommi, while Tõnu pulled his trousers up over his belly and set off. Our sauna is way down the hill and the hill is very steep. I wanted to go too, but Mother urged me not to – they'd tread me underfoot. So I didn't go. I watched the men rolling down the hill. Then Mother said, 'Go and offer Tiina some redcurrants.' The bushes were already red with berries, and it wasn't time for the jays yet. But we already had lots of scarecrows. We ate those berries and Tiina's mouth was red with the juice. Her cheeks were too. I said very softly: 'Your mouth's red.' She wiped it away with her arm and went on eating. There among the bushes it was dark and warm. The sky was still glowing over the park. In the park there were very many burnt German cars. Suddenly a terrible howling could be heard from the yard. We rushed out of the garden and looked down the hill toward the sauna. The men were shouting in front of the sauna, a couple of them were completely naked, and Father cried: 'Look at that bloody barrel!' Then we understood that fat Tõnu couldn't get up the hill any further. Kravchenko and Blumberg's boy were pushing from behind, Father was pulling from the front and Tõnu himself was straining, but it was all to no avail. After about a minute Tõnu sat down on the fence and wiped away the sweat. 'Worked up a good steam, but now I can't get up the hill any more,' he said. Then he collapsed, and so did the fence. The men were very sorry and didn't know what to do with Tõnu. Blumberg's boy said: 'Peace – life!' That's what the Forest brothers had said when they'd made off with the milk from the Aravu dairy. Now Blumberg's boy was saying it again. He'd never been a Forest brother. It had got quite dark, there was no moon, only stars, and Kravchenko was screaming up toward the house for the lady to bring a lantern. Mother was indeed coming with a lantern, and at first she laughed at Tõnu's predicament. Then she brought the light down and Tõnu noticed it. He said: 'Excuse me, I'm naked.' What's more I saw that Tiina was still standing there, and I thought she must be cold, because by now a mist was rising off the river. But see, I didn't do a thing, I only had time to think, because now Kravchenko was demanding a rope. Mother and I fetched a rope from the wall of the barn and brought it down. Tõnu was now much less agitated. He was already cracking dirty jokes, but he was still sitting on the ground, almost in a nettle-bush. When you sit down suddenly on nettles, they sting. But if you sit down slowly, it may happen that they don't sting. Father took the rope and they tied it around Tõnu's belly. At the same time Blumberg's boy had to lift Tõnu up a bit. And then they started tugging violently. Tõnu puffed a lot and said he had an itch. But the men were tugging like Volga boatmen or like those who in one or two pictures were supposed to be pushing their way out of the earth. Kravchenko and Blumberg's boy pushed from behind, while the whole family of us pulled from the front. About ten minutes passed, then the man was up. He himself said that not every day could be like that, or he'd be worn out. One other boy had arrived there meanwhile, and he remarked that not every day is Saturday either. At that point everybody went terribly quiet. Ivi the neighbour came, and Mother went to the sauna with the women. Tiina went too. Tommi came up to me and licked my hand. It was completely quiet. Only the birch was soughing high up in the darkness. The unknown boy was standing under the birch. He had a strange face.

The Man with the Green Rucksack

Arvo Valton
Estonia

Into the station waiting-room, around midday, came a heavily-built man. He wore a tie, and a faded suit. He stepped through the rows of seated people to the furthest corner of the waiting-room, and removed a green rucksack from his back. He put it down on the grubby parquet floor and asked the people on the nearest bench to sit somewhere else. He then pulled the vacated bench into the corner. Thereupon he took a book out of his rucksack, climbed up onto the bench and began to read the book in a loud voice, with declamatory passion, so that the whole waiting-room could hear it.

At first only those nearest to him took any notice of the strange orator. They watched the man standing on the bench and were forced involuntarily to hear his words. The man's voice was so powerful that whenever the noise of the crowd died away his voice was carried across the whole hall, and everyone was forced to hear him.

But immediately the noise swelled back, following its own irregular pattern, and the man's voice was drowned in the general hubbub. Life went on as normal in the waiting-room. Some people came from a train, some went to one. Masses of people were passing through the waiting-room all the time, to the platform and back again. Some spoke loudly amongst themselves, gesticulated, some ran anxiously from one door to another. On the benches on both sides of the hall were seated those who had to wait a long time. Someone was eating a snack. Another was sitting a child on a potty, another was nibbling sunflower seeds to pass the time, another was sleeping. It was an international mixture. Beside the counter that went under the name of a 'buffet', hefty, middle-aged, careworn women were selling tepid, dirty-coloured coffee and 'railway buns', which kept their shape for weeks.

The man who was reading loudly from the book was disturbingly extraordinary in the tiresome ordinariness of the waiting-room. Although the captive audience had nothing to do, and the reader standing on the bench made up for the deadly boredom of waiting, nevertheless it seemed strange, for they were not used to such a thing. The people hurrying through the hall were also disturbed. They tried to find out what important message was being announced there in the waiting-room. Some of them even stopped for a moment, but then hurried on their way. For what was being read was a quite ordinary work of fiction about imaginary princes and heroes, exciting adventures with lyrical or philosophical asides, emotional love-affairs and strong passions. In places the book was boring, in places amusing, as this world is. And these worlds, these passions, flowed through the big man's powerful tenor and his forced pathos, into the humming mass of people that was drawn to him or sat impassively. Great truths, brazen lies, panaceas for the world and illusory consolations, all settled over them in the same way.

Some of the audience eventually started to listen keenly,

once the surrounding diversity no longer distracted their thoughts. Perhaps some were drawn into the fates of these non-existent heroes and even missed their trains. But the majority were just rushing past, and a brief snatch of it might provide one with a wild chase, fill another with great truths, another with sweet tender romance, another with an abstract discussion of sophistries. And all of them went their own ways, because they absolutely had to go. All the more so since the man on the green station bench had not announced anything of such vital importance that you couldn't live without it for another minute.

But people also appeared in the hall who began to take an entirely different, a more active interest in the matter. First of all came two cleaners in blue coats, whose job was to scrub the dirt on the floor all over the hall twice a day. When they saw the man declaiming, they looked at each other, and both felt that the place was disorderly.

'What a place to give a sermon,' said the elder woman.

The other one was a woman of action, and she went with firm steps up to the man and asked angrily: 'What's the meaning of this?'

The man took no notice of his interrogator. The part he was reading from was amusing, and the man was smiling. The cleaner took a step backwards, put her hands on her hips, stuck out her chest and struck what she thought was a warlike pose. She bellowed: 'Get down off that bench! The bench is for sitting on, not for climbing on!'

The man got down off the bench, still smiling, and did not break off his reading for a moment. But the cleaner dragged the bench back to its former place, in a row with other benches. Thereupon she surveyed the hall triumphantly. But no special notice was taken of her act. No-one commented or applauded. She went back to her fellow cleaner and they looked at each other. The one who had set things in order was not satisfied. Naturally she was not about to start listening to what the man was reading. She had a job to do there; she was almost the administration, not some train passenger who could hear the sermons of a tramp.

Clearly, reading out loud in a railway waiting-room was a criminal act. But the old women were not specially expert about written matters, and they could not find an appropriate law that forbade reading aloud. They didn't dare make up a new law of their own – they were just working for the railway system.

So the old ladies went straight to the station superintendent and said in unison: 'There's a man reading out loud there in the hall.'

The superintendent took his red cap off, scratched his forehead and asked: 'What's he reading?'

'Don't know,' the women answered firmly.

'Who is the man?' asked the station superintendent.

'Don't know,' the women answered, again unanimously, and in their voices could be heard a patriotic vigilance.

The station superintendent now became thoughtful, as the matter seemed to be serious. He put his red cap on, and went to the waiting-room door. Indeed, there in the far corner of the waiting-room stood a big man with his face to the hall, reading out loud from a book, so that in the quieter moments the words reached even the superintendent's ears.

The superintendent withdrew into the doorway. He couldn't show himself in the hall, because being in public he would have had to take a stance regarding the orator, but he couldn't do that because he didn't know what sort of stance to take. His experience up to now had not once included a case of someone starting to read aloud from a book in front of everyone in a waiting-room. And so now he had to think over the situation.

He assured the cleaners that the matter would be looked into, and sat down behind his well-worn table. He took off his cap, and scratched his brow. But nothing sensible came to mind, so he rang the station patrolman.

The patrolman was a phlegmatic man, like keepers of the peace everywhere: he stepped into the room, announced that he was in the middle of his billiard game, and asked what was up. The station superintendent said: 'There's a man in the waiting-room there who's reading aloud from a book. Go and find out what he's up to.'

'Sure enough,' replied the patrolman and went off to the waiting-room. He walked through the rows of benches, looking around with an air of authority. A rustle went through the hall as the patrolman appeared. The people shuffled their things about with embarrassment, hid their sunflower seeds, and those who had their feet on the benches took them off. The figure of authority also circled around the orator, closing in, following him with a meaningful look. Thereupon he sat down on the bench opposite the man, stretched his legs well out in front of him, folded his arms and carried on looking at the man quizzically. Those sitting down watched with interest to see what was to happen. They were all listening to the reading without understanding much of it, because their thoughts were on the patrolman.

The only one who remained completely undisturbed was the man himself. At that moment he was reading an exciting bit: the hero had got into an impossible situation from which he of course had to escape. The man was swept along in the excitement, he was reading quickly and making vague gestures with his hands.

The patrolman at first didn't find anything particularly dangerous to society in the man's reading. When he had sat

111

there for quite a while, he began to feel ashamed of the ambiguity of his attitude. Perhaps it was also because the people had so quickly got used to his presence; they didn't stir any more, nor did they take any notice of him. And he had the feeling that he had descended to the level of an ordinary train passenger, as if he had come there like some little boy, to hear a story. Therefore he shambled back to the station superintendent, and said: 'I don't have any reason to bring him to book for this. There's no brawling, no racket, no hooliganism. No spitting on the ground, no putting feet on the seats, no stink.'

The station superintendent had meanwhile had a dozen jobs to see to and had quite forgotten the man. Now he became aware of him again; he took off his cap, furrowed his brow and lifted the telephone receiver off its hook. Then he looked around helplessly: who should he ring?

'You mean, no racket and no spitting?' he asked, making sure, and looking the patrolman in the face.

'Exactly!'

The superintendent rang the railways' lawyer and asked: 'What do you do in a case where a man isn't spitting or causing a disturbance in a station waiting-room, but is reading aloud from a book to other people?'

After that clear statement, the superintendent had to give the lawyer a long and rambling account of the circumstances. Thereupon the lawyer let forth a mass of foreign-sounding words and legal terms, which made no sense to the superintendent at all. Obviously the lawyer had nothing pertinent to say, and had therefore to resort to science.

The superintendent replaced the receiver and scratched his forehead. He had the feeling that he had been abandoned on all sides and would have to resolve the matter himself. He even thought of simply going straight up to the man and saying:

'Listen, don't read aloud, why don't you go out into the square in front of the station and do whatever you want to there, that's somebody else's area.' But to such a reasonable statement the man was bound to ask 'Why?' Try to explain it to him then, when you don't know it yourself. In itself, yes, it probably doesn't matter so much what he's reading, but it would still be better if he wasn't there.

Nobody would actually start saying anything, so the superintendent asked the protector of public order: 'So what should we do now? Who should we ring?'

'Don't know,' replied the patrolman, succinctly. 'I don't have any instructions about such a thing.' He thought for a moment and added: 'But perhaps the city authorities could do something about it?... There should be a couple of men right here in the square in front of the station.'

The superintendent took up this idea and asked him to call in the town police.

Soon the railway patrolman brought in two men with him. The superintendent told the men: 'We've got a man reading aloud there in the waiting-room. Perhaps you could do something about it?'

The railway patrolman added: 'I don't have any instructions.' One of the uniformed town policemen asked: 'Is he disturbing public order?'

'Hard to say,' replied the superintendent evasively, shrugging his shoulders. 'He's reading aloud from a book.'

'That's your territory,' said one of the visitors reprovingly. 'If he was making a racket out in the square in front of the station then we'd take care of that.'

The railway patrolman bent over to the superintendent's ear and whispered: 'Perhaps he could be coaxed outside.'

This whispering didn't please the visitors, but the superintendent frowned. Then he shook his head and said to the men:

'At least take a look at the matter, perhaps you could give us some advice.'

The visitors looked at each other. The first one asked: 'Is he a strong bloke?'

Now the railwaymen exchanged glances.

'I don't think he'll give any trouble,' the superintendent assured them.

'A respectable-looking man, reads books,' the patrolman added.

'But why did you ask us here at all?' the guests wondered.

'We don't have any instructions,' shrugged the railwayman.

'Perhaps he's reading something that's banned,' the superintendent offered uncomfortably.

The visitors whistled.

'There are quite different men who can check on that,' they said.

The superintendent reflected. He looked at his guests and said quietly: 'Sorry to have troubled you.'

The visitors marched out.

'You can go too,' said the superintendent to his patrolman.

The latter sighed with relief, made a gesture with his hand, as if striking a billiard-ball with a cue, and vanished.

When the superintendent was left alone, he went to the waiting-room door, so as to peep in secret at the orator. At that moment he seemed to be reading a funny bit, because some of the people were laughing. The man himself was making broad gestures with one hand. I ought to ring, thought the superintendent with a sense of regret; ultimately he wasn't competent to decide whether the text the man was reading contained something forbidden; there are responsible organs for that, so let them decide; anyway he was responsible for the station (and wouldn't it just have to happen while he was on duty!) – otherwise any of the passengers might – there are all sorts of people there! – do it first. And that wouldn't do. They might even make out that he had been encouraging it, exploiting his professional standing, giving opportunities to dubious persons, and so on. On top of all that he had a wife and little children.

The superintendent hardened his heart and went to his own room to telephone.

Soon some men in civilian clothes came to the station. They disappeared into the chief's office, came out of it one at a time, and quite unnoticed became a couple of new passengers in the waiting-room, listening attentively to the reading of the book. One of them pretended to be sleeping, but in fact was peering vigilantly from beneath his eyelids at the extraordinary reader.

In the chief's office telephones were ringing, work was going on smoothly and faultlessly. A messenger went into town a couple of times. Soon there were various sorts of messages on the superintendent's desk, photographs and a copy of exactly the book the man was reading.

It turned out that the book was permitted to be printed by the relevant authority and in this respect there were no hindrances to reading it. But such conclusions were not much help to the station administrators. The man went on reading. The superintendent asked: 'But what is to be done?'

This time the visitors were very helpful and said they would assist if needed. The station employees need not worry. Of course they would check on matters that came within their sphere of competence, and would not get involved if the station administrators wished to adopt any other measures in relation to the orator.

The superintendent sighed. It would have been better if they hadn't made that last remark – this way the matter was at least partly still in his hands.

The visitors left. But the superintendent didn't know that one man did stay in the hall, with a book in his hand, following the text that was being read, making sure that the man didn't add anything of his own devising. At every point where the reader would make a mistake, the listener would make a mark in red ink, so as to be able to define later with certainty the nature and deliberateness of the mistakes.

The superintendent was stuck with his old problem. Again he was left alone with the obligation of responsibility. He involuntarily thought that it's bloody difficult to manage such a big mechanism as a station. Especially when you're confronted with incidents. He rang the representatives of the directors and voluntary bodies of the Railways Board.

'This reading, was it arranged with anyone?' the representatives of the directors and voluntary bodies of the Railways Board asked.

The superintendent sighed. 'No, it wasn't,' he had to admit.

Meanwhile the representatives consulted amongst themselves and then announced to the superintendent: 'We'll convene a consultative meeting and reach a decision. But you are to keep us continuously informed if there is any change with regard to the reading.'

The superintendent sighed with relief. At last someone had removed the basic responsibility from his shoulders. Of course, it had happened while he was on duty and he had to be clear about it. But had he not acted correctly and informed all the proper quarters?

The working day was nearing its end. The man was still reading. The superintendent went to the door to peep at him furtively. The whole crowd of people in the hall was listening to the man's tenor voice, receiving the ideas from the book and the emphases from the reader's mouth in a completely spontaneous way. And the superintendent did not know that somewhere in that crowd there was a certain person who was unwaveringly keeping watch on the spiritual well-being of the users of the station and the railway in general.

On leaving the station the superintendent informed the patrolman who came to relieve him about the situation, and ordered him to ring him at home immediately if anything new happened. And indeed the telephone did ring in the middle of the night. The sleepy patrolman informed him that the orator had just left the station. He had gone into town, to an unknown destination. One of the people waiting had also followed him to the same destination.

'What could be the reason why he left?' asked the superintendent.'

'Apparently because he'd finished the book,' the patrolman informed him. 'It was about half past two. Passengers were dozing on the benches, and some of them grumbled about him reading aloud. But I must say the man was quite a help to the night duty.'

According to the regulations, sleeping in the waiting-room was forbidden. Particularly at night, this point was observed rigorously: a special officer went around, prodding dozers up with a long stick. This was done with a view to the passengers' well-being – so that no-one would miss their train by sleeping.

'Well, thank God for that,' said the superintendent. 'So that is now settled.'

In the morning he rang the representatives of the directors and voluntary bodies first of all, and announced cheerfully that there would no longer be any need for consultations. But the representatives replied that a commission to look into the matter had only just been formed, and its work could not be left incomplete.

117

'But what will they investigate if the man isn't there any more?' wondered the superintendent.

'That is for the commission to decide,' the representatives replied. 'He's not there today; he will be tomorrow. The problem, as such, still exists.'

The superintendent had to admit, on reflection, that in some respects the representatives were right. Until yesterday, such a thing had never happened. And about the future one couldn't be certain. Privately the superintendent admired the deep theoretical considerations of the representatives at the Railways Board.

Around midday, the man with the green rucksack turned up again. He remained standing in the same place he had occupied yesterday, and commenced reading aloud from a new book. The humming was the same, the people who had not been allowed to sleep during the night were dozing on the benches, hordes of travellers were passing through the waiting-room; the majority of the passengers were new ones. But the general picture was the same. They were eating, sitting children on a potty, conversing, making feeble railway jokes and thinking unconsciously about their obsessions – in a word, they were living.

Once again it was the cleaners who brought the news of the orator to the superintendent. The man put his hands to his head and moaned. The patrolman, who was in the room at the time, said quietly and calmly: 'I thought he'd come.'

The superintendent looked at him inquiringly.

'Why did you think that?'

'He'll come tomorrow too. Perhaps he'll keep on coming,' the patrolman replied with the complacency of a prophet.

The superintendent moaned once more.

'Why?'

'Psychology!' the patrolman stated mystically.

The superintendent looked at him incredulously.

'Fixations. Desire to improve the world. Popular enlightenment. And other things,' the patrolman catalogued confidently in response to his superior's inquiring look. The latter was truly astonished at the pregnant meaning of the patrolman's words.

When he had recovered from his astonishment he rang the representatives and stated in a weak voice: 'He's come back.'

'Very good,' the representatives replied.

After that the station superintendent hesitated a long time, but finally he did ring the visitors who had been there yesterday as well. They replied that they knew about it, and there would be no need to inform them in future.

... And so it went on for several days. The man would read in the waiting-room from the books that were in his green rucksack. When he had finished them all, he brought new ones with him, or repeated some of those he'd read. The staff at the station began to get used to him. But somewhere far away in the Railways Board, the commission carried on with its work. The only ones who remained passive were the passengers.

From time to time the commission would inform the station superintendent of the progress of its work. As a first step, the commission had issued an assessment of the phenomenon being investigated. Such a so-called 'spontaneous phenomenon' had its good and bad sides. Among the first group one might mention the fact that the reader, who had appeared of his own accord, was offering the train passengers cultural entertainment and to a certain extent educating them in the field of literature. Of course, on the debit side, the main thing was that it was being done without consultation with the directors and voluntary bodies of the Railway Board. Besides, it was apparently being conducted on a methodologically false basis, without any scientific organization of the reading.

As a second step, a decision was made with regard to the future. If it was found that the amateur reading in a station waiting-room was an undesirable or even damaging phenomenon, then strategies and tactics to combat such phenomena would have to be worked out. But if the matter was deemed generally positive, then it would have to be based on scientific principles, and the ideological effect of the reading would have to be assessed. In fact, when the work was at this stage, one young member of the commission came out with a proposal to organize their own readings from books in waiting-rooms, so as to release the public from the dubious effect of amateur readers. (The aforementioned young member of the commission was noted, and was subsequently elected to all other commissions.)

As a third step in its work, the investigative commission spawned a set of new commissions. The Repertoire Commission began gathering a list of suitable works for readings. Of course, a number of educational factors were taken into account in this. The Executive Commission for Organising Readings began drawing up instructions for reading procedure, timetables, specifications for strength and expressiveness of voice. The Commission for the Selection and Training of Cadres began organizing special courses for readers. In addition to these, there was also a group of sociologists, who had to study the effect of the readings on the audience; a scientific research group, which for the time being didn't know what it was supposed to do, but which had a very broad scope for expansion and further development; an aesthetic group, which had to consider several specific phenomena; psychologists, mathematicians, and finally several less pertinent special commissions, of which a couple were secret.

Several months passed before the repertoire was settled at

the various instances, including a couple of committees in the capital; before the readers were trained and instructed; before the workshops had constructed the special platforms; before a reading procedure had been assembled and fixed, on a scientific basis. Thick volumes of the minutes of their work were assembled. Prior notices of the railwaymen's estimable initiative were published in the paper.

But all the time the man with the green rucksack kept on reading books in the waiting-room as before. Unscientifically, in the way he knew. In the course of time he had gained several regular listeners, who would sit in the waiting-room without having a train to wait for. This fact was reported to the commissions, and there arose a whole mass of problems. There was a danger that in taking the event to the masses there would be no room in the waiting-room for the passengers. It was proposed that readings be organized elsewhere, but in that case it would no longer be for people waiting for trains. It was suggested that instructions be drawn up for those waiting, and that entrance to the station for those not waiting be forbidden.

Finally things had proceeded so far that a start could be made with the readings. The first thing was to put on a reading in the same waiting-room where the man with the green rucksack was doing his readings, so that the unqualified competitor would be ejected – the success of which action was not doubted by any of the scientific organizers.

But just before it was to commence, the man with the green rucksack suddenly disappeared. One noon, he simply didn't turn up at the waiting-room any more. No-one knew where he had gone.

The station superintendent reported the matter to the representatives of the directors and voluntary bodies of the Railways Board. It created general indecision. The railway patrolman tried to find the man and bring him back to the station, but the search was fruitless. The commissioners decided to wait. It was no use putting on any new readers if there was no-one to be ideologically ejected.

But perhaps that was not the main reason why the enterprise, so gloriously set up, did not finally get off the ground. No doubt it was affected by a very general and natural law. The man did not turn up anywhere. The specially trained readers looked for suitable work. The platforms lay in warehouses gathering dust, the instructions stayed in safes. Gradually the commissions folded up. New things came into the world, and onto the railways, and the members of the commissions had for a long time been participating in new commissions. They were cut out for that sort of work and they no longer had any time for the work of the old commissions, which were seemingly biding time and whose dispersal was a fact.

The waiting-room went back to its old way of life. People ate, slept, chatted, discussed life, and recalled old times. The superintendent was satisfied when everything went on from day to day in the old way. The night patrolman prodded sleepers with his stick. From time to time the cleaners tried to seize power in the administration and to take out their anger at their failure on the waiting passengers. It no longer occurred to anybody to read aloud from books in the waiting-room.

The matter was of interest only to science. Some wrote dissertations on the history of the failed experiment, some on the new opportunities, outlining their hypotheses for the future. And some wrote stories on the subject.

Thirty Pennies

Orvokki Autio
Finland

Jaska pulled the outside door open, but at the same time he let go of the handle and let the door shut. He stood on the steps with a small, flat, zippered briefcase under his arm and looked at the pile of newspapers in front of him. He calculated that there must be at least thirty separate bundles there, and probably more, but the lowest ones could not be seen, because someone had brought their newspapers in a loose heap and they had spread everywhere – one of them was already fluttering in the wind towards the street. Jaska raised his collar and started walking to the Tankard, a couple of blocks away. There he drank four beers in quick succession. After that, he went back to the same building he had just come from: the newspapers were gone. He walked up six flights of steps and rang the doorbell.

'You're late,' said Elli, surveying Jaska, a cigarette with a long column of ash between her fingers. 'We said three o'clock.'

'Well, you seem to be home anyway,' said Jaska, stressing

the word 'home'. Just a month ago, Jaska and Elli still shared the same house and home, and in that home, little Onni, one and a half years old. At least, that's the way it seemed. But now Elli lived with Mauritz, and Jaska had been to the lawyer, and the divorce was just about through. Now all that was left was the matter of Onni. The lawyer had told Jaska that he could have Onni if he just put on the pressure, because Elli was the one who had left their shared home. Their shared home. That's what the lawyer had said. That the evidence was quite clear. But Elli had threatened to do herself in if Onni was taken from her, and she had even decided that she could kill Jaska too, and so finally Jaska had decided to give Onni to Elli. Jaska had now come to draw up the document in which he would declare he was handing over responsibility for Onni. Elli seemed a bit pissed.

'Well, come in anyway,' said Elli, stepping back shakily.

'Where can I write that contract?' asked Jaska.

'There's a typewriter in there,' said Elli. 'In the bedroom.'

Jaska walked in, sat down by the typewriter, his cap on his head, his coat still on, took a piece of paper from his briefcase, fed it into the machine and turned the cartridge. Elli stood next to him, smoking a cigarette.

'There ought to be witnesses for this too,' said Jaska. 'To sign their names underneath.'

'Well, there's Lehmonen and Alholinna in the kitchen with Mauritz, having a beer,' said Elli.

'Who's that?' boomed Mauritz's voice behind Jaska's back. 'The husband himself! What brings you here?'

'Now Mauritz,' said Elli. 'Don't you remember? We agreed that Jaska would come to settle about Onni.'

'I see! Making a contract behind my back! That's how it is: you arrange things together, you don't just start doing things off your own bat – you bloody do things together!' Mauritz explained, swaying, trying to enunciate every word, every letter, as clearly as possible.

Jaska started tapping the keys.

'That's my machine!' said Mauritz, taking Jaska by the arm. 'Ex-husbands don't write on it!' Jaska shoved Mauritz away and continued writing, looking all the time at the paper.

'God!' threatened Mauritz. 'You don't play it with your elbows!'

'This has got nothing to do with you,' said Jaska.

'It sure has! I'll decide what's to be said, and I wear the pants around here!' yelled Mauritz.

'It's not a question of pants now,' said Jaska. 'It's a question of my son.'

'Mauritz, go back to the kitchen,' said Elli. 'We'll deal with Onni.'

'Okay,' conceded Mauritz, noticing that his bottle was empty. 'I'll give you a quarter of an hour!'

Jaska remembered Mauritz's old corner cupboard which was still at the place on Oikokatu. 'Farm-hands' cupboards' they used to call them. It had appeared in the corner of the bedroom about three months ago, with pipes and lumps of tobacco in it, and Jaska had asked Elli what it was.

'Just Mauritz's cupboard,' Elli had tossed over her shoulder.

'What's that thing doing here?' Jaska had asked.

'The cupboard or Mauritz?' Elli had asked.

'Well, both,' Jaska had said.

'Don't suppose he has room at his own place,' Elli had said.

'For the cupboard or for himself?' Jaska had asked.

'Not really for either of them, I guess,' Elli had answered.

Elli stood behind Jaska, reading what he had written.

'No good,' Elli said. 'There's a spelling mistake right at the start, there – "we hearby agree" – you don't spell "hereby" like that!' Ash fell from Elli's cigarette onto Jaska's coat.

'Don't bloody drop ash!' snapped Jaska, ripping the paper out of the machine, throwing it onto the floor and taking a new sheet. 'You'll set it on fire!'

'It's better to marry than to burn, as they say,' purred Elli.

'Did you really have to go and get pissed when you knew we had to work on this paper?'

'You're pissed yourself.'

'It doesn't mess up my thoughts,' said Jaska. 'But bugger it, this isn't easy.'

'Oh, you poor thing!' said Elli, sitting down by the desk and stroking Jaska's sleeve.

'Look at this billing and cooing!' exclaimed Mauritz, slamming the kitchen door behind him and pulling Elli by the arm against the other wall.

'This is far from billing and cooing,' Jaska asserted.

'Is that contract ready?'

'No,' said Elli. 'It's not two minutes since you came in and interrupted.'

'Interruption seems to be what's needed here – straight away you're at each other like a pair of fleas!' slurred Mauritz. 'All this promising and talking of love, and then God help you as soon as your back is turned!'

'There's nothing going on here but a bit of correcting,' said Jaska and took out yet another sheet.

'Oh, "correcting" you call it now?' teased Mauritz. 'Having trouble spelling our name, are we?'

'You just learn to write your own name,' said Jaska. Mauritz's name was actually Matti Maijala, but he wrote his name as Mauritz, always with a 'z' at the end.

'Look, pal, don't shoot your mouth off!' Mauritz began.

'Mauritz darling,' said Elli, 'Look, Mauritz, darling, try to understand. We're just doing this paper.'

'Well, what were you doing dangling off the edge of the

table there?' demanded Mauritz.

'Well, because of the spelling – an official document has to have no mistakes,' explained Elli, pushing Mauritz back into the kitchen.

'Come on, Mauritz,' said Alholinna at the door. 'Come and have a jar.' 'Give me one too,' said Elli. 'Jaska like one?' asked Alholinna. 'You seem to be having some problems with the contract?' 'Why not, it'd be nice,' said Jaska. 'I'll try and keep Mauritz over there on the other side,' said Alholinna and brought two glasses, which smelt of brandy. Jaska poured half a glassful into his mouth while tapping the keys with the index finger of the other hand. 'Now you've made another mistake,' said Elli. 'Start again.'

'Fuck and bugger it,' said Jaska and ripped out the sheet.

'How about leaving it for another time,' suggested Elli and sat down opposite Jaska.

'I'm not coming here another time,' said Jaska, and pulled out yet another clean sheet from his briefcase.

'Just write it out somehow,' said Elli. 'You're always such a useless pedant.'

'Hell!' snapped Jaska. 'You're the one who's whining on all the time about mistakes!'

'Yes,' said Elli. 'But I mean, you always were such a stupid sort of pedant.'

'I can't be bothered talking now about yesterday's problems,' said Jaska. 'I just want to get this paper done.'

'Papers, papers,' said Elli. 'Papers, clauses and paragraphs – they were always important to you. You've always imagined that if all your papers are in order, then so is your whole life.'

'Yes, and so my life has always been in order, as far as my papers are concerned,' said Jaska.

'Do you mean to say that right now your life is in order, once you get that paper done?' asked Elli.

'I do,' said Jaska.

'Then your whole life depends on papers,' said Elli. 'Don't you see that if you'd arranged something else besides papers in our marriage, you wouldn't be having to draw up that paper now?'

'I think I've done my best,' said Jaska. 'You're the one who took up with Mauritz.'

'You don't even begin to understand!' said Elli, lighting a cigarette from the previous one. 'You just don't understand, you really think you've done all you could.'

'And so I have,' said Jaska. 'You're the one who smashed the whole system up! You're the one who pushed off.'

'But why?' said Elli. 'Don't you even wonder why?'

'I suppose Mauritz is more considerate and tender,' said Jaska. 'Statistics show that wives usually leave their former life behind for that reason.'

'Oh, heavens above!' said Elli. 'You and your statistics! Can't you see anything more than statistics in this?'

'What else is there to see in this?' said Jaska.

'I can certainly see something else!' shouted Elli. 'You pigeon-hole and make statistics about everything in life! Is there something missing completely from your head, or is there something extra? It's as though you don't have any feelings at all sometimes!'

'Do you have any?' inquired Jaska. 'Even in bed you never showed a flicker!'

'Did you try to do anything about that? No! You just pigeon-holed me among the frigid women and left it at that, but I can tell you, I'm not frigid. Comes as a surprise to you, eh?'

'Look, we're supposed to be doing this paper,' said Jaska.

'Don't you want to talk to me even now? Don't you?'

'We've done the talking now.'

'We've never done any talking! You just thought that if your bills were paid, then everything's all right and I'm satisfied.'

'Well, weren't they always paid on time?'

'They were paid, they were paid! Everything was taken care of! Everything was taken care of on the outside, and we were an example, at least you were. I suppose I've lost my reputation and made a slut of myself, since I left our household – where the bills were always paid.'

'And who asked you to leave? You would have had a place to live, a life, somewhere to be.'

'Don't you understand that I can't live with receipts and talk to them?'

'I was there, and so was Onni.'

'You! You were like a wall – if I tried to talk, you'd go off for a drink!'

'Look, I always took care of Onni.'

'You did, you did. I never denied that either. That boy is your life. That's what that boy is to you – and your mother. I always got the feeling that I had nothing more to do with our son than that I'd produced some new Jaska. Little Jaska, to your mother. And yet that boy is just as dear to me as he is to you, and still you and your mother are prepared to take even Onni away from me. Just because I left you. If I leave you it doesn't mean that I'd leave Onni.'

'Well, now you're getting Onni,' said Jaska. 'That's what I'm trying to do with this paper, and there's even a new father for him, there in the kitchen, all ready. If you just get married, then Onni will have a mum and dad again.'

'I don't think Mauritz will change into a father just because of some marriage certificate – you're his father. And Mauritz and me, we haven't planned to get married.'

'The law says, at least, that the new spouse has the duty to maintain the child,' said Jaska.

'The law says! The law says! You've got it all worked out, haven't you? Even though we haven't even got the divorce through yet.'

'I have to look after my interests.'

'This is a question of Onni's interests.'

'You're looking after Onni now.'

'And you're his father.'

'But not looking after him any more.'

'Doesn't fatherhood matter to you? The fact that the child is your son? Doesn't it mean anything to you at all?'

'That's all changing now, for good.'

'Obviously it's no use talking to you.'

'And I didn't come here to talk either!'

'Now that I know – ' said Elli wearily, 'Now that I know what that little boy means to you, then why do you have to turn things upside down, things that are quite clear, just because we didn't get along?'

'With this paper I am handing over my son,' said Jaska curtly.

'You can't do it with a piece of paper, you just can't give up your child and everything. And you don't even have to.'

'The law is the law,' said Jaska. 'And I didn't start this business.'

'No,' said Elli. 'I don't suppose you have anything to do with anything, you're quite innocent and perfect.'

'As far as the law is concerned, the fault is yours, anyway,' said Jaska.

'And you've done everything right. Is that what you're saying?'

'According to the law I have.'

'So you're satisfied and happy, then, now that you've done what you think is right and according to the law?'

'You're the one who's looking for new happiness.'

'And I hope that you'll find happiness too.'

'You do, do you? So we're starting all over again, finding happiness, are we?'

Mauritz had come into the room, without Jaska and Elli noticing. 'Out of here, and make it snappy! You come here with your documents and your briefcase and make as though you're going to discuss the kid, but you don't get round to it, oh no, you both start getting all warmed up again! Well, I'm not looking at pictures of old husbands under my roof any more!' roared Mauritz.

'The paper's not ready yet,' said Jaska.

'Ready or not, out you go! Get your lawyer onto it, but just don't come here messing around with other people's Saturday evenings!'

Jaska got up, and his eyes chanced upon the picture of Onni on top of the cupboard. Onni was smiling with the two-toothed mouth of a child of a year and a half, and pressing a bright-coloured rubber ball in his chubby hands.

'Well, are you going or aren't you? because I'll soon put a bit of speed into him, if this knight doesn't clear off out of the house!' bawled Mauritz, tottering against the door-post.

'Where's Onni now?' Jaska asked Elli.

'He's in the country,' said Elli, alarmed. 'At my mum's. Now go, go!'

Jaska began zipping up his briefcase and remembered how, just a week ago, he had carried Onni on his lap through the town. Onni liked walking in town and looking at the cars; when Onni saw a Deux Chevaux he squealed with joy. Jaska had run his lips across Onni's cheek, and Onni had slapped his little red mittens onto Jaska's cheek and shrieked with excitement the word he had learned: 'Face!'

Mauritz came up to Jaska, pushed his nose almost against

Jaska's, and shook his fist at him. Elli came and tried to draw Mauritz away. Jaska let his briefcase fall to the floor, pushed Elli aside and took Mauritz by the lapels, without saying a word.

'Let go of me, you hear!' said Mauritz, and swiped at Jaska's face. Jaska flung Mauritz at the wall, grabbed an empty Coca-Cola bottle from the table at the same time, hit Mauritz on the head with it; the bottle smashed into splinters, and Mauritz slumped to his knees, his eyes elliptical with shock, rubbing his head with his hands, staring at the blood on his fingers. Jaska stood panting, the neck of the broken bottle in his hand, and took a step toward Mauritz.

'He'll kill me!' squeaked Mauritz, and half-ran, half-crawled, to the kitchen, slammed the door and cried out again: 'He'll kill me!' Jaska threw himself against the door and tried to push it open; Elli tugged him by the hem of his coat; Jaska kicked her away.

'Jaska!' screamed Elli, biting her knuckles. 'He's gone mad!'

'I'll tear his throat open with the neck of this bottle!' said Jaska in a low voice.

'Jaskajaska,' faltered Elli. 'What are you doing, surely you'd never do that what's come over you oh God put that bottle away!'

'Shut your mouth!' bellowed Jaska. 'The paper isn't ready yet, the boy's still in my charge, and no-one else better talk about it.'

'Don't open the door, Mauritz, keep it shut oh Lord what's happening here!' howled Elli. 'Police!'

Jaska backed away from the door as soon as he heard the word 'police'.

'Police!' cried Elli again.

Jaska let the bottle-neck fall from his hand, turned, took his briefcase under his arm and went through the other door into the hall. Alholinna ducked quickly from the kitchen, out of his way. 'Me and Lehmonen, we didn't see or hear anything, if this gets out, remember that, Jaska, sure, we understand,' he mumbled.

Jaska looked past Alholinna, growled something and walked to the stairs. Having reached the street, he put his hand in his pocket, thought for a moment, and went back. He rang the doorbell. Elli came to open it.

'What now!' Elli burst out, backing away in fright.

Jaska counted thirty pennies from his wallet, and gave them to Elli. 'That's for the bottle. It broke.'

'I'm not going to give you a receipt for this,' said Elli venomously, and threw the money back in Jaska's face.

Jaska stepped calmly downward, the coins rolling about his feet. Once again, he had paid all his bills.

The Storm

Bo Carpelan
Finland

I remember dreaming about the great storm which, one October evening over forty years ago, shook our old schoolhouse by the Seaside Park. My dream is full of driving clouds and plaintive cries, of thundering echoes and odd coincidences, a witches' brew which still bubbles and steams in the memory of that day of the great yellow clouds.

Our mathematics teacher – a little wiry woman who seemed to have swallowed a question-mark and was always wondering where the dot had gone, and therefore with low voice and downcast eyes conducted us as though we did not exist -: even so, her small black eyes observed everything that went on in class and were as quick as a weasel if someone disobeyed her – was standing and writing the 7 times table on the board when a strange light filled our classroom. We looked toward the window: it seemed as if the whole schoolhouse was suddenly transformed into a railway station. It shook and trembled, a whistling sound penetrated through the cold thick stone walls, and gliding past the tall windows at a furious speed were streaky clouds of smoke, hurling our classroom forwards as if we were sitting in an aeroplane. Our teacher went over to the window, and raised her dark thin head. Without a word she ceased writing and stood looking out at the driving clouds.

Out in the corridor, doors being flung open and shrill cries could be heard. The desks shook slightly, and as if at a common signal, we rushed to the windows, climbed up into the deep window-bays and followed the progress of the wind. It had a deep dark voice and another, higher and shriller, and both voices were intertwined like ropes, and struck against the trunks of the old maple-trees, tore at the last leaves and made the park look like a collection of black, whirling brooms, bending like arches before the mighty boulders rolling in from the sea. 'Back to your seats!' shouted our teacher in a sharp voice, but we clung to the spot. The driving clouds vanished, and outside there now reigned a thundering darkness, and the six white lamps in the ceiling were lit, only to go out again. 'To your seats!' cried our teacher, and reluctantly we made our way to our desks. 'Write!' cried the voice from the corridor. Suddenly the lights came on with full force and the door was flung open. We rushed toward it, and were sucked into the dark corridor, where we pushed our way to the outer door.

Suddenly we heard a terrific crash, which drowned out the tinkling of the glass, the murmur of thousands of voices from the great yellow wind. Through the stairway window we could see the shiny metal roof of the school being torn off its beams with a shriek and flying out toward the sea like a billowing sheet. On its way, it tore off the treetops in the avenue of maples and vanished with a roar above the observatory up on the dark tottering hill which rose out of the swaying park. And immediately after the roof there followed a cloud of white leaving certificates and essays which had accumulated for a hundred years in the school loft. Like feathers from an infinitely big eiderdown – that is how this whirl of white flakes of paper looked as it rose above the school and was driven out to sea or swept at a furious speed toward land. How strange nature is! As it turned out later, those compositions – 'My summerhouse', 'A sunrise', 'What I feel about the sea', 'My favourite author', 'Flowers of house and garden' and other similar subjects, were blown out to sea, where several generations of fishermen found them diverting reading by the oil-lamp in the autumn. They spent a long time – so my mother told me – carefully trying to dry out the soggy blue exercise-books which suddenly came floating down from the clouds over rocks and skerries, and making out their beautiful calligraphic script, while hunters and farmers up north, in their turn, could read about 'Karl XII, the Hero King', 'Europe's Influence on America's Culture', 'Mussolini: Portrait of a Leader' and 'Electricity as a Source of Energy'.

When the cloud of compositions and leaving certificates – nobody was interested in the latter really, they just vanished and were no more, perhaps used as fuel – was seen to rise above our shamelessly naked school, the Headmaster – a tall thin man who could contort himself into the oddest postures – rushed up the stairs to the loft, and the whole school loyally followed him. In vain did the school's old caretaker try to stop us: like a river we streamed past him and stormed up to the loft, where it suddenly became absolutely quiet. The school was in the centre of the cyclone, and an awful silence settled over the meagre remains of the archive. But along the walls stood case after case of the school's pride: the stuffed birds donated by the former headmaster. Climbing onto a table, the headmaster called to us to convey the birds to safety. 'The storm will soon be on us again!' he cried, his white hair standing on end, as in an altar-piece I once saw in a church. In

136

that picture the old man had had a sword in his hand, but the headmaster had a pointer.

How right he was! We had scarcely opened the doors of the cases of small birds, ducks and tits, swans and razorbills, ibises and storks, crows and horned owls, gulls and eagles, before the wind struck again. In the sky, which shone brilliantly above us, there now blazed a fiery red glare, and with a howl, a thunderous flapping vortex passed through the gigantic open room and ripped the birds from our hands.

And the birds! It was as if through all these years of dust and silence they had only been waiting for this signal for departure! With one unanimous cry, as if from a huge, many-stringed harp, they flew along the familiar walls, and rose crying and twittering, wailing and chirruping, calling and moaning, piping and cooing, from our sight. With rumbling wings, fluttering wings, swishing wings, with flashing eyes and outstretched necks, with legs stretched backwards and talons wide apart, they wheeled in a whining circuit around the Headmaster, who stretched toward them a long, pale, powerless arm, and then they vanished, like the leaves of the trees, away and out, into the depths of the heavens, and their cries died away in weird waves of echoes, while we, crawling in the heavy, silent loft, managed to get out and down the stairs.

Suddenly we noticed that the only things we could hear were our own voices and booming steps, that the wind had ceased just as abruptly as it had struck the second time, and that outside there reigned a great, milky-white silence. The schoolyard doors glided open as if by themselves. The lamp-posts around the yard stood contorted into the oddest positions, and our strict gymnastics teacher shouted: 'Don't look at the lamp-posts! You hear?' But his voice was solitary and powerless – why should we not look around at the destruction, at the old school with its thick, scratched, dirty walls, at the roof-timbers which stuck out like the ribs of an old whale against the light pink sky, at the trees which stood stark and leafless, with broken branches, and the world which had been destroyed and resurrected? If I closed my eyes I could see them all, the boys in plus-fours and jackets too small for them, the girls in checked cotton dresses and sagging stockings, with plaits and sweaters – I could see them all if I closed my eyes, how they stood there in the schoolyard, how their faces lit up after the storm, the great yellow storm, the one which I later heard was only local and did not affect any other school at all, no other part of town than ours –

I was awakened by my mathematics teacher standing beside my desk with her supple little ruler, and I got up, drowsy with sleep.

'Sleeping in class, Carpelan? Do you know what happens if you sleep in class? Answer!'

It was deathly quiet in the classroom; all eyes were on me. I whispered: 'You dream.'

'Louder!' cried our teacher, quite desperate. 'Louder!'

'You dream!' I shouted.

'You dream!' shouted the whole class, exulting and clamouring, 'you dream! You dream!' And the class broke up in cries and laughter and I had to stay behind.

But in the dark schoolyard, on my way home, I found a soggy blue exercise-book on which was written, in a graceful hand: 'The great yellow storm'. I stood under the street-light, under the straight, intact street-light, amidst the flaming maples whose every leaf waited to fall calmly at the first hard frost. My heart pounded, as I read: 'I remember dreaming about the great storm which, one October evening over forty years ago, shook our old schoolhouse -'. Then blank white pages flashed before me. There was no name on the cover. I took the book with me and hid it in the drawer of my desk. But I was forced to show mother my report: 'Sleeps in class and answers insubordinately.'

Mother looked helpless. 'What am I supposed to do?' 'Sign your name.' 'Yes, but what did you say?' 'That I dreamed.' 'Yes, but so does everybody when they sleep.'

I could not reply to that. We looked helplessly at each other.

'What did you dream about?'

'About the great yellow storm.'

'About the great yellow storm? Oh, that!'

And mother nodded and wrote: 'Have seen the great yellow storm myself.'

And then she signed her name.

But every time the wind rises and the clouds scud across the sky I remember the day the school's roof flew away and the birds vanished, when the Seaside Park became a threatening darkness and everything cried and trembled under the pressure of the great wind, that wind which still prowls around, waiting to change and shake everything that gets in its way.

That Summer the Clouds Hung Low

Rosa Liksom
Finland

That summer the clouds hung low, just above the hills, and nature stood motionless, as if on guard, from one week to the next. Small birds shrieked occasionally, and the swallows had been eating their young since the early summer. On some days, the sun tried to pry its way behind the cowshed and on the other side of the lake, but before six o'clock it would take fright and hide behind the grey, heavy clouds. It wasn't necessary to take off the double windows all summer, and the door was not opened before Midsummer. Hay grew poorly and in constant fear of rain, and in the heavy, oppressive conditions it was stuck on grey stakes, only a dozen or so to a strip. It did not rain all summer; the rain skulked above the village like a wasting beast, ready to spring, but the attack never came. Flowers withered on the window-sill of the porch, and in front of the veranda, and the grass in the yard rustled.

In the first week of August the hay-gathering began, and then the rains came. Black clouds came from beyond the lake early in the morning, and encircled the village until eight in the evening. It rained for three weeks at a stretch. Drops struck heavily at the window, and gathered in huge puddles in the yard and in front of the sauna. The sand in the yard took on leopard-spots, and the flowers snapped and rotted on the lawn. For a few days at the end of summer the sun shone hotly and intensely, but not two days in a row would be dry. The hay turned yellow, then dark brown, and before long it was black and stinking on the racks, a sorry mess around the damp and decaying stakes, or in black lumps strewn along the fields. The people sat for days in the cabin with mournful expressions, waiting for the rain to stop. And when it did stop, it no longer had any significance. All had been lost. The hay was silently gathered and sprinkled with salt.

'During the war we used to feed the cows newspapers, at least this is a bit better,' said Grandfather when the last load was being carried on the dray into the shingle-roofed and gap-walled barn. Mother glanced expressionlessly at Grandfather and no-one said a word. Then the sun slammed heat at each house and at the tilting, huddled hut. It shone for a full day and night, the flowers crackled into new bloom, and in the vegetable bed the carrots and beetroot began to push up green shoots. Someone even said that three shoots had been seen in the potato-patch. Old men and women dragged themselves into the yard, and hobbled restlessly back and forth through the village. They went around speaking of bad times to come, of wars and shortages. They whispered behind the backs of the children, and would stand at the window, even before five o'clock, staring across to the other side of the lake, waiting for the arrival of the bombers of Jesus. They would waver in the windows of the cabin until nine in the evening, and then fall asleep, into uneasy twitching slumber.

The whole summer had presaged misfortune, and then, at the end of August, came the turning, the beginning of a new summer, the rebirth of nature, which brought a more suspicious expression to people's faces than before. The children stayed in the back room on the sofa, and the young men glanced anxiously by turns at their parents and grandparents, expecting an answer which was not to be found. The pine forest and the hill slopes were filled with blueberries, and a couple of weeks later the heavy red blooms of lingonberry spread in huge tussocks. The cows ate their fill of fresh grass and fungi which abounded in the forest pastures.

The old people were ordered off the village road into the cabin, they were snapped at and their complaining mouths were silenced. Nobody wanted to think about the end of the world in that time of strange August heat. The children splashed in the water at the lake's edge and hunted frogs with forked sticks. They would hang the frogs on a birch twig and carry them on their shoulders along the lake shore. The live frogs groaned, pierced through on the long sticks, and their goggle eyes gaped with alarm and pain.

That summer Arvi came.

In the midst of the heavy rains and the bad weather, he fell out of a taxi by the sauna, and walked in a drunken haze through the cabin door. He wore some blue garment, recognisable as a suit, and in his hand he carried a small brown cardboard suitcase. He opened the door briskly and threw the suitcase down by the stove. Grandfather raised his old gaze in the direction of the door and grimaced scornfully. Arvi smiled amiably and sat down on the bench.

'It's come again,' he said, seeking something with his gaze. Everyone knew what it was but nobody would mention it. I would have liked to say it all, right then, but I didn't have the courage, or any right. Arvi's suit bore big black water-stains, and from his black hair water dripped in little drops, down to his neck and slowly into his blue shirt. The hairs on his chest were grey stripes, and had sprouted while he had been away.

'What the devil are you doing here?' said Grandfather, staring at Arvi's old suitcase.

Arvi pretended not to hear, smiled to himself and winked at me across the cabin. I felt gooseflesh rising and pressed myself tighter onto the wire bed.

The rain clattered onto the roof and loft. Mother put plates on the table and a cauldron of potatoes in the middle. Arvi glanced inquiringly from the bench at Mother, but Mother avoided his gaze. A long silence descended into the grey morning, Arvi's expression grew darker and he got up from the bench and walked across the yard to the sauna.

Everything went on as though nothing had happened, and nothing had happened either. Arvi had come, and everyone had known he would, ever since the day Arvi had left: sooner or later he would be coming.

'Is it pissing down?' Grandfather had said on the first day of the rains, imitating Arvi, but as the rains wore on, the joking got less. Arvi had visited the breakfast table by way of Grandfather's mouth a couple of times in the winter, and then when the rains came; otherwise no account of Arvi was kept. I just felt all the time that he was present. Arvi's silly grin had been sulking at the end of the bench all winter, and after Lea left, a heavy, dark-blue-tinged shadow had remained in the cabin.

In the evening I peeped out from the little window by the garden plot at the porch of the sauna, and I saw Arvi sprawled out on the bench in the dressing-room. Arvi's blue shirt was undone almost to the navel. The stomach was quite invisible, but the jacket pressed at the arms and shoulders. Arvi looked unconscious and familiar. I would have liked to wake him and tell him everything Aunt Lea had told me before she left, but the words would not come to mind, and my legs would not

143

cross beyond the doors of the sauna porch. I tore my legs on a raspberry-bush, and I heard Grandfather shouting:

'Bloody bitch, get out of there behind the window, or I'll tear your eyes out!'

I ran across the yard to the playhouse and then at last I understood that there was something about Arvi, something Aunt Lea had told me, but which no-one else in the house or the village had grasped. Something, of which I had only a small inkling, united me, Aunt Lea, and Arvi.

In the evening Arvi came out of the sauna. He had washed himself, and was no longer either smiling or in a gloomy mood. He came into the cabin and read a newspaper with a fixed gaze.

'She died,' said Mother while Grandfather was emptying the chamberpot around the corner. Arvi didn't raise his eyes from the paper. I sat on the bed with a magazine in my hand, observing Arvi. A black shadow passed across Arvi's face, he swallowed a few times and finally his eyes sank to the floor.

'That poor thing couldn't get away from you before...' said Mother and turned away her eyes.

The subject wasn't pursued any more. Arvi stacked wood in the shed for the first week, came to eat his meals and drink coffee, but he would sit with his eyes downcast. The second week he made fence-posts in the shed, and fixed up old hay poles. Grandfather sat on the bed and listened to the pattering of the rain. Mother would glance anxiously toward the shed. She seemed to want to say that she didn't blame Arvi. What had happened was God's decree, it was he who held the reins in the end. It was left unsaid, and Arvi sat silently in the midst of the rain, a heavy sorrow resting on his eyes.

The old men and women whispered that it was Arvi who had brought the rains and the misery when he came. They shrugged in the direction of the shed and turned their heads away when they met Arvi's gaze. 'He's always brought trouble, he's a devil, he took Lea, and he brought the end of the world.' Mother heard the whispers, she hurled her sharp looks deep into the old folk's hearts and stifled the complaints. The old men and women tottered back to their folding beds and left Arvi in peace. In the hay-gathering, Arvi drove the horse, and almost single-handed stacked all the hay from the poles onto the cart and from the cart into the barn. I noticed that Mother admired Arvi, though she tried to hide it with extreme coldness. Grandfather knew it too, and spent sleepless nights. He would clatter around the room after three in the morning and sigh in his rocking-chair.

Arvi slept in the loft, with its white walls and low ceiling. Aunt Lea had feared that room, because below its window Grandmother had lain in her coffin under a canopy of spruce branches. Mother slept with us in the bedroom, wearing a long night-dress and scowling at Grandfather in the dark. Grandfather made sure that the bed arrangements did not get into disorder, and Mother was so fiery-tempered that I feared that one night she would kill Grandfather right there in his creaking chair.

At the meal-table, I sought Arvi's gaze, but couldn't reach it. He did not notice me at all from the day he arrived, and in my dreams I walked with him through the streets of a strange town, through fields of hay and on the river, catching frogs. I could not shake off the thought that I had to tell Arvi everything that Aunt Lea had entrusted to my heart. That it was my duty. I was tortured by a burning desire to meet Arvi's gaze just once.

With every step Grandfather was close on my heels. He kept watch over Mother and me. He counted every glance between Mother and Arvi, followed every movement of my feet, so that I would not get involved with Arvi in any way.

That spring I had stained the sheets and my pink underpants with blood for the first time. Mother had washed them silently, and Grandfather saw from the washing-line what had happened straight away.

'One more bitch we've got, does that bloody tart have to start lusting for cocks as a kid?'

I was ashamed in front of Grandfather, and in my humiliation I managed to scream: 'Nobody wants your cock any more anyway! You'd be better off dead!' As a reward for this I was whacked on the legs with the shaft of a pitchfork. Grandfather struck me with such force that beads of sweat stood out on his forehead. I stared at him, paralysed with hate: 'Bloody old bastard! Shrivelled old turd! Hit me again!'

Mother glanced from the window into the yard, and I caught her scornful look. Mother had chosen her side.

I knew that Arvi would get into the car in September. At the beginning or at the end. I had decided what I had decided.

When the rotten hay had been trampled into the floor of the barn and the sun had given birth to a new spring, Arvi moved to the barn by the lake shore to nail up a new shingle roof. He nailed from morning to evening, and only after nine o'clock did he come into the yard and go up to the loft. One evening, when the sun had painted half the sky with fire and the other half with rich violet, I went to the shore after nine. I sat under a big pine, and let my gaze rest on the calm surface of the lake. Arvi came down, sat down at some distance and lit a fag.

'You've turned into a woman,' he began, and looked at me for the first time carefully from head to foot. I felt a snatching in the pit of my stomach, and my cheeks glowed.

'Even your tits are growing before my eyes,' he said, smiling. I was ashamed and proud at the same time. I had big fine tits and a slim body.

A long, easy silence followed. The rushes were growing, handsomely green and sturdy-stemmed. Swarms of gnats buzzed on the shallow waters, and schools of fish swam in black flecks against the sandy bottom.

'About Aunt Lea...' I began, and looked sideways at Arvi.

'It's nothing,' said Arvi, and stubbed his cigarette.

'We can't...dead and gone...better this way...don't bother thinking...'

I let my long hair fall across my face, and everything Aunt Lea had said seemed obvious. Nothing of it had to be repeated. It was all inside me and would be until I died. There on the shore I understood that explanations were not needed. I didn't need to say anything, and it seemed to me that Arvi knew it all long before I did.

A good feeling came over me; I felt like making love. Arvi looked at me with kind eyes. I stripped off and went to swim. Arvi sat on the shore and looked at me closely. My nipples went hard and swelled and my heart hammered when I came to the shore and walked in front of Arvi.

'Would you lie with me,' I said.

Arvi looked at me without a word, got up, handed me my clothes and walked into the yard. I got dressed and the tears rolled from my eyes. In the night, lightning split the northern sky in two.

The thunderclaps couldn't be heard, and not a drop reached the pane. I stayed up all night, looking at Mother's empty bed.

The next morning Arvi got into the car.

The Aluminium Rings

Eeva Tikka
Finland

After a drive of fifteen miles or so, the whole thing began to seem ordinary. The hands on the wheel began to calm down, and then the thought, the bitter words, lost their sharpness – it was just, just the usual. Even the cause of the quarrel vanished under the miles, and he couldn't help it, although he had blamed Teija for it without reason. But then, what was said was said now, since they had quarrelled, and you do quarrel when you live together.

What the hell. In the evening we'll settle it all. But first, today's job has to be attended to. This is where you have to turn left off the highway – both sides of the road piled high with logs, you rarely see so many piled up. Somebody's been keeping them for himself, hasn't sold them – they say that even that is a crime nowadays. There are many sorts of criminal – is that the side road that leads to the house?

He turned into it; according to the instructions it wasn't far now. The spruces there on both sides of the road still bore dark patches under their eaves, but beyond them, in the open

148

fields, the brightness of midday and snow streamed out. And there, there was the house, just as it had been described to him on the telephone, and yet now, created before your eyes. A red house, or more of a cottage actually, in a white landscape; plenty of berries on the leafless rowans; old apple-trees. A cat on the steps trying to get in, the bustling of birds at their feeding-place.

There are idyllic places outside the Christmas cards too. He stopped the car in the yard, the cottage door opened slightly and the cat scuttled in. A man came onto the steps, old but still upright and sturdy, built for endurance – handsome when you really looked at him, anything but shrivelled. He was part of the idyll too, but without the white beard.

He got out of the car, and the man came toward him, hand outstretched.

'So the ringer's come, eh?' he said.

'Have you seen those nuthatches this morning?'

'Yes, they've been, both of them.'

'You're sure there are two then?'

'Oh yes, I can count as far as two.'

'I didn't mean – it's just that some people count the same bird twice. They're so mobile, those nuthatches.'

'Seen both of 'em at once. The wife'll tell you, her bed's just there under the window and she stares out for days on end, to pass the time.'

He glanced beyond the old man at the window, and the face of an old woman was visible now.

The man had rung about the nuthatches a couple of days ago, the same day as his piece about them had appeared in the paper.

'So come on and put rings on our Siberian visitors while they're still in these parts.'

And now he had come. The man asked him to come in

first, but he wanted to start straight away, look for a suitable place for the net; there, between the rowan trees, where the berries glistened. He put the net up there; the trunks of the rowans were the right size, so he didn't need stakes, they stayed in the car. He felt a familiar cool unease as he turned his back to the net and walked to his car, and took out his scales and his notebook. Then he had to turn round and look: a great tit was just fluttering into the net.

He took it out immediately, weighed it, attached a ring to its leg and wrote the details in his notebook. The man stood beside him watching, and somehow his presence disturbed him, though he could not order him away either.

'Ah, so these ordinary birds of ours are worth ringing too, eh?'

'Sure – in fact all birds are worth it, really.'

'Seems to be a male, with such a broad stripe on the breast.'

'Yes, it is, or rather a young male. Last summer's brood.'

'How can you tell?'

He explained, and remembered how he had once explained it to Teija. That was different, but the old man was more particular, and seemed to be taking note of the facts, not pitying the birds, sticking to the facts, as men do. Gradually his presence ceased to trouble him – he was just there, not a disturbance. Then the man went indoors; when he glanced at the window, there were two faces there.

Mechanically, he removed some birds from the net, great tits and willow-tits, there were quite a few of them, clean-looking and fleshy, two or three grammes heavier than usual. The old ones had been feeding well and started early in the autumn. He glanced again at the window and almost felt gratitude. He measured, weighed, ringed, took notes. A bird didn't weigh much, but when you let it go, it felt as if your hand had taken flight with it. Then it would sink down again, a part of his body.

He looked at the net; there were six or seven of them hanging and struggling there again. And something pale and rapid darted past the net to the bird-table – he was startled. It was a nuthatch, and he had already begun to fear that they wouldn't come. It plucked a sunflower seed from the table and fluttered lightly into the net. There it was. He went to take it before the others; it was the most precious. The old man came out and looked on while he inspected it, put it into a nylon stocking and weighed it.

'And then the rings,' said the old man while he attached the ring. 'Aluminium engagement rings. I guess we'll still get the other one too. Just for them I bought the nuts, although the tits won't leave them for them. Let 'em take 'em if they want to, they're all hungry after all.'

He let the nuthatch fly out of his hand, and it flew off nimbly, scolding as it went.

'Chirp away,' laughed the old man. 'But now you got a ring round yer ankle.'

Before dusk came, another nuthatch appeared, and tumbled into the net as if it were inevitable, hanging there helplessly, yielding to his hands. This was a female, the other one was male, though it was not easy to see the difference.

'Now they're engaged to each other!' said the old man, who was once again present. 'Or p'raps even married. Till death do them part, like me and Kerttu over there.'

He laughed. 'Till death do them part! – That's how people used to think when they got together. Times've changed now. S'pose you're not married yourself?'

'I haven't dared to take such a big step,' he said, letting go of the nuthatch. It flew into the same clump of spruces as the first one.

'Ah well, you're still young,' the man said. 'I mean, you've still got time. S'pose you've got someone in mind then?'

'Yes, I guess – someone.'

'You plan to, then.'

'You've got to at least plan to,' he said, hoping the old man would stop. Now that the nuthatches had been ringed, the main purpose of the trip had been achieved. In the dusk, he released birds from the net and ringed the rest of the tits and two bullfinches. It was mild and calm, and slowly the snow began to fall. The early nightfall felt calming, and so did the presence of just these birds, that had stayed here for the winter – one always anticipated the spring, the multitude of birds, and yet, when the migratory birds had left, it somehow felt better. The last tit was hanging in the net, in an awkward position, flapping a wing. He looked at it before taking it away, and felt no pity; its eyes looked straight at him, its imprisoner, its humiliator, and it understood nothing of ornithology. It weighed less than twenty grammes, it was feather and hollow bone, in the physical sense virtually non-existent. That was why it was easy for it to fly: there was nothing mystical about it, neither in its flight nor in its song. And yet sometimes one would start to look at it as a poet would: as something which one would never achieve oneself nor ever find in another.

The last bird left his hands in flight, fluttering a little – perhaps it was slightly injured? No, hardly, its wing was just momentarily sore – after all it had looked bad in the net, perhaps it had been there too long.

The old man offered him coffee with fresh buns in the house. He followed the man's efforts, as he took the coffee to his wife in bed and took care of her in every way. In their company he was somehow inadequate, dumb in a strange way, and suddenly he began to miss Teija.

'About five years our Kerttu's been like that,' the man said. 'Sometimes sits in a wheelchair, sometimes lies down. They'd take her away to a home, but I won't let 'em, how could I let the old girl go when I could still look after her? Or do I look so bad that I couldn't do the lifting any more? I asked them when they came here. They had to say I don't look too bad. I can still look after one woman, and the cat, and the birds.'

'It's best to be at home,' said the woman from her bed. She was quite fat; he thought that she would take some lifting, and looked sympathetically at the man. He will have to carry the shapeless woman to the grave. But then he does want to. He has chosen his burden himself.

'It's no problem being at home when you've got a good man,' said the woman. 'Someone used to come here once a week to give me exercise and look after me, like. But what exercise do you need any more to get to the grave. Funny how me legs gave way, just like that, and I've got other troubles too. I don't want anything more than just to die at home.'

But she didn't seem to be dying, and the man said: 'What's all this about dying, you're not dying yet. I'll still be looking after you when you're a hundred.'

'May the Lord take me to him before that. Without legs.'

'Now don't go on like that. Want more coffee? What about the ringing man?'

'No thanks, no more for me. I ought to be going.'

'What's the hurry when you ain't got a family? You can take another cup. After the job, like, out there for hours with your bare hands in the cold. Those birds are fun for us, you know, we follow their lives now that our own kids've flown the nest.'

'Got many of them?'

'Five left – one died young and one died as an adult. And one of 'em's going on fifty.'

When he finally left, he had the feeling that he had dropped in on one of the good moments of his early childhood – one of which he had not retained the image, but which had left an impression once inside him. Snow was falling softly; forest surrounded the road.

The peace of the stretch of forest lay behind him when he came to the main road. Snow flew at him swiftly, bitingly; the red cottage at the edge of the open field sank to the fringe of his consciousness, flashed into it sometimes and caused him irritation. What an idyll it had been – the sick woman in the bed, and each of them clinging to the other because there was nobody else.

Fifty years together. He laughed, stepped on the gas, overtook the car in front of him. His hands on the wheel were suddenly tight, stiff.

Fifty years. How could you know how much they must have taunted each other, like people everywhere, in the night, even at night. In fact most likely at night, away from other people's eyes.

He overtook another car and then tried to relax, slacken his hands. There was no hurry, he said to himself, staying close behind another car to overtake it too. But it wouldn't let him pass and he saw a woman in it, her blond hair waving as she glanced. She wouldn't let him pass, so she drove above the limit as well. But Teija in his arms, soon, unless – he gripped the steering-wheel, his hands trembling.

As soon as he opened the door he knew that something had happened, and he also knew what it was: Teija in bed with someone else! He went straight to the bedroom and laughed wryly when he saw the bed was empty: they were trying to cheat him! But the bed really was empty – he touched the wooden slatted mattress with his hand; where was the mattress, the mattress and the covers? Surely not out drying in the yard, when it was snowing and dark?

He opened the wardrobe door. Teija's clothes were not there, and her jars were not in their boxes – had she gone? The living-room looked bare, half the books were missing, the mats, the picture from the wall, everything that was Teija's.

He understood. It was true. As if a dream had ended, and dreams are always short. He found a note on the table and read: 'If you don't happen to remember, I paid for the bedclothes when we got the broader bed. So I took them with me. You've made your bed, now lie in it.'

What did it mean, made your bed? He no longer understood. He remembered Teija's best girlfriend, she must know something. He found her number in the telephone book and rang.

'Who did she go with? Who did she have?'

'Nobody that I know of.'

'How do you mean, nobody?'

'Nobody, I mean nobody. With you she – '

'You mean she went with no reason?'

'I don't mean anything. You ought to know the reasons better.'

The girlfriend hung up – he didn't get the chance to ask where Teija had moved to. But what was the difference – since she wasn't here, she could be anywhere. She was light; it was easy for her to fly away. He wasn't able to hold her by the legs like those nuthatches just now.

He laughed dismally when he remembered the old woman in her bed. Now there was a woman who would stay. She had lost her legs.

Later in the evening he fetched his old narrow mattress from the cellar. It was stained and thin, bought long before

155

Teija's time. He put it on the base of the bed, and it was only two-thirds as broad as the bed. He hurled himself onto it with his clothes on, and the slats felt hard through it. But he had to lie on the bed as he had made it.

It had all started too well; it was painful to recall it now. The night in the tent there at Siikalahti, and the next morning, with the sun rising out of the red mist, where the bittern boomed. Then the mist turned pale and the nightingales started singing all around them. He listened, looked, then put his binoculars on a stone when Teija called him back to the tent. She was there ready for him, and glowed against him in the cool morning. And with that, the best time for birds was past. But it wasn't wasted.

It came back like something from his youth, though it wasn't more than two or three years ago. Then, in the beginning, Teija used to go on ringing trips with him. But soon her company became tedious; she disturbed him, claimed that the birds were suffering, did not believe him when he said that ringing did not harm them. And then one of them died once, got stuck in a net so badly that nothing could save it, and Teija looked on closely while he put it out of its pain. Such things happen sometimes in this job, but rarely to him; he was a careful and efficient ringer, and it was wrong of Teija to avoid his hands that evening. And she no longer went with him, and it was better that way.

At that time she had become somehow withdrawn, and often waited for him to fall asleep before she came to bed. But he would wait too, staying awake out of spite, and when she did come she would bring with her the memory of that night in the tent and at the same time the knowledge that it had not been repeated – she brought that red mist down into the bed as if to dazzle him, and yet he could see: Teija never completely accepted him, she was always on guard about something. Was there somebody else that she did accept and merged with? Did somebody else have her time? He asked her, asked with his mouth, with his body, but she did not answer.

Yet now he wanted her back again. And she did come, before midnight, before sleep – she came unseen but tangibly, came to avenge everything, but most of all his love. Her hands were small and hard, and with them she aroused his desire and then fled.

In the small hours, when sleep had still not come, he took out his ringing diary and began examining it. It calmed him, and he noted that yesterday had been moderately good: twenty-eight ringings in the old man's yard, of which fifteen were great tits, nine willow-tits, two bullfinches and those two nuthatches.

He saw the thin net against the white snow and in it a tit, the one that stayed till last, whose wing was fluttering, stuck fast in the net. Yet it did fly away, though more poorly than the others; you had to hope that it wasn't permanently injured.

A nice day, nearly thirty ringed. And not a single one died.

An aluminium ring stays on a bird's ankle all its life. For small birds, that is not long, two or three years on average for a tit – roughly the length of time he and Teija had lived together.

The Wrestlers

Alberts Bels
Latvia

It happened in Latvia in the thirties.

Jānis Rūsa owned a farm that hadn't been paid off – or strictly speaking, the farm had been paid off, but Jānis had borrowed money to rearrange the farmstead, to buy some implements. The money he invested did not bear the fruit he expected, and Jānis was faced with a serious dilemma – to pay or not to pay? If he didn't pay, there was the threat of an auction and all the unpleasantness that that implied. Be that as it may, he did scrape together the necessary sum, by borrowing from his father-in-law Arvīds Petersons, by taking a loan from his neighbour Linājs, and by – shame to say – incurring a debt to his farmhand Vecbebru Rūdis, and yet – he was still short by sixty lats. Now sixty lats wouldn't normally be a large sum if it were just that, but unfortunately he just didn't have those sixty lats, and try as he might, Jānis couldn't think of anyone in the district, near or far, who might be able to lend that kind of sum.

One Sunday morning, while putting hay down in front of his two horses, he speculated sadly that perhaps he ought to get rid of one of the beasts. Now what put a silly idea like that into his head – who would go in front of the plough?

All the same, this Sunday he was going to make one more effort to get the money together.

So he found himself sitting in the tent. The huge tent loomed above the edge of the village – now just how did that tent come to be there? But the fact was that the tent loomed above it just like Jānis' thoughts about the sixty lats. Hell of a business, with many beautiful young women around, at any other time he would have been glad to look at them – why is he sitting here at all? – but now, from one side – interesting, only you don't know from which side, maybe it's more interesting from that side, the back side, where the circus people are getting changed, smearing their faces and powdering themselves, probably talking among themselves too – interesting, what do these circus people talk about before the show, and where do they come from, and where are they going? In a way it's obvious – they come from Slītere, go off to Pabērze, but where do they come from in the deeper sense? What drives people to do somersaults across a sawdust floor? They might be better off growing wheat or rearing horses! Or working in a factory. They don't have proper houses, no families, and there probably aren't any rich ones. What do they do in their old age? How long can a person flop about on a cross-bar upside down – well, another five years? – then he gets squeaky, stiff, falls down to sweep the arena or be a joker. Perhaps there's some deeper ailment that drives you to do tricks in front of other people. Work itself is the wheel that turns the days. Where does a simple peasant get such ideas? But then a peasant isn't simple at all, if he's got a double bottom, like a smuggler's bag? There are double chins, double accounts – but a double bottom I haven't seen yet. But wait a minute – what if I did somersaults on a mat to earn my keep? For others to look at? Just yesterday, and as recreation for them – as you see, there isn't any – anyway, yesterday: I went to the post-office to ring the bank about that promissory note, and there behind the tent, at eight in the morning, stands a knife-thrower, throwing half a dozen of them all around his head, like a potato-masher, like a hand-grenade; I come back, I see he's just throwing those potato mashers around his head, and this evening there he is standing in the arena, again throwing potatoes around his head, and that's probably how he spends his whole life; what sense is there in a life like that – interesting, could he say that himself? Perhaps we don't understand one another – he goes past me in a covered wagon, see, I'm tilling the soil, walking behind the plough and so on from morning till night, and another day, when he comes back, he sees me behind the plough and thinks: how monotonous a peasant's life is. And what is there to show for it? That grain, that bread? Or rather the smell of the earth, that soft warm sod, those birds behind the plough and the horses in front? Perhaps I plough because I like to? But how about those old people, with lumbago in their backs, rheumatism in their knees, pains in their shoulders? My grandfather, as long as he didn't have his hand on the handle of the plough, used to groan, moan, mutter and splutter, but when he started the first furrow, he'd fall silent and go on until evening without tiring. How he moved! If he hadn't moved, it'd probably have been the end of him.

But it wasn't curiosity that had brought Jānis to the circus. On the poster the owner of the circus had proclaimed that after the performance, anyone who wanted, if they paid a deposit of ten lats, could try their strength at wrestling with a bear. Whoever could beat the bear in a match would get a prize of a hundred lats. Now Jānis was secretly hoping for this prize, though he didn't really have any expectations. He had heard reports that no-one in the district, near or far, had managed to get this bear to the ground, and the circus owner had been pocketing these sums each time, not actually running any risk. And Jānis wasn't a paragon of strength either – his only trump cards were his dexterity and his twenty-seven years; but where others could carry a bag of grain a hundred paces, he was staggering after fifty; where others would be heaving rocks, Jānis could usually only manage to give advice. Anyway, when the circus owner announced that the moment had arrived, everyone could try their hand, Jānis went into the middle of the arena.

He needed the sixty lats, there was no getting away from it: the audience was making a noise, whistling, stamping their feet, some were applauding, but the ringmaster had already gone off to fetch the local doctor some time ago, and nobody could think that Jānis would have the courage to fight the bear. He paid the deposit.

What did Jānis know about bears? Only that bears are strong. This one must have been four or five years old, big, with combed brown fur, growling, unfriendly, doing everything reluctantly; his grandmother had said that evil spirits vanish when a bear growls. A bear could also be a bewitched person – perhaps even this one wasn't really a bear, but some strong man dressed up; well, if so, then perhaps all the better. The circus owner scrutinized Jānis with a certain anxiety, so that he felt quite uneasy; then he handed him a thick cloak of tarpaulin to put on and lace up crosswise, like boots – 'and I've about as much sense as a boot', Jānis thought, while the manager and his assistant tied the jacket at the back; is he going to tear me apart?

They worked slowly as they laced him, chatting between themselves, and suddenly the manager said, as if in passing: 'But if you get scared you don't get your money back.'

'Of course,' snarled Jānis. 'Why would anyone get scared?'

'Well, with such a ferocious beast,' said the assistant.

'Has he mauled anyone?' Jānis enquired with interest.

'Has happened,' the manager replied nonchalantly.

'Well, he's met his match here!'

Having tied on his tarpaulin jacket, they left him alone in the middle of the ring, and all around him the audience was screaming and bellowing; some wished him luck, but one burly mug in the front row shouted breathlessly: 'Jānis, he'll beat you black and blue!' and laughed like an idiot at what he'd said, which in the general hubbub probably only he and Jānis heard. A few seconds before the fight, Jānis' senses became heightened and exaggerated; he could clearly hear the circus owner behind the curtains letting the bear out of its cage, irritating the beast, hitting it on the snout with the whip-handle, and then the brown bear appeared, walking on its hind legs like a real wrestler, and everything fell silent around them, though in fact the noise grew even louder; it was just that Jānis no longer heard anything but the bear's wheezing breath. The closer the bear came, the more the beast's acrid stench filled Jānis' nose. Well, the rain didn't last long, and you won't wash it off in a tub; for a moment quite unseemly thoughts entered Jānis' head, but now the bear was right there pawing at him, and keeping some distance behind the animal was the circus owner, still egging the bear on. The bear's snout was tied up with a leather strap, but its claws shone sharp, black, as if sharpened and lacquered. The two wrestlers stood facing each other. A gong rang out. The audience fell silent.

Jānis was quite unable to seize the bear; it kept pushing him away with its paw, and the black, shiny claws each time squeaked on the canvas cloth, leaving white scratch marks. And then Jānis grabbed the bear and brought it to the ground.

It happened so quickly and unexpectedly, for both the

audience and the bear, as well as the circus owner and Jānis himself, that the whole circus seemed to be paralysed. Jānis nimbly jumped further away from the bear, but the animal remained lying for a moment on the sawdust, awkwardly moving its paws. And then the audience started to roar like a many-headed dragon that was hired to make a wind, and the circus owner's voice was quite lost in the roaring of the dragon.

'It wasn't the right way, it wasn't right!' shouted the circus owner.

'It was right!' howled the many-headed dragon. 'Now pay out!'

So this battle of words, this wrestling match, continued for some minutes, and meanwhile the bear fled and hid in its cage, but the circus owner announced that the performance was over and Jānis could collect his money when the audience had dispersed.

So all right then. No-one helped Jānis to untie the tarpaulin cloth, and when with great effort he had struggled out of his wrestler's clothes, the audience had already gone. The circus owner was waiting for Jānis in his little tent. After a moment's hesitation the owner started speaking:

'Look, you'll have those hundred lats, no question about that, but wouldn't you rather have this beautiful kerosene lamp instead? It's foreign, brighter than any decent electricity and costs a hundred and sixty lats.'

'Just the money,' Jānis said firmly.

'But this lamp's made of brass, gilded, you can hang it on a chain over the table, and these little hanging bits are gilded, they come at no extra cost.'

Jānis looked at the lamp. It really was oddly beautiful, but Jānis remembered having seen one in Riga, in a shop on Marija Street; it had cost twelve lats there. No, but Jānis would be ashamed in front of the whole village because of that lamp; if someone does tricks with a bear, he ought to get a hundred lats.

'A hundred lats,' Jānis said. 'If not, I'll call a policeman.'

'I see you want to ruin me,' the circus owner replied in a quite dejected voice.

This was getting silly!

'Where's the money you got for the tickets?' Jānis asked.

'That's already been paid in wages to the artistes in the first interval, and it wasn't very much anyway, so I'm still in debt to the troupe. There's no hope of getting that money back. I tell you, have pity on me. I haven't got ten santīmi in my wallet. If you call a policeman I've got a lot of unpleasantness in store for me.'

The circus owner seemed to be speaking the truth. Jānis didn't know what to do next.

'Okay then,' he said, 'nothing but swindlers! Then at least give me back the ten lats you asked for as a deposit.'

The owner, quite ashamed, shifted his feet and replied:

'I don't have those ten lats any more. The wife ran off with them to the shop to buy the kids something to eat.'

So now Jānis set off for home with the lamp under his arm and a halo of glory round his head. He couldn't say to anyone that he had been cheated, because you can't escape from people's mockery for the rest of your life. He said that he had got the lamp into the bargain along with the promised prize, and the very next day he sold his horse, because now he was seventy lats short – but in the evening, when Jānis was returning from the bank, he was passed by an old rattling van with a caged bear on a trailer. Behind the bars languished the great beast which Jānis had unexpectedly beaten, only because the brown artiste had not had a decent square meal for a whole week, and that evening the creature had resolved to wreak a nice revenge on its master and trainer by deliberately losing the fight to a weakling like Jānis Rūsa, whom, if he had only wanted to, the experienced wrestler could have knocked to the sawdust with one blow of his mighty paw.

The Fatherland is in Danger

Valentīns Jakobsons
Latvia

Not two years have passed yet. Not even two years have passed since our brother, father and teacher abandoned us and left this wonderful world for another, better one. Not even two years have passed yet, but unheard-of things are already happening in our country. Unbelievable, wrong things are happening in our country. Really, mad things are happening. Absurd things, you could say. Detainees are being allowed to grow their hair. The iron gratings of the huts' windows are being broken and torn off. They're ripping the fastenings and the weighty bolts off the doors. The urine tubs are being thrown on the fire. Now is that in order?

In the former isolation unit, or should I say the lock-up, a shop has now been set up. In it the prisoners can spend their money on rose-hip jam and fine 'Kazbek' cigarettes. But they may and can also buy rye bread there – as much as they want. As much as they want! In the former Severe Punishment Block, at one end of the old hut, they've set up and equipped a library. Tell me – is that why hundreds of thousands had to be rounded up and conveyed huge distances – so that they could read little books here, is it? As for what is going on at the other end of the hut, I'm ashamed to speak of it. Set up at the other end of the hut is a broad green table, and around it the convicts drive a little ball. Watching that kind of activity, it's enough to give you a fever. Here in the North, are there to be no more new buildings or mines, are there to be no pickaxes, spades and sledgehammers? The mind cannot comprehend such deep moral degradation.

The prisoners have been ordered to strip off their numbers. They've been ordered to strip the numbers off their jackets, their trousers, their cotton vests, their shirts, their caps, their ... Off everything. If there's a number inscribed on any item of clothing in oil-paint and you can't get it off, it has to be cut right out of the garment and a patch sewn over the hole. Numbered people are not allowed to work, they're no longer let out of the zone.

'Let the smart-alec who put the number on come and take it off himself,' bluster the stubborn ones. These undisciplined types just smirk at the commandant's order without batting an eyelid. And they jeer, you know, they jeer at the decent supervisors, who have to maintain order in unprecedented circumstances, who have to appeal, who now have to ask a convict to go off to the sewing workshop to stitch up his clothes. Can there be order if the barrack windows are left without gratings and the doors without bolts? Can good order exist if a prisoner doesn't have a number?

It can't.

Because of that, because of that lack of order, let's say because of the lack of a firm hand, one day convict Voskoboynikov is visited by his wife. The wife arrives, as they say, from the Great Land and brings her husband a uniform. She brings a brand new one, received from the hands of a tailor, with a colonel's insignia on the shoulders, and four rows of shiny baubles on the chest. And she also brings with her a new army cap to put on, laced boots to wear, and a dozen white handkerchieves to blow his nose on. The man nimbly slips off his tattered rags, gets changed, puts on his boots, scrubs his nails and, pure and smiling, appears before civilized humanity. At a stroke, he is no longer a prisoner, not a starveling, a louse-slaughterer, but officially Air Force Colonel Voskoboynikov. After that he goes to the airport ticket office and buys himself some tickets, because he's rehabilitated through and through. But before flying far away, he and his wife go to the Sever restaurant to have a meal. And at the door of this establishment he bumps into Captain Zamogilny, the camp commandant. The rosy-cheeked captain wants more than anything to refresh his parched mouth, and standing by the buffet table, to whet his appetite a bit.

'What the devil – Voskoboynikov? It's Voskoboynikov, the louse-killer! Really, I wouldn't have recognized you! ... Look, Voskoboynikov, now do you finally understand what Soviet power means? And that's why you've got to respect it ... Respect it and love it ... You ought to go on and on doing your term ... you ought to sit it out just like all the other stinkers. You ought to sit it out, but Soviet power, you see, takes you and squeezes the life out of you. So it lets you out of the nick before your time! ... Before your time!' – the camp commandant effusively tries to explain the noble circumstances of release to those around him. 'So let's you and I go to the bar and down a couple, eh – a double measure! Make that a couple of large ones!'

'Captain, obey my command! About turn! Quick march! Keep going!'

That the colonel isn't joking is obvious to the captain right through his hang-over, and so he turns about and briskly steps out of the bar. But there's only one bar in this town.

Sometime Later

Aija Valodze
Latvia

On coming out of the lift, Jānis Krūmiņš didn't go straight
past the doors of the secretaries' and editors' offices, but
described a semicircle, past proof-reading, the typing pool and
both sexes' toilets. He felt independent enough to think of
calling out a playful 'Hi, mate!' to the Editor – though he
didn't like to meet 'the boss' face to face; it was already
approaching half past nine, so he had to sneak cautiously into
his room. Jānis wasn't usually late, especially in recent times,
since he'd given up smoking – nowadays he woke up so early
in the morning that he went to work on foot, and he had
grown very much to like strolling unhurriedly over the bridge.
There he could always feel the wind, and all around there was
such a vast expanse that his breast filled with exhilaration.

That day, too, Jānis walked at a steady pace over the
Daugava, feeling the breeze on his face, though the water
looked quite smooth, with the clouds mirrored in it. This
time, though, the vastness of the scene created quite the
opposite effect on him from the usual. Involuntarily it

occurred to him that today, as he walked in just the same way, the same place as yesterday, he himself had grown older. Jānis was twenty-six years old, and this was the first time such a thought had entered his head. He immediately calculated, too, that in a normal human lifespan, say seventy years, a total of 25,500 such days passed imperceptibly by – and he had already lived nearly ten thousand of them. And yet he didn't feel that he was really living at all! Frightened and shocked, Jānis stopped, pressed his palms against the railings of the bridge and lingered in thought until two pretty young women going past, shop assistants or students, laughed as they said something to one another, and then both looked back at Jānis. Their light dresses billowed in the breeze, and the echo of their laughter was borne on the wind: will he jump or won't he? The girls' amusement confused Jānis, yet in his imagination he self-confidently blew them both kisses, while his physical self could only with difficulty turn around and finally resume its way to the tower block of the Press House.

Jānis left his office door fully open, so everyone could see he was there and already working. The misunderstanding about the bottle still depressed him; Jānis never wanted to go through anything like it again. Later he himself didn't understand why the water for the flowers was kept in a brandy rather than a milk bottle, and why he had shoved the bottle under the desk, because just at the moment when the editor came in to warn him about the fire inspection, Jānis accidentally kicked the bottle with his foot. The editor watched silently as it rolled along the floor. Jānis would have liked to say: 'Listen, mate, you didn't think I was having a swig on the sly, did you?' – but he kept quiet too, staring sombrely at the flower that the Letters section had given him on his name-day. And it wasn't even a real flower, but some floral super-monstrosity that grew in a pot, whose fronds were reminiscent of long shaggy hair – Jānis had anyway only held onto it because the huge flower-pot wouldn't fit into any of the editorial waste-baskets. 'Clear away all the heaters, please,' the editor said at length – so icily that he had not been so icy even that time when, in the paper on Jānis' day on duty, by the item about the fishing bans (forbidding fishing from boats or with a rod standing in water), the illustration that had gone in was a lovely sketch in which, against the background of the setting sun, one fly-fisherman was sitting in a boat, while another had waded up to his knees into the river. 'And other inappropriate objects,' the editor added, after an agonizingly long pause. Jānis didn't have any heaters: someone had taken away the 'Little Sun' back in the winter and hadn't brought it back, and the electric kettle had a burnt-out contact – but he hid the bottle behind the curtains.

The usual morning hurry and bustle had now died down, except for the excited voices still to be heard at the end of the corridor: a bit of sport taken out ... another corpse just come in, thirty lines ... get the swimming out, do away with half of the football ... where the hell is the chap on duty? This time it had nothing to do with Jānis, he wasn't on duty for this issue. As always in the morning hours, he had opened the telephone book, and drew it closer to the telephone.

This moment was the most unpleasant one – each time he felt as if he were about to throw himself from a high tower into unfamiliar waters. To be blunt, Jānis wanted to write only about poetry days and poetry evenings, about the exhibitions of poetry books and memorial events for dead poets, but he wasn't allowed to. It had all gone so far that Malda, the head of the department, would immediately put on a martyred expression as soon as he let slip, even by accident, the names Plūdonis, Poruks, or Čaks. In theory, Jānis too realized that life isn't one long poem, that the city's paper had to inform its

171

readers about industrial news, voluntary farm work and masses of other things. Still Jānis believed that one day the time would come when he could write about what he wanted to. Perhaps someone in the Culture section would retire and they would take Jānis on there. Perhaps he would put a full stop to his long planned dramatic poem, it would be printed in *Karogs*, would later be published as a separate book, Jānis would get a grant and become a free artist. When he was independent and famous, another dream would become more possible too: perhaps Jānis would win the heart of one of those bold and beautiful girls that he had always been afraid of – a bit like one of those who had earlier walked past him on the bridge, in a longer, pink dress. And then, no doubt, even the girls in proof-reading – who called Jānis the Shortest Legs in the Press House behind his back, as he well knew – would be proud to know him at all and even sometimes call him by his first name.

There, on the bridge, ever receding from the two beautiful girls and the place where the thought had been born in his mind of how imperceptibly time passes and how far away the fulfilment of his dreams still was, Jānis had suddenly felt helpless and insignificant; he wanted his dreams right now, not sometime later; he didn't want to wait, damn it! Yet now Jānis was again sitting obediently at his desk in the News section of the city paper, with the long-haired plant that was no longer watered turning yellow on the window-sill. He leafed through the telephone book, speculating on whom to ring amid the jungle of names of companies and institutions.

If he was lucky, he would write two or three news items a day, of no shorter than ten and no longer than twenty-five lines, because short ones were sent back from the secretary's office, while when she saw the longer ones, Malda would start to look at the ceiling and her face would say quite unmistakably: 'I know you're an imbecile, but at least don't show it!

I've got enough work to do without crossing out your eternal wafflings!' There was nothing for it but for Jānis to write it himself, because Malda had long ago ceased giving him the freelance writers' material; Jānis didn't know how to correct or abridge as Malda could. She regarded all the freelance writers as blockheads and graphomaniacs and treated them accordingly: change the headline, a line over the introduction, chop off the end, full stop. If any of the blockheads and graphomaniacs later felt offended, Malda would purse her lips and chirp into the receiver (because the editorial staff were protected from the physical presence of irate outsiders by a militiaman or woman who sat at the entrance of the Press House tower day and night) so tenderly, just as if she didn't at all regard the importunate subject at the other end of the line as a complete cretin, a verbal diarrhoetic, something like: 'Delighted that you remember us ... what did you say ... But dear sir! The character of the paper! No, no, very valuable material, write for us again, we'll be glad to, we'll look forward to it, good luck, bye!'

Wow, that Malda! Jānis had been told that Malda was a widow, and after a few years of marriage her husband had gradually started to get more and more weak and taciturn, until he died, and no doctor could tell what he had really died of, perhaps some still undiscovered disease. Yet Jānis felt he knew why Malda's husband had died, and felt a quiet but indissoluble solidarity with the dead man: Jānis would definitely have chosen death too! Malda was like an American. True, Jānis had never known an American, but he pictured them clearly enough: they were exactly like Malda, the gaze of whose steely eye sent a shudder down Jānis' spine every time. Always very alert, energetic, dressed in flowing, gathered dresses, hearty on the outside and ice-cold inside; she exuded for Jānis something perhaps not quite deathly, but that often

173

robbed him of his appetite, and recently, when shaving in the morning, Jānis began to notice anxiously that his cheeks, too, were starting to get thinner and paler. Jānis knew what immense contempt this woman had for him because he longed to write picturesque meditations on long-dead poets, not brief, concrete, contemporary news about new products and city workers doing work on affiliated collective farms and state farms in terms of 'man-days', weeding the beet, preparing cattle-fodder troughs and otherwise helping country people. It seemed to Jānis that he could read Malda's thoughts when, wreathed in cigarette smoke, she sometimes looked long and hard at him, and Jānis was obsessed with a fear that one day Malda would suddenly be unable to contain herself and would pat him on the bottom with her hand – just like Granny in the old days, when he was afraid to go through the woods to the neighbours' house for milk, because the bigger children said an Old Man lived in the woods. 'Nowww!' Granny would say, 'a real man isn't afraid of anything!' and would look at Jānis as derisively as Malda did. And although Jānis had long since ceased to be a credulous little boy convulsed with fear, for security he always, even when in the queue in the Press House bar, tried to stand with his face rather than his back to Malda, because now he could no longer stand such a great humiliation. Despite everything, in his heart Jānis felt like a real man.

However, when quick and lively steps approached along the corridor Jānis started up just as in his childhood, and hurriedly began to dial the first number that came before his eyes – it was a secondary school. Telepathically he strove to inspire Malda not to come to him. 'Just keep further away,' he said mentally, 'you can believe me, I don't want to see you!' And the steps stayed in the adjacent office, while in the receiver a distant voice replied:

'School.'

This voice was infinitely gentle, almost singing, so Jānis, suddenly encouraged, introduced himself as a newspaper correspondent and immediately asked whether anything interesting was anticipated in the new school year there, such as a meeting or a Young Pioneers' working-bee. Perhaps the children had undertaken to tidy up the school grounds? Meanwhile with one ear he was again listening to the familiar footsteps and, raising his eyes, felt something like a blow in the chest: in the doorway stood Malda. Around her fantastic dress, as usual, wafted rings of cigarette smoke. 'It is not permitted to smoke on editorial premises, madam, there is a balcony for that!' Jānis contemptuously rebuked her in his imagination, while Malda, having met Jānis' gaze, immediately waved her hand in a lively way – 'hi, baby!' – and nodded approvingly: young pioneers' life, not bad, a little report like that, none of your fancy newspaper lyrics, okay?

Marija was brushing the dust off the bust of Makarenko when the telephone rang. The headmistress was downstairs, in the kitchen, so Marija, pressing the plaster bust to her breast, reached for the receiver herself. Although she had already attained her fifth decade, Marija retained something of a child's mentality; as she washed the long corridors, she shrilly sang about the green forest and the three twined roses, she made eyes at the handsomest boys in the older classes and generally felt young and joyful. Yet even the cheekiest boys would hardly make fun of Marija and, if they sometimes did tease her, they did it without malice, because they had known this nice woman since their first class: Marija was already working at this school before even the kids in the eleventh class were born. Marija immediately took a strong liking to the young journalist's voice in the telephone receiver. He spoke so courteously and shyly, almost appealingly. So Marija couldn't refuse him and agreed to everything he wished – the meeting?

of course! planting greenery in the grounds? of course! the Pioneers' working bee? that too! because no man had ever talked to Marija as tenderly as this boy from the paper – except for that foreign railwayman, who long years ago had treated Marija to chocolates in the coal-shed and then seduced her; and then there was the fireman, who gave her a big brass brooch set with violet stones.

But the headmistress, who at that moment was fishing for maggots in a soup cauldron, already had bad experience of newspapermen. That was just why, each day, she would go down several times to the cellar to carry out a curious ritual amid the smells and fumes of the kitchen: she would pick out a barrel of pickled cabbage with a long stick, sniff the beetroot and carefully stir the contents of all the frying-pans and saucepans. Because of this daily act the kitchen staff regarded the headmistress – just as they did Marija – as a bit touched, and to an outsider it really did look odd that a grey-haired, reserved lady, whose eyes always – even when smiling – betrayed some hidden, heavy suffering, would resolutely, puffing with the effort, rummage about among the heated and unheated foodstuffs. During the past year the staff of the school kitchen had entirely changed, so none of the heat-reddened, white-clad creatures who, when the headmistress appeared, immediately started flapping about like a flock of startled seagulls, knew what a heavy blow the headmistress had suffered about ten years before. As if out of spite, just when her enlarged photograph, in which she looked so good, had been set up in the local scroll of honour, something unthink-able happened: there arrived at the school a pitiful-looking little man with a grey, wispy beard, who spoke smoothly and flatteringly and eventually, in a roundabout way, came to mention some letter of complaint, which he didn't even give the headmistress to read. But a month later a shocking article appeared in the young people's paper: 'Maggot soup for lunch today'. The school cook took offence and went off to work in a restaurant, but the headmistress' photograph promptly disappeared from its place of honour by the path through the park, opposite the fountain.

When Marija, beaming, warbling and beating time with a brush, welcomed the headmistress on the landing with the joyful announcement that a newspaper correspondent was about to arrive to inspect how the Pioneers had planted shrubbery in the schoolyard on the day of the working bee, the headmistress clutched with both hands at the banister and closed her eyes for a moment: why, oh why did she still expect dangers only from the kitchen? For years now the green patch at the school had been a real nuisance: there on the lawn, surrounded by hedge, bounded by the street on one side, there had been regular visitors with sandwiches, serious men with pale bluish faces - you might almost think they were the miraculously revived corpses of drowned men. The cover of the hedge was also sometimes used by one or two members of the fair sex, who, to tell the truth, didn't differ much from the other corpses: they also had men's shoes and long trousers, as if pulled out of a rubbish bin, but the upper parts of their bodies were covered by something not really dark or light, buttoned right up to the neck - a sort of cape. The lawn, of course, was trampled and yellowed, and even in the middle of summer covered with leaves from the two maples. The wonder was that it hadn't withered away yet. You couldn't say that the headmistress hadn't struggled against the local alcoholics - she had. On several occasions she had complained to the Internal Affairs Department, reminding them that 'after all, our pupils, young ladies, have to walk past there!' The headmistress had even organized a sort of voluntary law-and-order corps, whose appointed leader was young Miss Gulbe, and it incorporated

Miss Gulbe's class, which had then been Class 10, but was now 11C. But despite everything, they hadn't managed to preserve the grass. That day, when Jānis Krūmiņš rang the school, the lawn looked more wretched than ever.

'Come here!' the headmistress said to a little boy on his own who, halfway down the stairs, was kicking off his gymshoe.

'Come closer!' she repeated kindly, when the boy, alarmed, stretched his hands out straight by his sides and looked up. And as he slowly climbed up the stairs, the customary hint of silent, repressed suffering around the headmistress' mouth impressed itself deeper still. He would be about the same age as her little grandson in the distant town, from where she had received one single letter – a little postcard of gnomes, and on the other side, in childish Russian writing, 'New Year greetings to Grandma. Seryozha.' Yet this shy appeal for reconciliation only raked up her sense of offence more forcefully – never, never! She had let her son choose. And when he chose his Sonya with the pyramid of peroxide blonde hair which even in the wedding photograph rose up tilting halfway over her head like the Tower of Pisa, she had told her son once and for all not to bother trying to come back, that she could have loved a simple shy girl such as Dacīte, Mudīte or Ilzīte as her own daughter, but this Sonya with a haystack on her head, this vulgar, hard, faded woman! It was only in her dreams at night that her son sometimes still came back to the headmistress as she had loved him – a puny, pliant and sickly child, for whose life she would have sacrificed her own without a moment's hesitation, her little kid, her laddie, who was only connected to the big, foreign man he was now by her own sense of injury and suffering. Everything had burnt out – all that remained was a heavy sorrow.

'Go and get Miss Gulbe,' said the headmistress to the boy,

when he came up to face her, still turning his earnest child's face up toward her, without saying anything. And suddenly she was overcome by such an inexpressible desire to clasp to herself at least this strange boy that she clenched her hands together and turned away – and only after a moment did she add, still looking not at the boy but at her own hands: 'Go, go quickly!'

The correspondent might turn up at any moment. So as not to waste time, on her way to her office the headmistress called in at the stationery room for brushes and paints, and while she waited for the young teacher, on the edge of a newspaper she herself mixed with the green a little yellow and blended an almost natural-looking tone.

'Come in, Astrīda, sit down!' she called, when the young form-mistress, evidently alarmed, as she always looked, heaven knows why, popped her head in the door. 'If you recall, last spring your class was given the job of looking after the lawn,' the headmistress continued, more forcefully now, with this reminder anticipating possible objections, and she immediately saw with satisfaction that a blush of fear slid over the teacher's face. Although Gulbe was in her second year here, the headmistress still perceived in her some kind of strain or awkwardness. The headmistress had also noticed a couple of times that Gulbe's pupils laughed and made faces about their teacher behind her back, although the teacher herself hadn't complained of any differences of opinion with the class. So the headmistress realized quite well in what an unenviable position the teacher now was, with her authority not held in very great esteem by the class even now. Yet there was no other way to avoid yet another public shaming in the press – the law-and-order corps would have to paint the grass.

As the headmistress spoke, the usual look of anxious agitation on the young teacher's face was replaced by horror, and suddenly the headmistress realized that all the time, from her very first day, since Astrīda Gulbe had come here, her perpetually frightened face, with the restless, lurking, painted eyes which aroused suspicions that she had something to hide, or did not have a clear conscience, had been getting on her nerves. Should a person with such an appearance really be working as a teacher at all? 'Don't keep making such a silly face!' the headmistress wanted to shout, when the young form-mistress, rapidly blinking her ink-daubed lashes, finally reached reluctantly for the brushes.

'No, anything but that', Astrīda wanted to call out, imagining for a moment the amusement of the beautiful Helēna and Marika and the other twenty-seven, all smirking, quietly sniggering and coughing. She had often been thinking anyway that she wouldn't last the time till 11C broke up. One or two were already daring to chuckle to her face; only yesterday Helēna, before Astrīda had had time to say 'Stand up, Mihailova!' piped up in a little high voice: 'Stand up, Mihailova!' – and when Astrīda asked with annoyance 'What did you say?', Helēna muttered with feigned fear, 'Sorry teacher, I must have been thinking aloud ...'

Now Astrīda understood where she had permitted a mistake right at the beginning, when just a year ago the headmistress led her into class 10C and introduced her as the new teacher. Astrīda was scared when she saw how mature her pupils were, how well dressed. Most of them didn't really look like secondary school pupils, but reminded her of the young, wealthy idlers who swanned through Old Riga in the evenings and smoked on the benches by the Planetarium and opposite the Luna café – from their arrogantly scrutinizing looks as Astrīda walked past, her steps always faltered, she felt like a poor, clumsy peasant, and she could never regain her lost self-confidence, even with her conviction of her own superiority.

For it wasn't written on her brow that she was a thinking woman with a higher education, who could only spit on all kinds of mass-produced idiots. So the first time she stood face to face with her class 10C, Astrīda was unable to deliver the free, friendly talk she had been rehearsing on her own down to the finest details. She felt only uncertainty, yes, almost enmity, because she herself had never managed to feel – or at least look – as self-confident as, for example, the strikingly beautiful girl in the first bench in the row by the door, who, putting on an innocent face, tried with a metal ball-point pen to make the sunbeams shine in the new teacher's eyes. Nor had Astrīda ever been able to save money to dress with the same nonchalant chic as her audience on the periphery of the class. Instead of the expected interest, she saw in her charges' eyes only a bored superciliousness. And suddenly Astrīda realized now ridiculous her secret dream of being Pupils' Pet had been. To them she would always be just a 'teach', leading her insignificant grey life for a pittance of a wage – because what normal person goes to work in a school anyway? The normal ones head ministries and travel in luxury Zhigulis, appear on television, make films and get scientific degrees. And at least for the present Astrīda did not have the power to demonstrate that in a couple of short years quite a few of these snobs, instead of the college auditorium and the laurels, would be having to put a gun across their shoulder and march 'left, left!', or weigh sausages behind a counter, but that is what Astrīda wished for them with all her heart. 'Stand up!' she said to the girl with the metal ball-point pen.

'What is your surname?'

'Mihailova', retorted the girl, with a broad smile.

'Well then, on your feet, Mihailova!'

That is how Astrīda's quiet struggle against her class had begun.

In the four years since finishing university, Astrīda had managed to work at seven different jobs, four of them at technical trade schools, two technical secondary schools and an evening college. Something had always happened to make her leave, because everywhere it ended up with a humiliating talk in the rector's office of each institution: 'very sorry, but ... the moral attitude ... authority ... pedagogical ethics ...' In fact it seemed terribly unfair to Astrīda that she, a free Soviet woman, had forced on her by others all sorts of monastic restrictions, that there was always someone sticking their noses into her personal life. For after all, didn't an unmarried teacher have any right at all to personal happiness? Was it Astrīda's fault that she felt a spiritual kinship with, say, the father of one of her pupils?

And yet at this school, where Astrīda had been working longer than anywhere else previously, her reputation had remained irreproachable. Here she had not happened to fall in love with any married colleague, with the father of any pupil, and the pupils themselves were still too green, not like they were at the evening college. So Astrīda had not been faced with having to write a resignation letter. Here at last she could start her new life; she only had to hold out until class 11C broke up, and then everything would be different. She would get to be mistress of one of the smaller classes and within a year she would be Pupils' Pet. And when the time came to part, there would be tears in every eye. 'That was my literature teacher Astrīda Gulbe, whom I have to thank for making me what I am now,' one of her former pupils, a People's Writer, would one day write in his memoirs.

'Now we've got a little practical job to do,' Astrīda began, at once amused and malevolent, because she had long since ceased to hide her real feelings from her charges. 'Mihailova, Kalniņš, Šmits, Apsītis, here's a brush for each of you. Balodis will run off and fetch an empty bucket, ask Auntie, fill it one-third full of water, and everybody down to the yard on the double!' – Astrīda clapped her hands. She knew very well how much she offended the feelings of these future professors and budding film stars if she treated them like kindergarten kids. 'Since we don't know how to look after the lawn – hold on, Mihailova, you can rough up Kalniņš later – now let's see how our yard would look if we had been a bit smarter at doing our duty!'

For a moment there reigned a silence the like of which Astrīda had not experienced for ages with this class. No-one was quietly humming, no-one shuffled their feet, no-one even waved a hand calling 'Please, Miss, may I go to the toilet?' And only then, finally, did Helēna – it had to be her again! – sweetly whisper: 'Please, Miss, will we be tying the leaves back on the trees too?'

Meanwhile, correspondent Jānis Krūmiņš was meandering among the endless utterly identical houses, until finally, having got out of the labyrinth of the new estate, he sighed happily – the building to the right of the lilac-coloured Siamese-twin blocks must after all be the damned school he had been seeking for a whole hour. There weren't any balconies to hang out babies' nappies and women's underwear, and in the yard, behind the low hedge, stooped many figures dressed in bluish hues – they must surely be the Pioneers, the working-bee. In the foreground rose a peculiar metal shape, something between a stylized artificial earth satellite and perpendicular sewage pipes. Sitting on this shape were three youths, two of them smoking, and the third, conducting himself expansively, was singing – not, as Jānis ascertained on coming closer, some Pioneers' work song, but only 'There's a light on in the whorehouse, think I'll drop in for a while'.

'Hello!' Jānis greeted the boys, in a sudden fit of weakness greedily breathing in the cigarette smoke. 'I'm from the paper – they told me you've got a Pioneers' working-bee going on here ...'

Countless times Malda had told Jānis that you have to talk persistently and self-confidently, to inspire immediate respect for a representative of the press, for after all the paper really is something. Any fool ought to understand that a newspaper is capable of lifting you up or dashing you down at a stroke, so a representative of a paper is always a special person, the sort of person who sets the tone everywhere and at all times – even interviewing an academic or a minister. 'Can you really not learn to speak?' Malda had asked, as Jānis at once pressed his bottom against the wall. She herself knew how, oh, she sure did! But Jānis kept on hesitating and getting embarrassed, and it wasn't only his voice, but his whole demeanour, the eyes and the mouth, and the hands plunged into his pockets that mutely screamed: 'It's uncomfortable for me to barge in and disturb you, but I have to do it, sorry, forgive me ...'

Some of the working-bee were raking, but others were treating the garden with a bright green solution – apparently pest control, Jānis surmised. One of the boys, sitting on the artificial satellite, generously handed him a packet of 'Kosmos', and Jānis, being a man of weak character, after ten days' abstention once again voraciously smoked – and how infinitely pleasant it was!

'How are you getting on in general?' he inquired, pleased that he had already partially found a common language with these boys. 'I mean – with life as a Pioneer?'

'Can't complain!' jauntily replied the one who had just been conducting himself. 'As you can see, today we're pain – er, our Swan is swimming!'

'Get off the sculpture straight away!' called a young woman piercingly. 'What are you doing there again! Throw away

184

those fags this instant! And what are *you* looking for here?'
This was unmistakably aimed at Jānis.

'I'm from the paper,' he mumbled, startled.

'So you can fling fags on the ground then, can you?'
growled one of the boys in a quiet bass voice, while the other
repeated victoriously: 'Off the sculp-ture!'

'Sorry,' said the woman. 'Oh, so it's you! My boys are
fooling around, I'm sorry, but you really mustn't give them
cigarettes! Still schoolboys, you understand ... Now get down
quick – you heard, on the double! I thought you were some
friend of theirs, or ...'

Jānis really didn't like this woman. From moment to
moment she'd start laughing first at this, then at that, tossing
back her head and baring her teeth as if for biting. The girl, on
the other hand, who was looking at Jānis, bent over a tin
bucket ... She was even more beautiful than the one on the
bridge in the pink dress!

'I'm the teacher, the form-mistress, Gulbe,' said the woman.
She came closer and closer to Jānis, so that he involuntarily
moved backwards, but just then a voice rang out, clear as a
silver bell: 'Oh, don't go on the grass, the grass hasn't dried yet
...' And without even looking, Jānis knew clearly that that
voice belonged to the heavenly creature by the zinc bucket.

'Mihailova!'

'But I'm already standing, please, Miss!'

Jānis rode the trolleybus pensively back to the Press House.
Gradually a suspicion arose within him that there was
something not quite right about this Pioneers' working bee.
The unpleasant teacher had talked convincingly about the
young people's initiative and activity, but somehow the
Pioneers themselves didn't seem quite so serious. The
staggeringly beautiful girl had unexpectedly mentioned some
drunks who came to the school to pee. But the teacher had

185

immediately sent the girl away. Jānis had been unable to avert his eyes as long as the golden-haired angel was visible on the path covered with concrete slabs. In his confusion he didn't really know what to think. Jānis, to tell the truth, felt unpleasantly offended by the word 'pee' coming from the mouth of such a young, lovely girl.

Depressed, Jānis looked out of the window. Malda was expecting a report on the Pioneers' life at the school – brief, pithy and lovely. And Jānis did know how to write – in three and a half years' work he had mastered the special style of the paper. So why was his heart suddenly so terribly sad this time? The trolleybus mounted the bridge and in a little moment was already gliding past the place where Jānis, sunk in thought, had been standing in the morning. And just at that moment he again caught sight of the girl in the pink dress. Her hair was billowing in the wind. And again she was walking, walking away, until she vanished from Jānis' view. And suddenly he knew quite clearly – this girl would always be going away and would never belong to him. And perhaps he would never write his dramatic poem either. Time just goes and vanishes – like the girl in the pink dress – and doesn't look back at Jānis Krūmiņš, who goes on consoling himself with dreams, that sometime, sometime later ... He vividly remembered what he had experienced: he had entered the schoolyard through the low wrought-iron gate, seen the boys on a bright metal monster, heard a song that he too, Jānis, had once sung when pissed in his student days, heard the silvery voice of a beautiful girl. And then with sudden cynicism which surprised Jānis himself, he saw the conclusion of his report. It would be so ringing and optimistic that even Malda would find nothing to cross out or correct. 'Tired but satisfied after the work they had done, the clever pioneers gathered by the garden sculpture – a symbol of the upward thrust – where one of their

186

classmates, at first quietly, but then ever louder, began a patriotic Pioneer song.'

On the way home Jānis, just as in the morning, went to the bridge railings and gazed down. Only this time there was no-one nearby to comment: will he jump or won't he? And he wasn't going to jump either. The water there, deep below, looked threateningly dark, and it was probably quite cold.

A Christmas Story,
Half a Century Long

Martiņš Zelmenis
Latvia

It was snowing. Sonny would now go upstairs; Sonny had
drawn the caretaker woman and her cat on the wall, in the
place where the rubbish containers used to stand, when the
caretaker noticed him and, shouting something, rushed up after
him, a broom in her hand. Sonny would now go upstairs.
While his mother was away at work, he couldn't even get into
the flat – not even if the neighbours let him in, it made no
difference as the door to the room was locked; he would have
to sit in the kitchen, which smelt of cats, or in the corridor,
which smelt a bit of blubber-oil and pickled cabbage. Sonny
had nobody to play with – one friend was still at school,
another – in the next staircase – was sick, and mummy
wouldn't let him go near sick people, and the boy's mother or
grandmother wouldn't let Sonny through the door either, and
the one with all the parents seemed to be gone for good, and
those two who now lived in his room, it turned out, had no
children. Sonny had never ventured upstairs, he was afraid of

heights, and mummy wouldn't let him either, but the snowflakes were so big that it occurred to Sonny to have a look at the view of it from right up on top – whether it was any prettier than on the ground, at Sonny's level, where you only had to stretch out your hand and it would silently settle there, in a few imperceptible moments filling the outstretched palm of a mitten – perhaps that happened faster up there? Or perhaps they were even whiter? In the yard the caretaker was rushing about with her broom and shovel, unable to sweep it all up – could you even sweep away so much snow? She just walked around with her broom, driving away the little boys who drew her riding a broomstick, a cat on her shoulder. The caretaker was a witch, Sonny knew. That was why no-one would have anything to do with her, they'd turn on their heels and vanish indoors, leaving her with her raised broom; she wouldn't go after them.

Sonny rushed quickly up the first and second flight of stairs: down behind the door of the staircase – whether it was wet or dry outside – there always lingered pungent-smelling puddles, so Sonny hurried past the 'uncle' who stood swaying beside a puddle, as well as past his own door on the third floor, only stopping to draw breath by the window on the fourth floor, through which he glanced outside: the world had thrown off nearly all its colours, and, looked at from the staircase warmed by the radiators, the huge white puffs of floss which, dampening the world's noise, slowly (even more slowly than usual, it seemed to Sonny) drifted past the window, were warm, not cold, even though his drenched mittens were no proof of that. Sonny took them off and stuffed them in his pockets: the left pocket of his overcoat had a sort of pocket of its own, and if you put something in it, it didn't slide through a huge hole into the lining. He pressed his bluish fingers onto the radiators; were they more warming than the snowflakes?

More than anything like that: so soft, fluffy and, here on the fourth floor, definitely warm, Sonny looked into - such whiteness! The beautiful flakes had covered up the sun, taken over the world, brought with them a silent, calm even light; the few vehicles down on the road were driving with their lights on, but from Sonny's height they looked like dwarves running around with lanterns. People were walking like white snowmen, like an army of snowmen dressed in military uniforms; it was happening further off, beyond the little single-storey wooden house - there was a road there that on other days was very noisy. The vehicles were rushing along it - no, the dwarves with lanterns - but without their accustomed sound. Sonny felt this was a special day in his life.

On this side of the one-storey wooden house - where the dwarves must live, Sonny was convinced - covered in white flakes, was the yard from which Sonny had just been driven. No, her form still adorned the yellowish wall, blanched by the wind and rain; Sonny saw it and was glad. He felt even gladder about the bushes, which in their snow cover reminded him of big round hats. Never in Sonny's life had these bushes, into which the 'uncles' would throw little bottles with corrugated sides, looked so beautiful; they didn't remind him of hats at all, but of the brittle white crunchy cakes that Mummy had brought for some occasion long long ago and which had tasted really delicious to Sonny, so that now, looking down from the fourth floor, he was in two minds whether it was worth running down and biting into at least one of the two snowy cakes - now what if someone just like him were to guess that these were sugary-sweet frozen cakes and gobble them up before he could gnaw off a bit? But when he caught sight of the caretaker's back, dressed in a smock unaccountably free of snow, bending over one of these bushes, he sighed as heavily as his little soul allowed him. What else could a witch be doing there but casting a spell on the dainties he longed for, making them into tasteless iced water the very moment when he would have taken a mouthful of the wondrous delicacy? No, he wouldn't go down. He hadn't gone up yet. He would go still higher up, up to where, looking out of the window, he would be even giddier. So he clutched at the window-sill, drew himself up against the glass and, pressing his nose against the cold blotches of translucence, went on peering into the yard. He caught sight of a snowdrift, a little snowdrift in the place where, his mother had once hold him, long ago, long before he was born, a little fir-tree had grown, until a man from their own building – he lived just a storey further up – one lovely winter's evening before New Year (round about this time of year, it occurred to Sonny), had cut it down and taken it off to his room. The man had been wearing green clothes and long boots, and when the caretaker and several other residents of the building had gone to harangue him, he had replied that the fir-tree was the property of the people, but he too belonged to the people, and therefore he had every right to that tree, so leave him alone! And he had slammed the door in their faces with his shiny boot. Mummy said he had done wrong, that man; the others had been afraid to wrestle with him on account of his green suit, but Sonny didn't agree with Mummy. He understood that it was the same with this 'uncle' and the fir-tree as with himself and the frozen white cakes (which other people who don't understand might take merely for snow-covered bushes). The 'uncle' had been afraid that somebody else might get to it before him; that was why he had cut the fir down and taken it away. If Sonny were bigger and the witch hadn't managed to put a spell on his cakes, he would certainly be down there helping himself to them – but it would take nearly a week to eat up a whole one that big. If Mummy said that the fir-tree had looked very pretty in the middle of the yard, Sonny would have gladly believed her, and might have mourned for it a bit with her, but he wasn't able to imagine how the yard might have looked with a fir in the middle and decorative bushes (whose name Sonny didn't know) at the sides. It was very complicated. And what had happened later? Later the 'uncle' had gone off to work somewhere else, nobody knew where; he'd vanished, as if the earth had swallowed him up, said Mummy. If the vengeful witch with the cat and the broom were already living in their building then, he had no doubt about what became of the fir-cutter.

The feeling of standing alone by the door behind which the vanished 'uncle' had lived was not the pleasantest, and Sonny had to cast a watchful glance over his shoulder before he could continue going upstairs. No, nobody was secretly observing him and pursuing him, not even those boys from next door who had not let Sonny go into the street today and pelted him with huge snowballs. Sonny climbed higher and looked again at the window over his shoulder; in its curved upper part there were some stained translucent, strangely wavy pieces of glass which formed a very interesting image, illuminated further by the sunlight. Since there was some similar fragment in the window of nearly every floor, except the first two, which Sonny climbed past every day, he thought that the repeated bits of glass might make up some exotic flower. Or animal. Sonny had never before climbed up so high. He looked at the semicircular upper part of the window on the fourth floor, but what was left of it was only a tiny green and a still tinier wavy transparent piece of glass, which wouldn't help you guess whether it was a flower or a beast. On the fifth floor, however, the window pleased Sonny very much – the funny little bits of glass were preserved intact almost throughout the upper part of the window, right to the middle; the other half was ordinary window glass. Well, what was it? Just like a flower, yes, almost definitely, but maybe it was an animal after all? A fabulous, very beautiful animal, never seen before? Green, blue, white. Have to go up further. And when Sonny did get up those two flights of stairs, he was a little disappointed. Yes, he was no longer in doubt: growing on the window was a funny exotic flower with bluish-white petals. Yes, it was beautiful, but in his heart of hearts Sonny was disappointed that the beautiful flower didn't look like a flower. Then with trembling heart he went to the window. How small everything was down there! Sonny pressed his nose to the glass and flinched with surprise: in the middle of the yard stood a fir-tree, a large one, not yet covered in snow. So the 'uncle' with the green boots must have just brought it back and put it in place. He must be living in Sonny's block again; the spell must be broken. Spells are broken just like that, aren't they? There on the staircase between the topmost floor and the attic, clambering onto the window-sill, Sonny looked at the fir-tree growing. Yes, you could see it: it was spreading wider, growing taller, and the snowflakes couldn't cover its branches of green needles – quite different to down below, where they had quickly filled Sonny's dirty blue mitten. He opened the window and stuck his bare hand out – icy water collected in his palm, it was freezing; but the fir, keeping away the beautiful white flakes, was growing before his eyes, and soon, to Sonny's utter astonishment, before his wide open mouth and eyes, a green branch of the fir was rustling along the window-sill, raising the snowflakes from it, and Sonny's bluish hands caught hold of the green, sharp and fragrant branch. He didn't know himself why he did it: probably to be the first to hold the unbelievable in his hand, and so that when he saw the reborn fir tomorrow, or maybe this evening, he would be able to say: 'But I was the first one to touch it, when it had already

193

grown above the roof.' The sweet frozen cakes down below could no longer be seen; the fir was so big that it took up the whole yard, its lower branches were already feeling their way up the wall, scraping against Sonny's drawing of the caretaker. The caretaker was no longer in the yard; she had probably been frightened off by the fir growing. The branch slipped out of Sonny's hand, and swept upward, and the next one was already brushing along the sill – such a fir!

How quickly it had decided to grow! Who knows, do they all do that in the forest? Without thinking about the consequences, whether he'd get a thrashing or not for it, Sonny clambered onto the sill, stretched out his arms and jumped onto the fir – he would climb even higher than the attic, where Mummy dried the washing and never took him with her, higher than the chimneys, where even Mummy never climbed, even higher than all the buildings in the town – the tree's springy branches held him up, he clambered onto the trunk, held onto the resinous and fragrant bark, and felt that this tree was trembling with its terrific effort. Sonny didn't climb at all, yet long ago he was already above all the houses, chimneys and roofs. Along with him the fir was rushing through the air, and Sonny became afraid – he mustn't fall off! So many snowflakes around him – you couldn't see anything – just imagine! Sonny was so afraid that he forgot to breathe; he screwed up his eyes and held on to the fir, his frozen fingers becoming quite white. He was rushing along.

And then the tree stopped trembling; Sonny understood that it was no longer rushing headlong. His heart sank to his shoes, he opened one eye, then the other. Around him it was bright. The snow had stopped. For some reason, too, the fir had shrunk – no, perhaps it hadn't shrunk. It proved not to be so huge after all, and Sonny slid easily down along the branches, to stand on a glittering, perfectly smooth floor in a huge room, whose walls could only just be made out in the distance, not discernible to a rather little man like Sonny. It was both beautiful and a little terrible – there was nobody around, the hazy silvery air was so clear that it made you giddy and stung your nose a bit. Sonny was still afraid – just a little bit – because there was nobody there – no, far away, someone seemed to be sitting at a table, tinkering with something.

Sonny started to go in that direction, where a person seemed to be slowly going through some papers on the table. Sonny, such a small fellow in a big place, walked along, and as he walked it seemed quite strange – his footsteps on apparently solid ground did not echo in the least, they made no sound, and the light, which from who knows what source lit up the spotless room around him – not a single dropped cigarette-butt! – was not that of a little star, even a lantern or a candle. When Sonny took a closer look at the person arranging the papers, who seemed to be well-dressed, with a brown jacket with blue checks which at first took Sonny aback, it seemed to him that the man had no face, just a skin-coloured spot, but that first impression passed and Sonny saw that he had been wrong. The man had kindly eyes and a smiling mouth, with which he addressed Sonny:

'Nice of you to come. Weren't afraid now, were you? You weren't scared?' – to which Sonny, just recently as frightened as a mouse, shook his head in the negative. Wow, what a moon! No, what kind of moon is that – maybe the bright light is coming from him? Sonny craned his neck – there was something shining up there, and Sonny pointed his potato-digging, nose-picking finger at it and said: 'Look!'

'I know, I know,' the man at the table replied, quite indifferent to Sonny's discovery, just like all adults, but Sonny was expecting such an attitude from someone like him.

'What do you do here?' he inquired.

'I work.' The man continued ruffling through and examining various writings piled up before him on the table. It looked boring to Sonny.

'And you do that every day?'

'Actually no,' replied the man. 'You see, now I'm doing everything so that it'll be easier for you to understand.'

'Then you've been waiting for me!' exclaimed Sonny, surprised.

'Who are you? Have you got any chocolate?'

'I have,' the man said, handing him a big piece of chocolate wrapped in shiny paper across the table. 'Of course I was waiting for you. Don't you recognize me? I'm your Daddy.'

The chocolate stuck in Sonny's throat – was his Daddy like this? And did he have such a clean job? Mummy always said about his daddy that it would be better if he didn't exist at all, but here he sat, smiling a little, and Sonny saw that he knew and understood all about Mummy.

'Why don't you help Mummy? Mummy always says that you've never helped her.'

Daddy seemed to sigh behind the pile of papers. 'I do help her,' he said, and took from a drawer in the table the first piece of paper he came across. 'You can read, can't you?' Sonny shook his head. 'What's written down here is all the help your mummy could get from me – all the time, every hour, if she wanted to. Yes ... Yes, if she was able to receive it.'

'But you ... You're not really bad then?' Sonny wanted to be brave.

'I don't even know any bad people.'

'The caretaker's bad, she's a witch,' Sonny proudly informed him.

'No, you'll see straight away that she isn't. And is it good to draw on walls?'

Sonny wasn't really sure that it was good to draw on walls, and so to reaffirm his words he embellished the scene more juicily: 'And at night she rides around with her black cat on a broomstick!'

His father now laughed out loud. 'I know she doesn't! And the cat has a white chin! I know!'

Sonny felt disappointed. Grown-up people always knew all about what he was only finding out, and it wasn't interesting with them, so Sonny began picking at his nose. He didn't even bother to hide it. 'But why did you leave Mummy?' Sonny didn't feel sure that he had anything more to discuss with the person who sat there and called himself his father. 'You aren't even a good person!'

'It's not like that. Let's leave me out of it, okay? Your mummy is very good, but she wasn't telling you the truth: we didn't really get to know each other. Not in the way people usually get to know each other, so they want to have children.' And Daddy went on and on talking, but Sonny wasn't listening; he had a big tasty block of chocolate, and he was showing it due respect: the paper was rustling, the chocolate was crackling.

'I suppose all your teeth are healthy?' Daddy asked, smiling.

'No, one hurts when I bite something or drink water. Mummy says when I go to school, I'll have to go to school, and then it'll hurt even more. So I bite with the other teeth, on the other side.'

'So then you mustn't bite anything or drink anything.'

Sonny turned away from the chocolate and raised his head inquiringly: was he laughing at him? Probably not, but just to make sure he changed the subject. 'What do you do here? Mummy says you don't do anything and you're a loafer. What's a loafer?'

'Mummy was exaggerating. She was angry with me. I do

197

work – can't you see? Work is natural for everybody, well, just like eating chocolate is for you; it's just that some jobs look like loafing to an outsider, like thinking for example. Sometimes – very often actually – those who think are called loafers. Do you believe me? But actually it's hard work, and besides, it's rarely paid for what it's worth. But the work is payment in itself, believe it or not.'

Sonny was not interested in paid or unpaid work. 'But you can always see work,' he reasoned, gobbling a big chunk of the sweet brown substance and thinking at the same time that the sweet white frozen cakes would have tasted good too. 'For instance, if I carry out the bucket of rubbish instead of Mummy, I'm a good boy, but if I make an effort and the truck has gone off by that time, I get a clip on the ear.'

'The trouble is, you're always in a terrible hurry, you're afraid of being late, but we do everything thoroughly, right to the end. Perhaps it's just that – doesn't it seem to you? – that people aren't meant ever to catch up, that you can't escape from that? What do you think, eh?'

The chocolate, however delicious it was, was melting, smearing Sonny's long since soiled hands with a reddish-brown, fragrant, sticky mass, which was getting more and more liquid and dripping in dark drops onto the floor.

'Now tell me, has Mummy brought you the fir-tree yet?'

Sonny was getting a bit sulky. The fir-tree. Licking his hands, he turned his back to the desk, where his inquisitor was still ruffling through and examining papers without stopping or hurrying, not hesitating at a single one, in a thorough, established rhythm. Sonny was a bit sulky; you couldn't really get to know adults. Sometimes they didn't know or understand the simplest things – they who were so sharp-eyed at catching the finest detail which Sonny would rather not reveal to them, wouldn't show them; sometimes they could ask the dumbest things, unbelievably dumb things. Besides – in spite of the chocolate – was the man at the desk all that interested in Sonny?

'Mummy doesn't have the money for that kind of thing,' he snapped. 'You ought to know that.' The man raised his head from the papers, looking at him with such cold eyes that Sonny lost the desire to sulk.

'But she's got enough money for booze?' – and, not expecting an answer, in an equally firm voice he added: 'You take too little notice of her, Sonny. Why do you sit in the kitchen when she has visitors? Or the corridor?'

'I can't stand them! They're awful!' said Sonny emphatically. 'When they call me in there, they stink, they dribble, their noses are runny.'

'Never say that people are awful,' said Daddy, and to Sonny's ears this didn't sound like an instruction (like 'Don't spit on the floor, you little pig!' or 'How many times have I told you that big boys like you don't wet their pants!') but like something significant, but it was hard for him to take in the words, for his father continued:

'You people are so tired of living, so worn out, that you no longer know how to love your own lives. Even a tiny little fellow like you. Straighten your back and relax. If someone just relaxes, that will be more serious for him than working. There isn't anyone to teach you how much easier it is to live if you don't feel life is a burden; if you live savouring every moment; because you can't – yes, nobody alive can know when and how it will end – nobody! You don't believe anyone who says they're content with little. Many people think that I oughtn't to be sitting here, but out among the trees, the lianas and the ferns in the garden, that I ought to have pretty flowers waving around me, birds singing and so on, that's how I should have received you, but that would be too much.' His father spoke in a way that Sonny had long since ceased to grasp. The sounds, the words, didn't reach his consciousness.

'Mummy will be home by now; I ought to be getting back. She'll be angry if she doesn't know where I've got to.'

'Mummy will be glad when she sees you; you've made her very happy today,' said Daddy, in a voice that seemed to have changed somehow. Sonny looked at him in surprise. His father was sitting here, yet his voice, as his mouth moved, was not coming out of it, but was resounding above his bent head. Out of the haze-shrouded distance? No, Sonny let his gaze wander round the infinite, boundless room: in the distance stood many lofty and stunted, decorative and plain fir-trees. Some had simple coloured bird feathers on them, others had mounds of cotton-wool and huge shiny balls. Much closer there were white-clad people all around in a row. 'Look, I know very well that nearly everything I tell you you can't understand, but you'll remember this talk of ours when you grow up, and you'll see it, so to speak, in its true light, and who knows,' (a roguish smirk) 'maybe it will help you to live. Actually I know even more. There will be a moment in your life when only this talk of ours will seem like a proper way for a person to live.' ('But we've only been chattering away for a long while,' thought Sonny, 'this is just the way adults talk. We haven't talked about a single video, which Daddy must surely have seen, or about makes of car, which he must have been a real expert on,' but he said nothing.)

His father waved his hand, and out of the distant row of lustrous beings one figure came forward with rapid steps. 'He'll take you back; you won't get anywhere on your own. You won't ever see me again, so I'll tell you something that you must remember all your life: I love you very much. Live well, Sonny!' And the white figure was already bending over Sonny to lift him carefully up, when Sonny, his breath taken away yet one more time this evening, noticed that he had the same face as Daddy. Above the white shoulder, through the two big white wing-tips Sonny noticed that the figure who had just quickly leaned over the table had no face. He felt frightened as the one who held him tightly by the hand said in a familiar voice he had recently heard:

'Don't get upset, don't be afraid, Sonny! It'll soon be all right, you'll soon be with Mummy.'

These words had not yet died away when Sonny felt a snowflake melting on his forehead, then another, and another. Around him was the sound of people, and through the others the voice of the caretaker could be heard, louder and more piercing than ever: '... and just think, he fell down right in front of me! And just now he was playing so nicely right here ...' Sonny could also hear Mummy's voice, but she wasn't speaking: for some reason she was crying loudly. Sonny opened first his left eye, then his right: he was lying in the snow, apparently right next to the snow-covered stump of the fir-tree, and standing around him were some familiar people, some less familiar: the book-keeper from next door in the same pyjamas that he used to carry out the dust-bin, and the fur-clad lady musician from the flat below. She had tears in her eyes too, for some reason, streaming blue-black down her ruddy cheeks. Why were they all so sad, the women crying, the men with incomprehensible terror on their faces? Sonny turned his head toward Mummy, who was crying just as bitterly: would she explain? No; she looked at Sonny with wide red eyes and sank down in the snow beside him.

'He's opened his eyes, he's alive, he's looking!' Sonny perceived rather than understood that that was what they were saying. Then someone was bending over Mummy and someone else was trying in vain to shove their shopping bag under his head, all the while asking:

'Where does it hurt, little boy? Tell me, little one, where does it hurt?' and 'Can you move about?' as well as 'Can you hear me? Do you understand what I'm saying?' – and above everyone the caretaker's voice: 'It's a miracle from God, no, I tell you, it's a miracle from God, it's a sign from God, and on Christmas Eve too!' That was the first time in Sonny's long life that he heard the word Christmas.

Wild Boars on the Horizon

Juozas Aputis
Lithuania

O rue so green,
Let me go home,
O rue so green.

That evening he was strange even to himself. Perhaps everything around him was strange, because Gvildys had never before felt his surroundings to strongly. Swaying a little, he made his way up the hill on which a white tower had been built last year, but you did not need it – you could see a long way into the distance from the hill itself. The sun was already setting without waiting for anything, hurrying without any compassion to plunge into darkness the forests and the peat bog where Gvildys had left the tractor, and after that Šatrija Hill rising in the distance, and the blossoming fields of clover. Looking in that direction, beyond the horizon, Gvildys felt a sadness which you experience seldom in the course of your life, such sadness that it seems that you are the clock of the world, and not the kind of clock which you wind up, but one on which everything turns: you radiate light and colour, you give water to animals in streams and quench the thirst of people, you build nests for birds and protect their young from hawks, you arrange matters demanding great wisdom, and, if you did not exist, everything – both living and not living – would fall apart. O Lord, Lord, you feel that the time will come when you will no longer exist. And so come the greatest pain and longing in the knowledge that you are god who knows that he will after all have to die.

Gvildys sat down on a large stone overgrown with lichen, his head swam, he had no desire to go home yet, he was a human being who still wanted to feel like a god, to return to his childhood. Childhood follows us every hour that we experience sadness and longing, we run to it like to a spring, where there is never any shortage of water, because only in childhood can we dig wells to give water to the thirsty. Then comes the day when we begin to realize that we are rolling a stone up a hill and that we will never succeed. But oh how we do not want to let it roll down again.

The man looked around him. You could see a very long way, the sun lit up the fields, and past the hills into infinity, on the horizon, tractors moved slowly. They were similar to the wild boars which at one time after the war, remembered Gvildys, would emerge from the forest and climb up on the mounds of potatoes that had been harvested. His head swam from the bottle of alcohol he had drunk, it became hard for him to put his thoughts in order, he got up and made his way down. He should have gone home, you could not remain on the hill indefinitely, you had to go down and return home. He quietly opened the door, went through the porch carefully in order not to be heard and tried to dispel his feeling of sadness, to appear happy. Two children came running in from the kitchen, got hold of his arm and began to pull him. Gvildys did not say good evening but only put his heavy hand on his wife's shoulder. An uneasy feeling went through his hot and dizzy head. His wife kept quiet, went on washing dishes, scolded the children, pushed a chair aside, while her incomprehensible anger grew and grew. All of a sudden she grabbed a broom made of twigs that was standing in the corner and slowly drew closer to her husband. Her eyes were terrifying, Gvildys had never seen them like that, he tried to laugh, but did not manage it in time – the sharp twigs stabbed him in the face, he felt a terrible pain in his eyes, while at the same time his wife screamed in a voice that was not her own. Holding his head in his hands, the man still managed to see her. His wife stood as if out of her mind, her arms hanging down by her sides, her hair dishevelled. Trembling she hissed 'That's for your drinking, that's for all the bottles you've drunk, for not caring about our home, for not caring about anything ...'

She probably did not hear her own words, she could not understand in any clear way why she had done what she had. Nor would she ever. She was a mother, she raised her children, many times she had looked through the small window of their cottage when the children screamed or when she became sick and tired of them. She had looked through that window many times, strange sounds enticed her to leave her home where almost nothing seemed any longer of any importance to her – not the forest, not the meadows, not the animals, and – horrible as it was to say it – not even the children. She remembered her mother who had also been young and as a young woman had raised her own children. She used to tell her daughter something similar, but what had her mother clung to in her moments of despair, what had she clung to?

Holding his head in his hands, the man sat down at the table. Terrible pain seared his eyes, the children stood in the corner cuddled up close together, with dirty faces and frightened, while their mother also did not move from where she stood. Gvildys got up, managed to find a towel hanging on the wall, wound it around his face and over his left eye, he was still able to see something with his right eye, then bent over, swaying, he went out of the cottage, found his bicycle in the barn and rode off.

It was hard to ride, the sun had already set, it became very dark, but Gvildys knew every little path, so he pressed down hard on the pedals through the field of clover.

At the dispensary he was told that he would certainly not regain sight in one eye and as for the other eye that was not certain either. If the nerve had been damaged then anything was possible. He should go immediately to Šiauliai or Kaunas, where there were more doctors. He should hurry, otherwise it might be too late. If he did not have any money with him, the doctor could lend him some, his wife could return it tomorrow or the day after.

Gvildys stood in the dispensary, looking through his swollen right eye at the small lamp under the ceiling and decided not to hurry, he would manage to get things done tomorrow, there was time. At the dispensary they bandaged his face better, but the sight in his left eye was completely gone, he only felt a terrible burning there, whilst with the swollen right eye he also could not see at all well.

Without saying good-bye, Gvildys wheeled his bicycle in the direction of the tavern where one could get spirits as well. There was no shortage of people inside, everyone noticed Gvildys, pestered him with questions, some tried to make fun of him, whilst others showed their pity, after all occurrences like this were not all that common in their village. Gvildys did not answer their questions. Perhaps if he had not gone up the hill today in the evening, if it were not for that terrible longing, perhaps he would have unloaded himself to his neighbours and told them the story, but now everything was not so simple. Gvildys found a free battered old table in the corner and sat down. If he had ever had the chance to see it, he would have thought how much he looked like the artist's self-portrait without an ear.

The people did not back off, they kept coming at him with their questions, but Gvildys did not open his mouth. When a young woman in a dirty overall came up to him, he quietly asked for a bottle and some bread, and then returned to peering through his white bandages over people's heads.

He drank a glass and held his chin in his hand. He looked terrible, in one corner of the ale house somebody was saying that it would not be a bad idea to call the police – could they not see that Gvildys had gone out of his mind, but someone else swore and made fun of the coward who had made this suggestion.

When Gvildys had finished his second glass, his wife's father came up to the table, his father-in-law, old and dry like a twig, with straggly grey hair and crooked hands. The old man sat down with his back to the people, and Gvildys felt better for that. He asked the girl for another glass and poured a measure for his father-in-law.

A good hour went by, those that had had more than enough to drink began to disperse, only a few people remained in the tavern, whilst the two of them remained sitting and drinking silently.

'How did this happen, tell me? For what?' the old man at last said breaking the silence, scratching his unshaven chin.

Gvildys downed yet another glass.

'I don't know, father. That's the whole thing, I simply don't know. Yesterday I brought home my salary for half the month, it was quite a bit, I kept some aside for a bottle and today during my lunch break I had a drink but not a lot, only enough to cheer myself up, you can go out of your mind with feeling so down, can't I have a drink, don't I earn a wage, is anyone starving at home, father?' He felt his tongue thick in his mouth, whilst the area of his left eye started to burn even more.

'She was like – an angel, my daughter.'

'What should I say, father? I don't know if we've ever had a really serious argument. As soon as I came in, she attacked me. You can see for yourself what she did to me.'

It seemed that only after his son-in-law's sad words did the old man see and understand what had really happened. He again scratched his cheek, finished his glass and did not notice how several large tears fell on the table. With tear-filled eyes he looked at his son-in-law, and the thought came to him that something strange, remote and terrible was walking through their forests and fields, no one had seen it yet, no one had come across it yet, but it was right here amongst them, it visited every farmstead, every home, it sat in the tractors or on the ploughs, but people could not see it, no one had made its acquaintance yet.

'I don't feel too good, son-in-law.'

'We've had a lot to drink, father.'

'I can't really understand any of it, son-in-law.'

'It seems to me it was for my drinking, father ... And look – she attacked me as if I was some stranger, as if I was some murderer. She scratched my eyes out, and all you can do is moan or drink like some good-for-nothing, and that's it. There's no way to get my revenge, no one to blame, there I was left blind in the middle of my own home and that's that.'

Gvildys became more and more drunk, there remained in him less of that closed-off masculinity that can bear the greatest misfortune, that can carry the greatest sadness through all one's life without saying a single word right up to the very end. He felt his fingers and his whole body begin to shake, while his right eye, not yet completely without sight, but not very far from it, began to close. He felt like a small harmless kitten which a child, hardly able to keep from crying, was carrying to a river to drown. The child looked for a long time for a stone. The kitten understood what was to come next, but could not use his claws to hurt the crying child ...

'What's happening, can you tell me that, father, can you? You old fool! You can't do anything, other than to keep quiet, and what am I supposed to do? Where am I supposed to go, what? Did you hear what they said at the dispensary? They said I could go blind in the other eye as well. Do you understand what that means?' Gvildys hit the table with his fist and his father-in-law, not knowing what to do, grabbed his son-in-law's hand and began to kiss it as if out of his mind, tearful and helpless, as if with his kisses he could erase this incomprehensible deed.

'You've never raised your hand against an animal or bird and now ...' his father-in-law started to say.

'It's easier to do that against a human being, father ...'

'The rye is blossoming everywhere,' said his father-in-law to himself, as if he had not heard his son-in-law, 'everything's in bloom, and you feel warm, good and sure of yourself. Even the cuckoo forgets itself and breaks into song in midsummer. Everyone sees you and you can see right through them. How can you raise your hand against another person when everyone looks at you as if you were the cleverest and the best?'

'Look, the rye is right here and the cuckoos haven't disappeared anywhere. There are as many as you want, nobody shoots them, father. None of that helps, for Christ's sake, it doesn't help; money doesn't help, nor bread ... I can hardly hear the cuckoo, it's as if its voice went straight into a barrel treated with tar ... Yesterday, when I climbed up on the hill, the tractors moved slowly along the sides of the hills like wild boars, moved slowly through the mounds of potatoes ...'

'Well, it helped me ...' sighed his father-in-law. 'What can I, a dry old stick, say to you now, how can I help you? I'm slobbering like a calf and can't find anything helpful to say. All those years have taken their toll ... My daughter Onute put out your eyes and now her old father is slobbering drunk at this table ...'

'What the devil could you find to say ...?'

'Don't think I didn't know that the first thing to do was to pull you out of here and take you to a town immediately. That's what I was thinking as soon as I found out, I ran like a madman to find you, and then the closer I got the more senseless did my hurrying seem to me. After all, by taking you to the hospital, I wouldn't have been able to help you anyway. I may be talking nonsense because of the drink, but if your wife has put out one of your eyes and the doctors are able to fix the other one, that means it's not the end, isn't that right?'

'So what do you want, for both my eyes to be bandaged up?'

'Don't you understand, you can't have it as if nothing at all had happened ...'

'What's the point of all this confusion! I feel as if I'm all tied up in knots – I can't control my feet, my tongue ... Perhaps time will erase everything. I remember when I was a child I was never able to imagine how I would live after my mother and father died. And look – it's been fifteen years and there are whole months when I don't remember them ...'

'That's how it is. Death – that's something else. You know you're going to die as soon as you learn to think. And you know that other people have to die, that that's the way it has to be ...'

'Perhaps that's how it had to be, for the wife to poke my

eyes out, only neither I, nor any one else knew anything about death, that that's how it has to be ...'

They had another glass, the bottle was already empty, only a few people were left, even though outside the windows one could see others walking and waiting. The two of them stood up – the old man and his son-in-law. The old man carefully took his son-in-law by the arm so that he would not bump into the chairs. Outside, against the wall, Gvildys found his bicycle, leaned on it for support, felt it as if to check to see that it was still in one piece and looked down at the ground: 'Well, I'll be off, father.'

'Where are you going to go, it's night, let's go to my place, you'll have time tomorrow or you can go straight from here to town.'

'Why do I need to stay over, father, as if I didn't have a home of my own.' Staggering, Gvildys pushed the bicycle and got on it.

The people parted to let him through. All of them had had a good bit to drink but they all had enough common sense to know that on the bicycle sat someone who was no longer an ordinary person, someone who was in some way different now. And so was the old man who stumbled after the bicycle.

Gvildys rode out of the little town, pedalled through the meadow, and his head showed white as a flag in the dark night, while his swollen eye found the way without any trouble at all. Pedalling away from the town and not in the direction of his home, he thought more than once of what his wife and children were doing, thought about why she had not run after him to town, about why she had not fallen to embrace his feet like those of Christ and had not begun to weep. After all the old man had broken into tears. He felt sorry for his wife, his home and his children, his sorrow was as if sacred, and a painful longing drove Gvildys on and on, as if he had decided to ride off into his childhood where all of us are gods.

Early in the morning the old man came speeding on horseback to his son-in-law's house. He found his daughter, Gvildys' wife, sitting outside in the potato field, with her eyes swollen from crying and full of sorrow. The old man fell into a fright, directed the animal towards the small town, then turned down the path his son-in-law had taken yesterday. The people also sensed everything and ran after the old man, some on their bicycles, some on horseback, and others on foot. The tractors stopped on the hills like wild boars, and the tractor drivers went running through the fields. The old man jumped off his horse and ran headlong like a dog sniffing for footprints.

They found the bicycle seven kilometres from the small town, tears were rolling down the old man's face, when he found his son-in-law's footprints in the marshy grass. All of a sudden everyone stopped as if paralysed: on a beautiful island, with his legs crossed, like a saint with a halo of white gauze sat Petras Gvildys, the old man's son-in-law, eating quietly. He had remembered that his wife, Onute, had packed some lunch for him. He had had a drink by the tractor and completely forgotten about the food.

Petras Gvildys sat at peace, as if he did not see all the people that had come running or the old man with his face white with amazement. Petras Gvildys was looking with one eye through the white gauze at a birch by the edge of the island and in which sat a frightened cuckoo.

Poor Peonies

Romualdas Granauskas
Lithuania

You don't always feel the same on waking, and you don't feel the same when you fall asleep either. Bružas went to bed without getting any sleep; he lay down on his left side, he put his palms together and placed his hands between his knees. He didn't even listen to hear whether his wife had already gone to bed, whether he could yet hear her quiet steps, whether she was clinking the medicine bottles in the other room. He lay without thinking of anything, but it just doesn't happen that you don't reflect on something before falling asleep. He just felt something – without words, without anything, without any images – he felt, and no more than that: he felt that he was feeling. Strongly, deeply, and he himself didn't know what. His heart was beating evenly, he himself could hear it beating evenly, yet before each stroke it seemed to be kicking, like this: ker-thump, ker-thump, ker-thump.

'It's lame', smiled Bružas to himself, and he was happy that he was thinking for once. 'Thoughts, that's good, now there'll be more of them; they don't usually come singly, so you won't have to lie any more without sleeping, without thinking of anything, only feeling something that you don't know yourself. Like an unshod horse ...' And slowly, as if down from a slope, the image of Einikis' forge came to mind: the shingle roof, all kinds of iron, a rusty tractor wheel ...

'The bugger isn't here yet!' – it suddenly pierced him, and Bružas at once sat up in bed, lowered his legs and clenched his toes, so that the cool of the floor wouldn't hurt them. 'He's cleared off with the car! Someone'll see, they'll tell the chairman, and there'll be hell to pay!'

By now Bružas was seriously alarmed. If only he would return at night, when it was still dark, when nobody would see – why doesn't that little bugger understand? He'd got that shaky milk-cart; he imagined himself as a terrible, Goliath-like being: I'll go where I want to, nobody is going to stop me! – Oh yes they will, my child, they will. The authorities have stopped bigger ones than you ...

'And I'm the one to blame,' Bružas reproached himself. 'I ought to have been stricter and ordered him to come back by dawn, but can you order someone of his age around? They've got – youth, cars, just think – they've got the whole world!'

Amid such frightening thoughts there loomed one more in Bružas' mind, but one which Bružas did not want to examine more clearly – one in which your own horse roams free in the autumnal alder-scrub, only you don't look in its direction, because you're too lazy to go and bring it back; let it wander, the fields are already harvested, the vegetables picked, it won't do anyone any harm, you can go and fetch it later, and if you turned back, you would make it out clearly enough: brown alder trees, the bay-coloured head, the glistening bay flanks, but the whole horse can be seen most clearly, because the trees aren't moving, it's the horse that moves: without direction, without a path, loose, and yet so sad. In such cases you can do nothing; you will go and fetch it, you will not leave the animal another night. And suddenly yesterday's table rose before Bružas' eyes: an empty glass, the window in the black and red striped sunset, the wrinkled hand of his wife, the box of matches showing the picture of a tawny squirrel and the inscription at the bottom: 'Don't set fire to our home!' Maybe it's as well that Juzis wasn't there, because nothing is worse than burning with shame in front of your child.

'I wonder what the time is now?' Bružas listened to the silence. The window was still dark, the dawn was not yet to be seen in it.

Bružas always woke up without any alarm-clock: as day broke, before the sun was visible over the ridge of the forest, but when it was just about to rise there; and he would go through the dewy pasture, looking back all the while: wasn't the bright and radiant rim visible yet? Bružas went on listening to the silence, as though this morning the sun might rise without rays, before the sky had whitened, spreading the sounds before it: the crackling, rustling and murmuring of the trees. Silence is nothing but silence. More exactly – a very great, black silence, such as you get on a summer night just before dawn. And especially when it promises to be misty and warm all day, and at noon the little chickens wobble around the well, mournfully chirping, and their yellow down is all flecked with silver tips: their fluff is thin, and drops of mist on its ends can hardly be made out. And here, in the silence of this summer night, Bružas' ear is assailed by a very quiet, very clear, very thin sound. To tell the truth, maybe the sound could be heard a little earlier: it was very similar to the cheeping of nestlings; that is why Bružas was reminded of those chickens. And when he realized where the sound was coming from, the image of a misty day and all the chickens at once fled from his mind, giving way again to fear and anxiety.

It was his wife, in her room, knocking against a medicine bottle. Bružas wanted to go to her at once and say something. He would lie down beside her, and in the dark the two of them would talk about their child, softly, without rancour, and afterwards dawn would start to lighten the window, and then it would be time to get up, but Bružas had long ago had the urge to relieve himself, yet he was too lazy, and that is why he was sitting on the edge of the bed, clenching his toes, and for a long time he deliberately contemplated in his mind's eye the warm mist over the yard, and the chicks, and the well, and he would have seen more, something nice, if it were not for the clinking of the bottle. Groping in the dark for the door of the hut, Bružas knew it clearly: he would return from the yard, he would not bolt the door, so he would not have to get up again just for Juzis' sake, he would go into his wife's room and lie down beside her thin, unsleeping, aching and unhappy body. No, first he would sit on the edge of her bed, he would rub his feet, sole against sole, so that he would rub the gravel off them from the path, he would stretch out beside her and would lie for some time like that, listening to her uneven, surprised breathing. And afterwards he would say something softly, so that she could scarcely hear it, so as not to startle her with his voice. Perhaps he would say: 'What was that you sang to me yesterday?' Or: 'Maybe, you know, it's good that Jonkus didn't come with Galdikas. Shit, I won't go to them either.' Can't start talking about Juzis right off. Bring the conversation round to it somehow from something else. But what the hell would be the use of that, when both of them have been thinking the same thing all night?

So, clearly knowing what he was going to do and how, Bružas took perhaps ten steps to one side, towards the garden fence. He didn't want to go any further: the grass in the yard was cold and very dewy. While Bružas stood there, contracting

216

his bladder in the dark, his ears perceived the distant humming of a motor. Turning his head as far as the veins in his neck allowed, he strove to make out two lights on the road, but he could see only one. In the darkness before dawn a motorcycle was coming, and Bružas quietly finished what he had begun, but sensed that the sound of the stream was wrong. It occurred to him that he had aimed at some clothing hung up on a tree by his wife. 'Perhaps it's a cheese-bag? ...' – he became alarmed and stooped to check it with his hand, but it found the heads of two soft, warm, moist peonies. How could they – such big ones – squeeze through the chinks in the fence into the yard? When he understood, he smiled to himself in the dark: they had put forth their buds into the yard while they were still small, and later they had blossomed, and could not get back – even if someone is peeing on you! 'Can't go back again, can't turn aside' – no longer smiling, Bružas thought of this, and grew angry with himself: 'Peed on the flowers and happy about it like a silly fool! ...'

And everything switched back violently to where he had previously peered into the darkness over his shoulder: off the highway and into his farmstead droned the motorcycle, and the bright headlamp jolted, trembled, jumped across the ruts, all the while approaching the windows of the hut like some malevolent eye. In the dazzling light Bružas ran headlong to the gate. He could not see who was arriving; the motor was droning very loudly, not a word of what was said to him could he hear. At last he collected his wits and went round the side of the motorcycle, and coming very close to it he recognized the stock-breeding adviser.

'Isn't Juzis here? Where's Juzis?' – he was shouting in his ear for the umpteenth time, and it seemed to Bružas that he was shouting back too, though in fact he was merely moving his wooden lips:

217

'Jesus Christ, my child, Jesus Christ, my child!'

The adviser finally switched off the engine, and the silence, like deep suffocating water, suddenly threw Bružas up into the blackness: above the roof of the hut, above the tops of the apple-trees, and there, at that height, he felt as if he were quite naked, like some speck, driven spinning along the chimney, like some insect fallen into a bright band of light and quite unable to get out of it.

'Trousers!' shouted the adviser. 'Trousers!'

Because Bružas was still being blown by this black gust along the chimney, he could not hear or understand anything.

'Get your trousers! Don't stand there pulling your prick!'

Hearing the swearing, Bružas suddenly found himself still beside the motorcycle, as if tumbling onto the grass with all his horror and incomprehension. He was not aware of going into the hut, or of coming straight out again, and not even later could he recall the several seconds during which the adviser turned the motorcycle around and switched on the engine again. Bružas merely jumped around barefoot, and he could not mount it at all, because both his hands were full: he held in them the dark lump of the trousers and pressed them tightly against his shirt-front.

The Dark Windows of Oblivion

Romualdas Lankauskas
Lithuania

Every time I came to this secluded village on the other side of an old pine forest, I liked to walk along the sandy path by the side of the forest that led to a pleasant little town with a small church solidly built out of field stones. It was pleasant to walk through the pine forest full of graceful juniper trees and breathe the air here. To the left of the pine forest stretched meadows and fields and further away flowed a stream winding its way past the banks overgrown with bushes and past another forest looking in the distance, probably larger and wider because it rose up to the sky as if it were a giant green fence that could not be scaled. Above the forest floated white clouds or when the days were sunny and fine a clear blue sky could be seen.

In the meadows and fields here and there grew oaks with their broad branches; my admiration of them never diminished - they were so mighty, so graceful, standing proudly in the ploughed fields or amongst the blossoming wild flowers. In early spring or late autumn, when the leaves had all fallen, the outlines of the branches stood out clearly, with hawks gliding slowly above the trees. The oaks were the last to blossom and turn green; they were also the last to have their leaves, the colour of copper, torn off by the autumn wind. I rejoiced that no one had yet cut down those wonderful trees. Perhaps the seclusion of the place protected them from the saw?

Yes, the place was indeed secluded and, one could say, completely untouched by modern times. Only the electric wires stretched out along the path reminded one that even here the twentieth century had penetrated, even though one could hardly have been able to tell from the old cottages - completely similar ones could have stood there a hundred years ago, dotted along the edge of the pine forest, only with smaller windows. Everything round about reminded one of the past, particularly those mighty oaks, everywhere there was a kind of solemn and incomprehensible mystery, as if by the riverside, in the meadows and the forests there still lived the benevolent spirits of nature.

But the village went into a steady decline year by year. Some of the inhabitants died, others moved to a new place, being built on the other side of the forest: a settlement built around a large state farm. The only people left in the village were several old women living on their own and only a few men still capable of work who also intended to move out with their families, so that they would not have to travel so far to work. Besides that, they were tempted by the new houses with modern conveniences. Yes, no one could stop the village declining, that is why many of the old but still solid farmsteads stood abandoned by their owners, with windows and doors boarded up. Weeds grew everywhere, in the farm yards lay wooden implements no longer needed by anyone, slowly rotting and decaying out in the open, pots and other household utensils thrown out were rusting away, roofs that had not been recovered or repaired had fallen in.

In fact there were two farmsteads which were well looked after: they had been bought by city folk who would from time to time arrive in their cars and make an effort to make things as nice as possible. In one of the farmsteads flowers even blossomed under the windows. In time only those two farmsteads were likely to remain standing.

I would often walk not just through the village and the pine forest, but also to visit those old women who used to go every Sunday to the church which was some three kilometres away. Neat, well looked after, with a new tin roof, it stood in the little town on a small hill, where down below flowed a river, the same river as in the village. The path in the direction of the town wound its way past the abandoned farmsteads.

Sometimes I would stop by one of these farmsteads, walk through the yard, look through the empty barn with open doors or the granary and on my way home bring back all kinds of utensils - a butter churn made of lime, a barrel for pickling cucumbers or a nicely carved wooden ladle which had probably been used to scoop grain. These things that had been thrown out were of no use to me. I had no idea what I would do with them but some strange feeling did not allow me to leave them there to rot out in the open. I intended to give them later to a museum if the museum did not already have them and if it wanted them. That is why I brought them back and piled them in the barn of the old woman I was staying with, surprising her with this peculiar pastime of mine.

She would ask, 'So what are you going to do with them? After all nobody needs things like that any more. Times are different now.' I would smile and answer that in spite of that I could not leave them thrown out like that, my heart just would not allow it, that was all. She would shake her head but, it would seem, approve after all, even though she could not see much sense in my behaviour.

On my way to town or just wandering around I would stop the longest at one particular house, quite a bit different from the others. That house was larger and more beautiful than the rest and stood in a wonderful location, on the edge of the forest not far from two old oak trees. From the yard one could see a stream flowing along the edge of the meadows and the church tower rising above the town. On a sunny day the river shimmered like a woven silk sash, while the tower would attract one's attention because of its extraordinary gracefulness. The house had two ends, wide windows with wooden shutters painted green, and two porches, one facing the path and the other the yard. I would often think that it would be pleasant to live in it, even though I had never seen a living soul there. Only in the yard here and there were strewn things no longer of any use, empty whisky bottles, old lorry tyres and similar kinds of junk. In the shed there stood a nice old-fashioned bed stuffed with straw, with hand-carved ornaments. The shutters were closed and nailed tight. The electric wires had been pulled down and left dangling down the wall.

The farm's driver had lived on the now abandoned farmstead, but he had moved to a new house a year ago. I got more and more interested in that farmstead and for that reason began to ask about it. I found out that earlier it had belonged to a family which right after the war had left it and moved to some town or heaven knows where, escaping from the fate that was to befall it, looking for a safer place; for some time the house stood empty; later on the driver made his home there, stayed most probably about ten years or so, until it was also time for him to move on to somewhere else.

The house remained empty and of no further use to anyone. In coming into the yard of the farmstead or in looking inside through the gaps in the closed shutters and boards that had been nailed up, one felt uncomfortable and sad - everything here gave off an oppressive grimness. One could see the signs of oblivion and decay everywhere. In the evenings no lights would come on in those windows. There was no sound of human voices or domestic fowl or farm animals. Sometimes there was the desolate sound of a field pigeon cooing in the forest - nothing else around disturbed the complete silence, unless it was the murmur of the forest when a strong wind blew.

But after all at one time the house had been full of life and activity, probably children had shouted with joy in it, fires had been kindled, bluish smoke had risen from the chimney, doors had banged open and shut, a cockerel had crowed in the yard, geese had cackled, cows had mooed in the cattle shed, horses had whinnied, a dog had barked ... But all of those sounds had long since disappeared and it did not seem that the farmstead could ever be full of them again. What did the future hold for the house? Would it be sold for demolition, and the buyer, after taking away the good timber, built a house somewhere else, or would he pull it down, dig a huge hole with an excavator and tip everything in and then level it?

I would sometimes try to imagine the sort of people that had lived here. What had they been like? How did they get on? What did they speak about in front of the fireplace on the long and dark autumn or winter evenings? They had abandoned the house and the whole farmstead, but in every step one took, in every room or in each thing that had been thrown out there were the traces of their past lives, a reminder of something and a witness to something; where a person has once lived his life, nothing remains without some trace. It was as if from everywhere there still emanated the warmth of human contact.

If I was caught in the rain while walking past that farmstead, I would go into the porch, sit on a rough wooden bench under a roof covered with wooden shingles and stay there listening to the calming patter of the rain and looking at the church tower off in the distance, which would become rather hard to see through the moving curtain of rain. When my glance travelled downwards I could see under the windows the tops of flowers that had withered; not all of them were dead - one or two kinds of perennial flowers would put forth blossoms of incredible colour and beauty.

Stopping here I would sometimes imagine that I could hear animals moving about in the cattle shed and the voices of people in the rooms, happy or worried, perhaps even the muffled sound of crying. I would become terribly uneasy, some sort of inexplicable disquiet would come over me, particularly if I heard the sound of a wood pigeon cooing and then I would hurry to leave the porch even though the rain had not yet stopped.

Then one golden day in early spring when the birch trees were still in bud, covering themselves with a gentle pale green, when the alder groves by the river's edge still looked dark violet and were still bare of leaves, when the forest rang with the joyful singing of birds, as I was walking past that house the thought came to me that perhaps I should try to buy it. In my mind I imagined that I would open the shutters, let in the light of the sun which would dry out the damp that had collected over the winter, how I would clean the dusty rooms and how well little by little I would get the house in order, and I would then spend my hours pleasantly there all summer until late autumn; perhaps I would stop by even in winter and light the huge stove decorated with beautiful glazed tiles - after all there were all kinds of dry trees that had fallen over close by in the forest, one only had to take what one needed and use them to heat the stove.

Having begun to fantasize more and more about the whole

thing, I could not stop myself any longer. Towards evening of the same day, I went to the state farm and found the director, a thickset man brimming with self-confidence, with the sort of red blotchy face that people have who like a drink too many, but he did not even want to hear about selling the house, repeating over and over: 'We can't. Besides, we need the house ourselves.' When I asked what they intended to do with the house, he could not say anything definite, just mumbled something under his breath; the question itself seemed to irritate him, because some kind of stubborn hostility suddenly appeared in his eyes and in his whole expression which he did not even attempt to hide.

And so ended our short conversation.

After that I would often go past the farmstead, noticing that some things were changing. To be more accurate, it was not the farmstead that was changing but only the house itself: someone had torn down the shutters, broken the windows, destroyed the nice stove and taken the glazed tiles; someone had started on pulling down the porch, the bench on which I used to sit was no longer there, uncaring hands had torn up the floor boards. The house slowly became a rubbish tip of no use to anyone, even though its timbers were strong, completely free of rot and untouched by bark beetles. It could have stood for many decades, but being destroyed as it was it came as no surprise that it went into a steady decline and fell apart. Just looking at it made my heart heavy. It was difficult to understand why somebody was set on destroying the house, why it did not give the destroyers any peace, what made them want to tear it down, smash it and demolish it. Where did this fever of plunder and destruction come from? Did it give these malevolent persons some sort of satisfaction? All kinds of depressing questions came to mind on seeing how the house was being progressively devastated.

Could it be, the thought would come to me, that it had already been consigned to its fate? Could it be that only the foundations would remain as a reminder that a fine house had stood here at one time? But perhaps it would be repaired, put in order and it would look like it originally did? After all the house could be of use, if not to me, then to someone else and not just of use but serve them well. I wanted to believe that. I just could not come to terms with the thought that the fate of the house was sealed, that there was nothing else to hope for.

It was a warm and sunny afternoon when I was on my way to town to buy some bread. Drawing close to the house, I noticed the door was open. What could that mean? Perhaps somebody had decided to live there and workmen were busy inside?

But my guesses were unfounded. Stepping inside I saw a table put together of bricks and boards on which lay scraps of crumpled newspaper and the remains of rotting food, while on the floor lay bottles of whisky, empty cigarette packets and cigarette-ends. Pieces of glass from broken bottles were scattered around. Most probably hunters or fishermen had come into the house and had eaten and drunk here, littering the room in a disgraceful manner. It was sickening to look at the remains of their feast, so I stood there for a moment, went outside and continued on my way. The house looked even worse and more empty than before. Probably even the mice had abandoned it long ago.

I came back to the village in late autumn. This was my last visit to the village that year since winter was just around the corner, the roads would be snowed under and blocked off because of snow drifts, and reaching it would become difficult. What would I do in such an out-of-the-way place with the forests and fields covered with a blanket of snow? Unless it was to visit those few old women who lived alone and to provide them with some diversion from their normal solitary existence.

Step by step I came closer to the house through the quiet forest which no longer rang with the song of birds. The last leaves were falling. Everywhere one could feel the end of autumn and the inevitable approach of winter.

The path turned beyond the bushes, I went around them, saw in front of me the farmstead and stopped in amazement. The house was no longer there; in its place stood a blackened pile of timber and a tall sooty chimney. The whole house had not quite been turned into ashes: perhaps firemen had rushed here to put out what was left of the fire, or perhaps a strong downpour had put out the flames.

I looked over the charred remains, prompted by some inexplicable curiosity, even though I did not see anything unusual there. However, before leaving the site of the fire, I noticed something sticking out amongst the ashes and bent down to pick it up; it was a reddish, somewhat sooty plastic doll's head with big sky-blue eyes; those wide clear eyes fixed me with such an intent and steady gaze, as if to demand some kind of clear and truthful answer, which made me begin to feel very uncomfortable and throw down the strange find that was of no use to anyone, as though it had burned my frozen fingers, and quickly walk away.

Shadow of a Marriage

Göran Tunström
Sweden

Two conductors stood tightly intertwined between the eastbound and the westbound local trains on the platform at Vara, kissing. One of them was Lars Nyponstigen. Here he was at last – in the autumn of heart-attacks and hair loss. He was holding his spectacles in his hand and kissing her mouth, and between the kisses he kept repeating 'At last!' This was of course the beginning of the end. The time was ten past one in the afternoon.

It hadn't started off so well, five years earlier:
Old lady with suitcase, her gaze wandering out over the deserted village and the fields beyond:
'I was supposed to be met by my sister. We were going to meet here, then I was to take the next train back, whenever it was supposed to go.'
'One moment,' said the blonde conductress, hunting for her timetable.
'Sixteen thirty-two,' said Nyponstigen.

The blonde met his gaze, then she turned a few more pages: 'That's right. Sixteen thirty-two.'

Nyponstigen sighed. Young people never learned anything. When he started on the railways he could pilot every single traveller both to Lycksele and to Paskallavik *with* the changes and waiting times without looking anything up. He regarded it as his job to keep the possible connections in his head. He hadn't become a conductor just to punch holes in bits of paper! There was such a pleasure to be had in timetables, in kilometres and distances in minutes; he could sit for hours with both the Swedish and the foreign ones – especially the Austrian ones. Ah, Madame wishes to travel to Mussgh: then change at Vänersborg at 11.36, you'll arrive in Gothenburg at... and so on down to Droppf, Kammerschlug, Bludenz, Pföls – even though he had yet to meet that lady going to Mussgh.

Actually Nyponstigen's peevishness was not really directed at his blonde colleague on the Herrljunga train, but it is hard for a married man suddenly to change his tone:

'It isn't impossible to learn those times...'

'I've only just started.' She had a lovely sing-song dialect.

'No wonder people are giving up the trains; they'll be laying us off soon.' He laughed bitterly.

'Then you can try something else. The main thing is to earn money.'

That was an odd attitude. Nyponstigen was a conductor to the very depths of his soul. Without trains he'd come to a standstill.

'You have to live. Live and travel.'

'I see,' he said. 'Where to, if I may ask?'

'I was in Venice last year. I heard a Monteverdi concert in the church of San Marco – it was fantastic!'

'Surely music sounds the same wherever you hear it.'

And the time was ten past one.

Because of their rolling shift schedule, twelve days passed before they saw each other again, between 13.08 and 13.10.

'Plenty of people?'

'Quite a few – after all, the summer season's started. The usual cat-transporters, tomato plants and fishing-rods.'

'They're a nuisance, those fishing-rods.'

'Are they?' she said, surprised, her brow furrowed and her eyes raised.

There was a package too, and then there was the station-master's bad knee, which had troubled both him and Nyponstigen for three years. Then time ran out again.

The next conversation, twenty-four days later, was a touch more intimate:

'Perhaps I should introduce myself. My name's Nyponstigen.'

'I know,' she said.

'Do you?'

'I asked. It's nice to know your colleagues' names.'

'I tried to change my name, but there was already somebody who'd taken the other name, in Västerbotten. And you? What's your name?'

'Mine's Pia.'

'Next stop Vedum,' said Nyponstigen three minutes later. There was only one person in the coach. As he passed, the passenger said:

'Thunderstorm brewing now.'

He spoke loudly and clearly; he'd got on at Vänersborg:

'I live in Stockholm. That's where I live. I'm off to see my brother. He's got a cottage in Borås. He's nine years older than me. His wife is my sister-in-law. It's so funny. Backwards and forwards we go, backwards and forwards. My fiancée's in Trollhättan.'

'So you've left her?'

'Yes. Now I can have a drop or two at my brother's place. His wife is my sister-in-law – backwards and forwards we go.'

There were plenty of passengers like that on this stretch; the big hospital at Vänersborg was just about the only source of passengers. Obviously there were others too. You sit hunched over a book – Nyponstigen read a good deal as they bounced along over the plains of Västgötaland, toward Grästorp, toward Vargön – you raise your head and find yourself staring straight into a smile, a pair of open eyes. You know you've seen them before, but that Before is only happening now. You dig around in your currant bushes, prune the trees and then you get a twinge around the heart, even if years have passed, you say to yourself: it might have been *her* instead. If you'd helped her off with her suitcase, brushed against her hand. Vedum, Vara, Grästorp, Vargön, Vänersborg. Backwards and forwards we go, backwards and forwards.

Thirty-six days later the train times overlapped again.

'Hi, Nyponstigen!'

'Hi, Pia – how's life?'

'So-so. Undramatic.'

'You live alone?'

'With my daughter. She's so beautiful,' said the blonde suddenly, and for the first time Nyponstigen noticed how 'inexpressibly' beautiful she was.

'And yourself?'

'No complaints. Kids flown the nest. Mostly pottering about in the garden.'

'Big one?'

'Red currant bushes, plum trees, lawn, mortgage payments.'

'Ah, currants,' she said, looking down at the ground. And once again the station clock showed 13.10.

Nyponstigen thought about her remark about the red currants. When twelve days had passed, he picked a bucketful of black and red currants and slipped them onto the train with him. But to be a conductor is to be subject to the vagaries of life; the trains coincided at Öxnered, and at Öxnered the platforms don't meet, and as one was pulling in the other was pulling out. Nyponstigen glimpsed her blond tresses and then the moment was over. He carried the currants home, and met his wife at the gate.

'What have you got in the bucket?'

'Currants.'

'Were you given them? I don't even know how we're going to use all of our own.'

'I didn't want to upset my colleague ... Any post come?'

That night he dreamed about her: they were walking across ice in the sun; the snow sometimes bore their weight and sometimes gave way. She was wearing a black fur and they were walking among yellow reeds and talking about old presidents who bred magpies. They walked faster and faster, then there was a staircase with icicles on it, they were sitting there talking about 'Zoo' – and about a Word that couldn't be mentioned.

'And then?' she asked when she and Nyponstigen at last met several months later, for now this At Last had taken root in him.

'I don't dare tell you any more.'

'Oh come on, it can't be that dangerous!'

'It was something about our shells breaking and then...'

'They're wet, chickens, when they come out.'

'Yeah,' said Nyponstigen, 'very wet.'

Nyponstigen had the greatest understanding of the medieval saints' ability to make their dreams materialize. Pia the conductress, who at first had been a little aperture in his universe who let in only an inkling of light, now became that universe, in which his wife was an aperture. As he was falling asleep in the big double bed, she would suddenly creep in beside him, caressing him. She was in his garden, in every doorway she stood and smiled; he started long silent conversations with her. And the trains ran in easterly and westerly directions, pulled in, stood still and set off again. And every time he approached Vara he was filled from within by a strange tremor. As if he were finally on the way to himself.

Nyponstigen knew that an undeveloped person's astral body is a hazy, loosely organized, vaguely outlined astral spirit-substance containing material from all the subdivisions of the astral plane, whereas love creates forms more or less beautiful in colour and design, in all shades from crimson red to the most exquisite and fine hues of pink. And now he realized that this also applied to the astral bodies of conductors: his own was now hovering over the platform at Vara, waiting for him and making use of his senses. This two-minute chink of central Sweden became his home, became the watchtower from which he could observe the past fallow years, the silence and stagnation. No, no, he was not complaining as he pottered in the garden, quite the contrary – his muscles were strengthened, he got the energy to extend his cucumber and squash beds; when the twelfth day was to occur, or might do, he took with him a bag of carrots, a few kilos of Reine Claude, asparagus when spring came, and if it happened that the big Intercity trains were delayed over at Platform Six at Herrljunga and the schedule was wrecked, then he might leave a package for her on the platform. The vegetables were eloquent. He wrote little recipes: 'should be eaten by candlelight'; and once, when she had a card from her daughter with her, he gave her chocolate cakes, but her daughter was allergic and couldn't eat them; he bought a lobster and a bottle of white wine at the same time as he and his wife, at the onset of the autumn storms, were sharing a similar meal.

'So nice of you,' said his wife.

'I think I've been so stingy,' said Nyponstigen. He felt rich, because he could sit in two places at once and in both places derive energy from the different conversations being conducted by his two bodies.

When his wife thought they had been sitting long enough, he discreetly wondered what 'long' actually meant.

'Two minutes – how long is that really?'

'Two minutes? We've sat here longer than that, and the news will be on soon.'

'Yes, but as an example. Two strong minutes are several years, if you look at it from another point of view. And where are those minutes – here or there, then or now? Like when you and I met for the first time. It's as if moments move sometimes toward us, sometimes far away from us.'

'Shall I put the coffee on?'

'That'd be nice. Did you know that as long ago as 1910 a certain Doctor Baraduc in Paris was well on the way to photographing astro-mental images? I really wish him every success in that job. He nearly managed to photograph musical images above a church where concerts are given; a piece by Gounod leaves – if I remember rightly – a pale yellow column thirty metres high which stayed in the air about twenty minutes, while one of Wagner's reached a height of three hundred metres for a duration of twelve hours.'

'Shall we have coffee by the TV?'

'If you want to, then so do I. You know, it's possible we're mistaking our categories when we talk about words like 'here' or 'there', 'long' or 'short', when we're dealing with concepts of time, that even the word 'I' is a linguistic trap. A two-minute chink is probably a place, not a time.'

'That's very likely,' said his wife. 'Can you take the cups

in?'

'And if music can remain in place, then surely so can one's feelings or thoughts exist in a place that one actually never left. Our actual selves are maybe standing like statues all over the place, if only we had eyes to see them with.'

'That wouldn't always be such fun,' said his wife, pouring the coffee.

'That was a good meal you made.'

'It was your idea. The wine has made you talkative.'

'Does it bother you?'

'No, no, not at all. It's just so unlike you.'

'We mustn't forget to ring the kids this evening. Before we go to bed.'

Even as he reached Vedum the scent of her hair came flying around a corner of time toward him.

'You're mad, Nyponstigen,' she said. 'Thanks a lot for last Saturday – I just wish you had sat at the table with us, though it was almost as if you were.'

'Did your daughter like the lobster?'

'Not much, but she thought it was pretty, she'd never seen such red food before. She's saved the shell, and she lies there looking at it every evening. I'd like it so much if you...came to visit some time...'

'The timetables make it hard. My wife would wonder...'

'Don't talk about her, it's you I miss.'

'Me too.'

It was now that they embraced each other and kissed until the clock had struck, and that, of course, was the beginning of the end. When he got home he wondered how he could invent some illness, a threatened strike, a guards' meeting. He pottered in the garden and time passed, but he never came up with it, though the light of the two-minute chink was becoming ever hotter and stronger, continually flickering

235

before his eyes, and in the middle of the flicker they stood, he and she, groping for each other's bodies; the bridge between them was broken down and the road led straight into Kamaloka, the Place of Desire.

'I'm going crazy with us never...'

'I'll try and come up with something.'

And the embrace of their souls on the platform at Vara was so strong that they left themselves behind for days and weeks; when they did meet on rare occasions – as brake failures and delays to the Intercity trains prevented many meetings – their astral bodies occupied the place their physical bodies would have taken up – behind the luggage trolley, which hid them from the view of any passengers. They were put off by the images, they were forced to stand outside them with their snotty noses, their colds and passengers' conversations about train times, which she had still not learned.

Nyponstigen became, if not a passionate, then at least a keen fisherman; a riverbank is a good place to give free rein to the laws of one's inner space, and his wife was a wonderful fish cook. No-one fried perch as crisply as she did, no-one's oven-baked pike tasted like hers, and her whitefish put any salmon in the shade, and Nyponstigen was dependent on her food. One day he took a pike with him for Pia. She was there.

'Oh!' she said. 'What kind of fish is that?'

'Well I never!'

'What do you do with it?'

Nyponstigen became indignant.

'Haven't you ever cooked fish?'

'I get so confused in the kitchen.' The pike dangled helplessly in her helpless hand, and she lifted her gaze. 'Anyway, I'm tired of your gifts. I'm tired of getting things from you, and not getting you. I can't go on with this any longer, longing, hoping...'

'Pia, the timetables!'

'Don't you understand what you're doing? Not one day, not one minute passes without me thinking of you, wanting to make love to you, wanting, wanting ...'

'I do too.'

'You can go on doing it – it's 13.10. You can keep your pike,' she said and flung it right across the platform. It hit him on the peak of his cap, struck his glasses and fell down on the asphalt.

That evening his wife prepared the pike that he claimed he had forgotten to give her the previous evening. She descaled it with practised fingers, sprinkled plenty of horseradish on it, popped some delicious knobs of butter inside and wrapped it in foil. One knows what one has but never what one will get.

'Fantastic!' said Nyponstigen. 'Not everyone can cook fish, to be sure!'

They shared a bottle of wine, and he got a record out of his briefcase:

'How do you put the gramophone on?'

'Press "start"!'

'Now listen to this!' He sat down in the armchair and closed his eyes.

'Monteverdi,' said his wife.

'What! Do you know it?'

'We've got it. I bought it a few years ago.'

'Why?'

She filled his coffee cup.

'It was recommended to me once...'

'By whom?'

'I don't remember. You can't go round in silence all the time.'

'No, no, you can't.' He sank back into the armchair.

'These holidays I think we'll go off somewhere.'

'Are you feeling all right?'

'There's a good connection at Gothenburg at 22.07. We change at Munich at 22.55 and arrive in Venice at 8.45 in the morning. For instance. You have to see Venice before you die. We've got discounts that we've never used.'

'No, we never have,' said his wife.

Immediately after that, Lars Nyponstigen's blonde colleague was transferred to the Intercity train, the one that pulls in over at platform three at Herrljunga. One of them comes rushing down from the direction of Alingsås, the other up from Falköping. The loudspeaker announces: The train will only make a brief stop. The train for Vara, Vänersborg, Uddevalla is standing at platform two. That's his.

And the big trains start moving, one to the north, one to the south, gathering speed, soon they have vanished. This evening he's going fishing.

Notes

Nyponstigen: This highly unusual surname means 'the rose-hip path'.
Västergötland: The area inland from Gothenburg (Göteborg), on the southwest coast of Sweden, is the setting for the train routes in the story.

The Trapper

Per Gunnar Evander
Sweden

1

The other day, the local paper reported that Kalle Sundberg had passed on. That was the wording exactly: it said he had passed on, in the exceptionally brief notice on the births, deaths and marriages page. The first thing I thought was that actually it's both a worn-out phrase and an incomprehensible one, 'passing on'. But there would certainly not be anyone who would misunderstand the report, even if in many cases they might want to.

My next reaction – just as remote, if one wants to be particular about it – was the one that you often have when friends or acquaintances in the past have gone away: for a few transitory moments you think it's strange that that person was still alive.

It was at Stockholm Central Station; I had eaten a tasty fry-up and taken two tots of snaps at the congenial restaurant when I was passing the kiosk and took it into my head to buy a newspaper from 'up home'. That's the way we people who've been living in the diaspora for so long like to put it when we're on the right side of the Dala River.

So I was standing still there outside the glass door while I browsed through the awful old house organ. Of course it was mostly rubbish and trivialities, as usual.

But then I found that Kalle Sundberg had got one last announcement and a notice. In both places it said that he had passed away and that he was eighty-two. A younger brother down south seemed to be the only relative. I read the announcement and the notice over and over again. Finally I felt a chill going down my spine; I straightened up, folded the rag under my arm and trudged off.

After a quarter of an hour or so I stopped at a street corner, unfolded the 'family page' again and read it. It was then that I finally comprehended that Kalle Sundberg was gone, and that he could no longer be counted among us.

2

One could write about Kalle Sundberg's life with exemplary brevity. As far as I know, he lived almost from the beginning of his life to the end alone in the house he was born in and very early inherited from his parents. During his working life he worked in the forest, firstly for the Kopparberg mining company, towards the end for the Forest Service. He was of small stature, and it was especially his legs that were so strikingly short; men used to joke among themselves about how Kalle Sundberg actually reached down to the ground with those stumps he called Shanks' pony. Perhaps you could even joke with him himself about it, I couldn't say.

But the fact is that Kalle Sundberg could not be regarded as any sort of lone wolf; he was far from unapproachable or bashful, and he was glad of company when others offered it to him. Perhaps he was shy and taciturn at brief and unplanned meetings, but otherwise suddenly open and almost talkative. Generally, though, he was thought of as lacking a talent for companionship, and that is the way he was seen and judged.

There was something obsequious about the figure of Kalle Sundberg; he was swarthy and grey, and usually came in the company of his dog, which he liked to pat and converse with. His walk was brisk; he stooped forward slightly as he moved; he hunted and fished and was known to be respected in both pursuits. It's possible that he didn't have a real friend, someone he was completely confidential with. But in that case I could easily count up a handful of people in his vicinity who didn't either. There wasn't anything so remarkable about that.

Sometimes it did happen that Kalle Sundberg would talk about himself, and then he would stand staring out the window and say that he was, when it came down to it, one of the isolated ones. If you asked him what he meant by that, he would start talking about something else.

3

I don't know if you remember when the Bjurboda gang was at the height of its terror. After all, it was quite a few years ago now, but some of the group's escapades became famous throughout the country, and not a few supporters of so-called law and order spoke out shrilly about it. With a few exceptions, it was hardly more than material damage that the gang caused.

Anyway it turned out that the Bjurboda gang consisted of seven youths altogether, all of them tearaways, aggressive and completely stunted by a neglectful and loveless upbringing. In other words, the same old story. Even today there are so many people who haven't got what is perhaps the most important

241

insight of all, namely that children need love and more love, limitless amounts of it. There are even those who delude themselves that a person is born somehow wicked, like some unmouldable, predestined prey.

But there was an important complication in the case of the Bjurboda gang, and that was its leader, who in both his actions and his attitudes was noticeably different from his mates. He went by the name of the Bjurboda Terror and – as those of you who remember will know – was guilty of two exceptionally brutal attacks, both of them on what they called defenceless women. It was known early on that he led, and misled, the members of the gang, sometimes with threats, sometimes with bribes. The Bjurboda Terror was a man in early middle age; when he got his nickname he already had a criminal record and was regarded as extraordinarily ruthless in his relations to his fellow men.

There is much more I could and would tell you about this unapproachable man, but it's not him we're talking about now but one of his many appointed pursuers.

By the time we are dealing with here, however, the Bjurboda gang had been broken up and its members taken in hand in different ways, yet the Terror, the leader, was still at large and being sought in our neck of the woods. One April day, when he had been tracked down to a particular area of forest, the police issued a quiet request for assistance from some members of the public. Inquiries were made as to how those who were more or less registered in the various hunting groups assessed the possibilities of helping with what they called 'chain surveillance'. In practice this meant that they would search for and encircle the wanted man but not actually take part in the arrest. This would preferably be done with the help of the owners' or other available dogs.

Among those who were asked about this was Kalle

Sundberg. In many ways he could be regarded as an obvious candidate. He had a dog, he possessed an enormous knowledge of the various hiding-places and nooks in the forest there, and above all, there could hardly be a man among us who had a better acquaintance with the wretched man known as the Bjurboda Terror. You see, they had gone around together about ten years before, doing clearing work, just west of Vallstanäs, and it was known that their work together had gone off without reported friction on either side. Nobody knew for certain whether they had met later or had any contact. But now he was asked, though last of all and with reservations expressed.

Kalle Sundberg was called to the meeting at the home of one of the most influential farmers. It was late one evening at the beginning of April, just before Easter, which fell early that year. It was a typical day in early spring, with mild, gusty, occasionally surprisingly strong winds. But the evening was dazzling, with moonlight and a faint play of stars, perhaps one or two degrees below towards midnight.

I have a very clear memory of Kalle Sundberg on that occasion. I myself had initially been considered as a dog-handler, but I had also taken on the job of keeping the minutes, and besides I would not be taking part in the final stage of the search.

Kalle Sundberg settled down on a chair in the farthest corner, looking shyly around when he wasn't staring at the floor; he greeted everyone there dutifully with a slight bow, in a way that emphasized the forward stoop of his form. He had brought with him his beautiful Swedish foxhound, which lay down softly but very vigilantly at his master's small feet. I remember that the dog's eyes were large and blackish-brown, with a temperamental expression; he was almost bronze-coloured, with a dark coat and a little white streak on the breast.

Eventually the farmer cleared away the coffee-cups and the plate of cakes and unfolded a faded General Staff map on the diningroom table. Before he gave the floor to the two policemen who were present he exchanged a few words with some of the others. Among other things, he told Kalle Sundberg, in everyone's hearing, that he had been asked to come because he was a good woodsman and perhaps, out of all those present, the one who knew the wanted man best. A trace of a smile dawned on Kalle Sundberg's face, his short legs shook slightly and the foxhound rose to a sitting position. Kalle Sundberg was surely not used to receiving compliments in this way, but he revealed his satisfaction with admirable restraint.

After running through the instructions, we broke up and each made his own way home. There was still a strong wind, and I suppose we all found that it was colder than the thermometer indicated. I dawdled a while on the farmer's front steps, watching the men trudging away, as gradually the clusters dispersed and eventually most of them had gone off each in his own direction.

I had occasion to later try to recall whether Kalle Sundberg was in the company of some particular person as he left the farm. None of the others had, they said later, spoken with him, but as a parting remark, the farmer had again pointed out that he and the police appreciated the fact that Kalle Sundberg had taken the trouble to turn up. The latter had looked away for a moment, and then at the farmer with a gaze, silent and calm, but slightly embarrassed.

A great majority of those present had dogs with them, all of the hunting kind. I seem to recall that there were fox-hounds, beagles, drevers, and, as I said, the Swedish foxhound. I don't know if it was for aesthetic reasons that Kalle

244

Sundberg's Swedish variety caught my eye, or whether I'm somehow just rationalizing after the event.

Anyway, perhaps that's of no interest just now.

4

As early as half past four the next morning we were all to gather and form into groups at the transformer kiosk just by the turning up to Skatfors. Since most of the questions of organization and tactics had been settled the evening and night before, the practical arrangements wouldn't take up so many minutes now; the idea was to get going before dawn had passed. Besides, the people in charge were experienced, so for most of them it was just a question of keeping the restless dogs in check and, basically, carrying out orders.

What was known was that the Bjurboda Terror was lying low up on a wide mountain pasture with a fairly large number of timber huts. No-one knew in which one he was hiding, and since he was armed and would hardly hesitate to shoot his way out, all of us were told to observe the greatest possible care at all costs, and to keep our dogs under control until an order to the contrary was given.

If I remember rightly, Kalle Sundberg was the last one to turn up at the meeting-place by the transformer kiosk. When he was spotted, someone called out to him from a few hundred metres away to hurry up. Some noticed that he looked surprisingly tired and worn-out, as if he had had second thoughts and didn't really want to be doing what he was, with such great reluctance, about to do.

Only when, silent and stooping, he had joined the others did the policemen notice that he did not have his dog with him. The observation aroused general irritation, and the farmer who the previous evening had lavished so much honey on

Kalle Sundberg went up to him and asked in a loud, provocative voice:

'Where the hell's your dog, man?'

Kalle Sundberg is said to have turned around at this point in surprise, to check whether his foxhound was with him or not. But he had no answer to give.

'Did you leave the dog at home?' asked one of the constables.

Kalle Sundberg became the object of everyone's interest, and they stared at him, waiting for him to say something. But he said nothing, and just looked down at the ground like a shamefaced schoolboy, and someone thought they noticed that Kalle Sundberg had never had such short legs as at that moment – as if the legs of his boots had suddenly grown right up to his crotch, as if he wanted to hide in his boots and let them stride away from there of their own accord.

'This is a fine thing!' someone sighed, amid all the swearing.

But one of the policemen gathered his wits and ordered an immediate departure, and while the groups worked their way forward and took up their allotted positions in a wide arc around the pasture, Kalle Sundberg was urged to go back home and fetch his bloody dog. After that he was to join, as quickly as possible, a waiting group, where the power-line cuts a path up to Skatfors. Before they left Kalle Sundberg and made sure that he turned homeward, they pressed upon him the importance of acting with all possible speed.

Kalle Sundberg never did come to the meeting-place under the power-line. They waited a good while; one member of the group said twelve, a couple of others fifteen, and a fourth at least twenty minutes, before they gave up hope and set off.

The reports of the length of time turned out to be of a certain interest; the delay caused by Kalle Sundberg's absence was later estimated as over half an hour. For this half hour was enough for the Bjurboda Terror to sniff out a trap and to slip through the chain just at the place where a link was missing, composed of the group that was delayed.

So the whole enterprise came to nothing, and the Bjurboda Terror managed to get far away to areas where he committed a series of desperate attacks, in which among other things one young couple lost their lives. Those with a good memory will probably have no difficulty in recalling this appalling act.

Just over a week after this event, however, the decision was taken to question Kalle Sundberg, and find out whether his breach of promise had any connection with the Bjurboda Terror's successful escape. It was mainly the others in the group who requested this measure, and several claimed that Kalle Sundberg should be put on trial for the incident if he could not offer a satisfactory explanation or otherwise defend what was regarded as a treacherous act.

There was something of the lynch-mob about the whole community's attitude to Kalle Sundberg on the day his questioning was to take place. For some reason – perhaps not unexpected, either – it was decided that I should keep the minutes of it. A lawyer in town who happened to have just qualified to appear in court took charge of the proceedings; as witnesses there were the aforementioned farmer and an elderly man in the biggest hunting team who was also a former lay assessor at the court in town. The hearing took place on the twenty-fifth of April; it was my birthday and there is no important day I remember better, or probably will remember better, in my life. For that afternoon, a chill went down my spine, and it was hard for me to straighten up for quite a while afterwards.

Kalle Sundberg greeted people bowing and silent as usual; in his arms he held an almost new-born foxhound puppy, which whimpered and floundered about, quite beside itself.

We sat down in the little living-room. Our host had laid out coffee-cups and fresh-baked bread; you could even have a brandy or a snaps with your refreshment.

It turned out to be long questions and short answers, and after three hours it was all over; the old assessor and I concluded the session with a couple of proper cups of coffee with brandy before we went off together with the other two. And Kalle Sundberg bowed and thanked us and stroked the puppy that was lying between his fists. I think we were all feeling foolish and devastated when we took leave of Kalle Sundberg.

When Kalle Sundberg had taken leave of the rest of us that evening of the gathering at the farmer's house, he was, he himself claimed, very happy and elated. For virtually the first time, he had experienced a sense of comradeship with the others in the community; all at once he had been given a task for the general good; it was clear he was wanted and needed, as he expressed it himself.

He realized that he didn't have many hours to sleep before his appearance the next morning. So he chose the short cut home across the Vallsta River, which would give him at least half an hour extra and the dog would not have to put up with the hardened slush and crusts of ice on the road. Scattered flecks of pale snow lay along the middle channel; otherwise it was sludge, and none of it reflected as much of the blue moonlight as one might expect. But Kalle Sundberg knew his home district; many times he had chosen the road across the river at this time of year, but perhaps he had never been quite as excited as now. He perceived a quite strange sensation, that his help was required – it was almost as if, in his solitude with the foxhound, he was embarrassed by his sudden pleasure.

It was when both Kalle Sundberg and the dog were in the middle channel that it gave way. At first, according to Kalle Sundberg himself, it felt like stepping into a swamp; he was so preoccupied with his bright thoughts that he was more surprised than frightened. A moment later, he had water and icy sludge up over his shoulders. His short legs automatically started treading, and he heaved his arms up in front of him, but only encountered a soft and porous mass, which gave way. He tried immediately to turn back the way he had come, but he soon saw that he was winding aimlessly about, finally completely disoriented.

After flailing about for a long time, he finally found some ice that held. But it was deceptively hard, and when he tried to get up, it refused to bear him. Falling backwards, he was sucked under the ice mantle several times, but every time grabbed hold of the edge at the last moment. Finally he managed to heave himself up, with great effort, so that he was holding on with his elbows a bit in from where it last broke. In this position he took off his gloves to get a better grip with his fingers. He pressed his nails into the soft icy surface as hard as he could.

He called his dog, but couldn't make him out. He listened for him, but could only hear the wind, dying away and returning, dying away and returning. Even though he kept moving in this way, treading powerfully, the cold of the water began to burn him all over, and he called for the dog ever more urgently.

For a while he hung on in this way, and struggled against the current. He says that the Bjurboda Terror came more or less involuntarily to mind: a thing like this wasn't going to stop him now. If anything frightened him, it was the thought of not being with all the others on the search in the morning.

He made renewed efforts to haul himself up, but the ice gave way, and when he finally had something firmer under him, and slowly heaved himself on his side, he lost his grip with his stiff frozen hands, and slid back.

Then he discovered his dog, suddenly standing just in front of his hands, just looking perplexed. Kalle Sundberg coaxed his hound to him, and fumbled for his forelegs and neck, but the dog kept lithely jumping away, and started to bark and leap about as if his master just wanted to play with him.

Nevertheless, finally Kalle Sundberg managed to get hold of one of the foxhound's paws and thus reach the other and pull the dog towards him. It struggled furiously, snapping at his wrists. But when Kalle Sundberg had got the dog to the edge, he quickly let go with one hand and gripped hold of the scruff of its neck, then let go with the other and joined his hands under the dog's belly. Kalle Sundberg pushed his chest onto the ice, and was sure it would all succeed, when suddenly the foxhound curled up into a ball and slithered with his master back into the water.

Kalle Sundberg immediately let go and pushed the foxhound away. It splashed hither and thither, and all its efforts to get up were in vain. It was then that the dog went on the attack, and for a while Kalle Sundberg didn't know how to defend himself. He chose, out of sheer instinct for self-preservation, to fend off the dog's attacks, hitting him on the head over and over again, but it hardly seemed to help. In one of the last assaults, he grabbed hold of the dog's throat with both hands and pressed its head under the water with the last of his energy. Kalle Sundberg told, with a slight stammer, how he kept his grip until his eyes went dim, and he himself was a good way down in the depths.

Somehow he finally got himself up – he could not explain how; suddenly he was lying up on the ice, and he slithered slowly and cautiously in toward the eastern bank, which is where he had been heading. He called out a few times before he heaved himself up, but he says that the only answer he got was the wind, dying away and returning, dying away and returning. Then he staggered home, frozen through and almost unconscious with exhaustion.

Kalle Sundberg then took off his heavy clothes and put dry ones on, draped himself in an overcoat, set the alarm clock and dozed off on the bed.

We all knew what happened after that.

But Kalle Sundberg added a conclusion that I couldn't resist putting in the minutes. When he left the organized force at the kiosk by the transformer with orders to fetch the dog, there was no longer any chance to turn back, there was nothing to add. The wind had died down a little; he just felt it lightly on his back on his walk home. He says that he was somehow moving mechanically, still with bad pains in his joints and hands. On the way past one of the slopes on the riverbank, he stopped short, and looked across the river, which in the fragile light of dawn was quite still, with sporadic blue-black openings.

An old woman delivering newspapers greeted him, and just for a change Kalle Sundberg felt that he wanted to stop and exchange a few words. But the woman hurried brusquely away. He was tired and hungry to the point of death, and suddenly afraid of getting home.

The last thing Kalle Sundberg had to say at the hearing was that he supposed he was one of life's isolated people, and that nothing much could be done about that. And, just as in a fuzzy photograph, I can make out Kalle Sundberg, in the middle of the death notice, standing at the entrance of his house, saying goodbye with the wretched little foxhound pup in his rough arms, tenderly and carefully stroking it. And I can hear his voice, too, I can hear it clearly, and at the same moment a chill goes down my spine, and I have trouble straightening up for quite a while.

The Wandering Cook

Marie Hermanson
Sweden

It was an excellent cabin. All year, Mr A had been saving for this holiday. On the workbench in the kitchen, he unpacked his equipment. He was well prepared. He had got hold of books from libraries and second-hand shops. He had been studying the subject virtually every evening during the winter.

Outside the window, the little lake glistened blue. From a bare hillock, a pier jutted out, and where it joined the land there was a well-stocked sauna. But he had other things to do than bathe in the sauna. He wasn't even going to row out and fish – even though fresh perch was a delicacy. The forest stretched for miles around the cabin. Perhaps toward the end of his holiday he could find mushrooms in it. Before that he would have nothing to do with the forest.

This had once been an isolated crofter's cottage. The owner had kept the old wood stove. Otherwise the whole cabin was new, big and modern. He switched on the big refrigerator, which began to hum faintly. He looked around for the freezer he had been told about, and found it at the entrance. A substantial-sized box, in which hunters could put the elks they had cut up. He started it up and went back to the kitchen. He liked the wood stove. That was what had made him choose this expensive cabin. But there was also an electric stove. With four hot-plates and two ovens.

He pulled out the kitchen drawers, moved all the utensils to the deep drawer at the bottom, and replaced them with his own things. Then he began to fill up the refrigerator and freezer. He put the books on a shelf in the main room.

When he had finished unpacking, he sat down in a pine armchair with wide arms for holding drinks, and looked into the empty open stove. An absolutely excellent cabin. A company owned it. It was for company entertainment. Germans with fat wallets would rent it for hunting. There was plenty of game in the area. The scenery was beautiful. In summer you could swim and fish in the lake. In winter there was a ski-slope half an hour's drive away. But he had chosen the cabin for its kitchen. And for its secluded position. Here was the calm he needed around him. This evening he would rest, have a cup of beef tea and a sandwich and go to bed early. Tomorrow he would begin.

His workmates at the office said Mr A was mad. Probably true. Mad about food. He had been born with exceptionally well-developed taste-buds.

Mr A lived alone. Women always got tired of him. What he would see as the high point of the evening – a supper made all by himself – they only regarded as a prelude. A prelude that gave them high hopes: the tenderness with which he cooked the vegetables (never too hard, never too soft), the sensitivity to the special qualities of every ingredient, the resolution with which he stirred a sauce, the narrow tip of the tongue with which he tasted, the cautious handling of a head of lettuce, which, after rinsing, was swaddled in a clean, ironed kitchen towel and was softly, softly, pressed dry – everything promised so much.

But for Mr A it was this that gave the evening its substance. The love-making afterwards was perfunctory, messy, lacking concentration. His senses were still full of the experience of the meal. His love-life was merely a physical necessity for Mr A, an emptying of the body, just like any other evacuation. When on the following morning he received cold looks from his lady friend, he anxiously wondered what he had done wrong. Was it the sauce? Or the dessert? He drew the conclusion that women were difficult dinner companions and from then on invited only gentlemen.

Despite his great interest in food, Mr A was slim, almost thin. He ate small portions and chewed slowly. Gluttony revolted him. His slender build, his cool relations with women and the intimate suppers with gentlemen occasionally led to the misconception that Mr A was homosexual.

During his previous holidays he had gone on an exclusive gourmet trip arranged by a travel agency in Paris. A small group of gourmets travelled around the Arab world for four weeks, acquainting themselves with the theme of the trip: 'The Cuisine of the Orient'.

They stayed at first-class hotels, were conveyed in air-conditioned cars, visited luxurious restaurants and palatial private villas. But it was in the market-place at Marrakesh, among maimed beggars and mangy dogs that, one evening, Mr A had the greatest experience of this journey.

Among all the merchants and performers fighting for the tourists' attention there was an old storyteller. He sat on a carpet and his face was lit up by a little charcoal fire burning in a dish. Those sitting around him in the dark were mostly local people, hardly any tourists. A Parisian companion interpreted the story for Mr A into French, a language Mr A knew well.

There are stories that go right to our hearts. Stories that make us blush, because it seems that our deepest secrets are being revealed. Mr A had never had such an experience in the European myths and tales he had heard. But now, in the market-place in Marrakesh, he felt 'Yes! This is *my* story!' During the trip, he later heard different variations on the same story, which only strengthened the sensation.

The next day they flew on to Cairo. From his seat in the aeroplane he took one last look at the city that lay below, dusty and ochre-coloured, as if the dunes of the desert had suddenly taken on architectural forms. Silently he retold the story to himself again and again, checking that he had not forgotten any detail.

And this was the story told by the old storyteller in Marrakesh:

Once upon a time there was a sultan who had a fantastic cook. This man's skill in preparing food was renowned far and wide, and princes and kings from all over the world would come to eat at the sultan's table.

One evening the cook prepared a meal that excelled everything he had ever achieved. It tasted so exquisite that the sultan believed he had left his earthly existence and thought he heard the angels of Allah singing. As a reward, he gave the cook his youngest and fairest concubine. But when the woman came to the cook's door, he refused to admit her. (Wise of him, thought Mr A.) So instead the sultan sent a beautiful youth to the cook. But the youth was not admitted either. So the sultan himself went to the cook's house to find out why he would not accept his gifts.

'I can't have anyone here tonight,' answered the cook. 'I need to be alone and undisturbed.' So what was the cook going to do that night? That he refused to answer.

The sultan went away, but after a while he returned to the cook's house and looked through the window. He saw the cook pouring soup into a bowl. Then the cook sat down and ate the soup very, very slowly. Between each spoonful he would sit for a while with his eyes closed, as if his soul were transported to another world. When the soup was finally consumed, he gave a blessed smile, went to bed and fell asleep.

Mr A understood this cook perfectly. But the sultan understood nothing. He was furious that the cook had spurned his gifts, and had turned him out merely to eat a bowl of soup! As a punishment, he had the cook's recipe book burned, and the cook himself was given thirty lashes. He received the lashes without a sound. With his back bleeding, he then went to the sultan. He said he was sorry for offending his master and that he would leave immediately. As far as the recipe book was concerned, it did not matter a bit that it was burnt. His father had taught him all his recipes by heart when he was a little boy and he no longer looked at the book. And so he left, without any attempt to stop him. (Quite right. One shouldn't throw pearls before swine, thought Mr A with a sting of bitter experience.)

But soon the sultan was deeply regretful. His new cook was nowhere near as clever as the previous one, and his meals were nothing like what his predecessor had concocted.

No longer did any mighty rulers come to eat at the sultan's table. Too late did the sultan realize the great value of their visits. In the cosy atmosphere created by the meals these rulers had settled disputes which might otherwise have led to war. Often these visits had resulted in trading links or an exchange of skills in various fields. Now the sultan had to observe how the other rulers would travel right through his country without stopping at his palace.

Couriers were sent out to seek out the cook and offer him a great reward if he returned. But it was as if the cook had been swallowed up by the earth.

The sultan tried to remember the dish the cook had served the evening before he left. It had been breast of pigeon, baked in a crisp creamy dough, served with a sauce. The sultan recalled that the sauce had contained beans and olives. It had also tasted of ginger, almonds and honey. One cook after another was instructed to reconstruct the dish. Apart from the known ingredients, they added various items that the first cook might have used. But they all failed. 'If only I hadn't had the recipe book burnt', sighed the sultan. (Barbarians! thought Mr A. That book must have contained the collected gastronomic wisdom of generations!)

The sultan never found his cook again. But once he did hear some merchants talking about an old man they had met in the desert. The old man had offered them some sort of pottage, which looked colourless and unprepossessing, but tasted so exquisite that they thought they heard the angels of Allah singing.

Long after the sultan had died and his empire had collapsed, people would say they had met the sultan's cook. He was known as 'the wandering cook', who turned up here and there in the huge Arab realm, served heavenly meals and disappeared without trace. 'Even today', said the story-teller of Marrakesh, 'one can meet people who claim to have met him.'

Shepherds in the mountains had told of a tired, emaciated old man who had asked them to slaughter one of their lambs. In return he would make them the most delicious meal they had ever tasted. Since they had intended to slaughter a lamb that evening anyway, they acceded to his request. The old man produced dried herbs from a cloth pouch, and out of the lamb's meat, the innards and the herbs, he prepared a meal that made the shepherds almost wild with pleasure. Some fishermen claimed to have met him on the shore, where he offered them heavenly grilled fish. In the bazaars of the towns he would turn up early in the morning, when there was the best selection on the stands. 'He has even been seen here in the Medina of Marrakesh,' said the storyteller. 'And the merchants fear him. Because he exposes any cheating. Nothing rancid, unripe or badly handled escapes him.'

And that is roughly how the story ended. The next morning, before going to the airport, Mr A took a good look among the stands in the bazaar. But it seemed that all the old Arab men were equally critical and scrupulous about their purchases.

Back in Sweden, he made up his mind not to go on any of the travel agencies' gourmet trips on his next holidays. Instead he would undertake his own gourmet trip within four walls. He had long dreamed of just this: to devote a long time to making one single dish until his skill was perfected. He had hesitated about which dish to choose. Now he knew: breast of pigeon, baked in pastry, with a sauce. He would imagine the pleasure that awaited him: the crisp, delicate pastry shell. Within, the pigeon meat, mild and rich at the same time. The aromatic sauce. The smell.

On the second day of his holiday he set to work. The wood stove in the cabin was better than he had dared hope. Outside the half-open window the pine-trees soughed. Otherwise it was silent. No telephone rang. No neighbours disturbed him. Now it was just Mr A, his faithful casserole and the juice from the freshly-grilled pigeon. He mixed in chicken stock, he put in the beans, the crushed almonds, the honey, the ginger. He cut out the breast of the pigeon. Rolled out the dough ...

The result dissatisfied him. But the next day he continued

259

with a new pigeon from the freezer. He tried various substances in the cause. Occasionally he left the cabin to get new provisions. Like a chemist in his laboratory, he experimented and made notes about his work. He felt his way forward with vegetables such as celery, tomatoes and artichokes. He used mushrooms such as champignons, chanterelles, morels and truffles. He also tried many kinds of fruit, such as apples, plums, apricots, oranges, lemons, chestnuts. He used spices, such as cinnamon, oregano, sage and thyme. He used smoked diced pork and the pigeon's own innards, the liver and heart. He used various kinds of flour and baking methods for the dough. He sent for Arabic specialties he had never eaten before. Every evening he sat down at table, and the menu, with certain variations, was the same, evening after evening: pigeon breast, baked in a crust, with sauce.

But instead of – as Mr A had expected – step by step approaching perfection, he became more and more uncertain that pigeon breast, baked in a crust, with sauce, was so fantastically good. And one day Mr A felt slightly nauseated as he took another pigeon from the freezer. He refrained from cooking that day. Instead he put on his raincoat and boots and went out into the forest.

It was almost September. The birches and aspens were already yellow; it had rained recently and it was cool. He wandered about aimlessly. Breathed in and out in deep draughts. It was as if the forest air washed away the cooking smell of the past month from his nostrils. He felt light and free. A cup of unsweetened tea and a rusk was all he had eaten that morning. He set off on little winding paths and wondered how old they were, who had trampled them down first. The paths led nowhere. Suddenly they were no longer under his feet. But he found new ones. And when he no longer found paths, he made his own.

He began to feel cold, and turned back. But as he went in the opposite direction, the forest looked quite different. Everything took on a different colour and form. He had to look back over his shoulder all the time to see that this was the way he had come. He became uncertain. The little paths had gone. He walked to and fro to find a place he recognized. Finally he realized he was lost.

Now he was walking blindly about. Walking to keep warm. He hoped to find a path or a road or a human habitation.

But he didn't have much hope. He had heard of the wilderness that stretched mile after mile north of his cabin. That was where he was now.

As Mr A walked, his hunger increased. Lunchtime had long passed, dinner-time too. Rain fell over the forest. Darkness gathered. Mr A crept in under a spruce. Leaning against the trunk, with fir-twigs as protection against the wet ground, he sat through the night.

When day dawned, he set off walking again. Hunger tormented him. He could have eaten anything. Pigeon-breast, oatmeal porridge, blood pudding, dog-food. Anything you could chew and swallow. There was nothing edible in the forest, though there should have been at that time of year. The fungi he found were inedible. He saw no berries. He drank from pools of water and ate a little moss. When another night was approaching he became desperate. No-one would miss him; he had said, after all, that he wanted to be left in peace in his cabin. Deeper and deeper into the forest he went. It was as if he had ceased to be human.

In the dusk, Mr A came upon a big marsh. On the other side he could make out smoke from a fire against the wall of firs. He began to walk around the marsh, and when he got nearer he saw a person by the fire. When he reached it he was at first a little disappointed. He had been expecting a hunter, a local farmer, a sensible person, who could take him home and give him a bed and a meal and some warm clothes. But this person did not look as if he could offer anything of the kind. The man by the fire looked like a tramp, unkempt and dirty. Loopy of course, thought Mr A to himself. Some sort of hermit.

He went up to the fire and the old man looked up. My God, he hasn't changed his clothes for a year, thought Mr A, but then he realized that he himself perhaps didn't look so fresh after his night under the spruce.

'I'm lost,' he said and crouched down as near to the fire as possible. The warmth was wonderful.

The old man was silently stirring a tin hanging over the fire. He had a beard and swarthy, weatherbeaten skin. Mr A smelled the stench from his clothes.

With a rag as a holder, the man lifted the can from the fire, produced a spoon and began slurping the contents. The spoon wandered between the tin and the filthy beard. A few black stumps of teeth were visible in his mouth when he opened it. Then the man offered his spoon to Mr A, who at first recoiled. But his hunger was stronger than his disgust. As if of itself, his mouth opened. Quickly the old man poked the spoon in, and Mr A swallowed.

What a taste! Mr A's tongue rippled with shivers of pleasure. His lips trembled. His gums called for more. The old man smiled and handed him the spoon. Mr A ate from the can. 'My God, what a soup!' he whispered. 'Mamma mia! Good heavens above!' His taste-buds vibrated with excitement. His sight became blurred. The marsh, the spruce forest and the cloudy sky merged into one heaving mass. And then he heard it: heavenly voices singing. The autumnal forest was drowned in a song of praise, full of blessing. Perfection. Perfection!

When he had emptied the tin, he felt a little drowsy. He

was sitting right on the ground, but did not feel cold. The old man had got up and was collecting his clean-scraped tin can, his spoon and few other things. He put them all in a sack and began to go into the forest. The fire died down, it grew cold, darkness fell. But Mr A remained sitting alone, caught up in a euphoric intoxication.

Suddenly a dog came rushing out of the forest. It ran up to Mr A, sniffed at him and started barking. Then he came to his senses. The dog was followed by two men from the village. They had noticed that the daily smoke from Mr A's wood stove was missing. People in the country notice things like that, Mr A thought later. With the help of the men he got back to his cabin. He thanked them and asked them if they knew the old tramp. To his surprise, they didn't. Surely everyone would know such an eccentric?

When he had got over his adventure in the forest, Mr A began to look for the old man. He rang the local social security office. Yes, they kept track of all the old people, and there were one or two recluses still left in the forests. Mr A went to visit them, but none of them was the one who had served him the heavenly soup. He checked with the police. At the supermarket in the village. With the old people in the retirement home. With the men in the hunting club. No. The tramp must have been from far away. He was not known in the area.

The fourth of September came, and Mr A's holiday was over. He packed up his kitchen utensils. For the past week they had lain unused. He had spent his time looking for the old man and had just eaten tinned food.

Mr A went home. He resumed his work at the office. He stopped making his own meals, and from then on he ate the dish of the day at the local cafeteria. His old friends sometimes tried to reawaken his interest in food. When they served him something succulent, at home or at a restaurant, Mr A would eat politely and silently. For anyone who has eaten a dish so exquisite that he has heard the angels of Allah singing can only smile at the efforts of other cooks.